The Sensitives

THE
SENSITIVES

Herbert Burkholz

Atheneum NEW YORK **1987**

Library of Congress Cataloging in Publication Data
Burkholz, Herbert, ———
   The sensitives.
   I. Title.
PS3552.U725S4   1987   813'.54   86-26545
ISBN 0-689-11842-2

Copyright © 1987 by Herbert Burkholz
All rights reserved
Published simultaneously in Canada
by Collier Macmillan Canada, Inc.
Composition by Maryland Linotype Composition
Company, Baltimore, Maryland
Manufactured by Fairfield Graphics,
Fairfield, Pennsylvania
Designed by Harry Ford
First Edition

For Bob and Camilla Teitelman

The Sensitives

1

T H E game was five-card stud, it was eight in the morning after a long night, and B. B. Thayer's suite at the Devon was filled with the aromas of freshly-grilled ham, eggs shirred in sherry, home-fried potatoes, and rich, strong coffee; all of it coming from the buffet table set against the far wall. You could count on Thayer for that level of hospitality. He lived in Houston, but he kept the suite at the Devon on East Fifty-seventh Street for his poker trips to New York. The buffet had been open all night and now the aroma of the coffee was enough to take my mind away from the business at the table. Breakfast time after a twelve-hour session, time to finish it off, deal once more around, and go home. I was ready for home. I had a head-ache splitting my skull from top to bottom, and the sharp edge of the axe was buried between my eyes.

Waiting for the next hand to be dealt, I stretched my arms and glanced around the table at the other players. On my left was Thayer himself, whose money came from natural gas. Next to him was Theresa Fabrikant, who ran an advertising agency that billed over two hundred million a year. After that came

Mario Villalonga, who owned a healthy slice of midtown Manhattan; Leroy Coopersmith, who had the keys to a union pension fund; and a man named Thuc, who had brought a load of suitcases slotted to hold ingots out of Saigon in the days before the fall. Not exactly a bunch of widows and orphans.

There were perhaps two dozen others wandering about, taking it all in. Some were the types who like to rub up against the heavy action even though they don't have the bankroll or the balls to sit in, and some were there on other business. Jaspers and Childress, who ran my security, were there, never far from me; and there was a woman dressed in black angora over black brushed Calvins. I had seen her around at other games, but never had spoken to her. She reminded me of Nadia, and I wondered how the woman I loved would look in a sweater and jeans. Probably terrific. I had never seen Nadia in anything but the businesslike suits and severe evening gowns that the Russians favored for working hours. I probably never would. The girl in angora saw my eyes on her and smiled before she turned away to the buffet table.

The other two people I knew were also at the buffet: Lew Meyerowitz and Carlo Vecchione, my backers. They were busy shoveling in breakfast, ignoring the game. They knew that they had nothing to worry about. At that point I was up forty thousand and it was one of my days to win. That was part of the deal that I had with my backers. I won only three out of every four times that I played. Any higher ratio would have gotten me barred from the better games in town. Carlo and Lew saw the logic of that, but only reluctantly. They were never happy on days when I had decided to lose. To them, it was like throwing money away.

"Ben?" Thayer's gentle voice pulled me back from my thoughts. "Ante?"

"Sorry." I corrected the oversight, chipping a white. Thayer dealt cards for stud, calling the up cards as they came out.

4

"Queen, trey, deuce, jack, nine, and a cute little four for the dealer. Queen bets."

I took a look at my hole card, a nine, which gave me a pair of them. Then I took a look at all the other hole cards, probing into the minds of the players. Thayer, Mario, and Leroy all had junk and would probably fold. Theresa had the ace of spades to go with the queen, and Thuc had the jack of hearts along with his king. The faces of the cards came to me clearly, reflected in their minds.

"Queen bets a nickel," said Theresa, and flipped five hundred into the pot.

As anticipated, Mario and Leroy folded. Thuc called, I called, and Thayer dropped out, saying, "I'll just deal."

As he dealt again, I threw up a block to keep out the random thoughts of the two players still with me. I knew their hole cards, and I didn't need to know anything else. Theresa bought the four of diamonds, I got a deuce, and Thuc paired up his hole card with the king of spades.

High man, he chipped a blue, and said, "Cost you a dime." Theresa and I called.

On the fourth card, Theresa paired her queen to go with the ace in the hole, Thuc looked down at a seven that didn't help his kings, and I drew the trey of clubs. With a pair of queens showing, Theresa chipped a blue, and said, "Bet a dime."

"Call and raise." With a pair of kings hidden, Thuc made it two thousand. I called the two. Theresa paused, and also called.

"Pot right," said Thayer. He dealt Theresa the ace of clubs to give her aces up. Thuc got the six of diamonds, no help. I drew my third nine.

I let down the block and probed around the table. From Theresa I caught the sharp yellow edge of greed. She thought a lot of her two pair. From Thuc came a resignation that showed itself in shades of cobalt blue as he realized that his kings probably weren't going to hold up. The rest of the table gave off brown indifference. That's the way I caught it sometimes, pure colors without words. It was easier with the words. I probed again at Theresa, and this time caught words as she figured the hand.

Thuc? Jacks, maybe kings, no threat. Slade, did he catch? Two small pair, small trips? No, never, wouldn't hang with that. So? Bluff. Hit him hard.

"Queens bet twenty cents," she said.

Thuc hesitated, knew that he was throwing it away, but slid two thousand into the pot. "Call."

"Call your two," I said, "and raise five."

Bullshit, thought Theresa. Her face showed nothing as she shoved a stack into the center of the table. "Your five. And my five."

Thuc folded.

I said, "Call your five, and raise ten."

Eyes opened around the table, and Thayer smiled thinly. *Bastard,* thought Theresa as she tried to decide what I was holding. She wanted to keep on believing in a bluff, but even in a game like that ten thousand dollars was not a casual raise. She had to call. She hadn't built her agency by letting people pick her pockets.

"Call," she said.

I turned up my hole card and let her see the third nine. She nodded. Her face was made of stone, but her head was seething. She had a sewer vocabulary, and she was the worst kind of loser.

"Mister Slade wins again," murmured Thayer. "Mister Slade thinks highly of a pair of nines wired."

I motioned to one of the waiters for a cup of coffee, and closed my eyes to ease the throbbing in my head. It was always that way toward the end of a game. The first few hours were all right, but after a while the strain of catching the thoughts and emotions of five other minds took its toll, and it was rare for me to finish one of those sessions without a skull-buster. A few more hands and it was over. There was no bragging from the winners, no moaning from the losers. Those people had too much money, power, and pride to show feelings in public. I doubt that they showed them in private. I could have peeked, but I wasn't curious. I had spent the last twelve hours roaming the ranges of their minds. It was dirty and wearying work, and I had had enough of them.

I went over to the buffet table where Lew and Carlo were waiting, and gave them my chips. It was no secret. Everybody knew that I played on their money. Carlo took the rack without a word or a smile, and went to cash in.

"How much do you figure?" asked Lew.

"About seventy."

"Beautiful." He grinned, and rubbed the back of my neck affectionately. "You're terrific, kid. I don't know how you do it."

He said that after every game, and what he meant was that he would have given everything he owned to know exactly how I did it. He and Carlo knew only that I could win or lose as I pleased. They had been backing my play for about a year, and making good money from it, but they had no idea what was going on. They were totally different types. Lew was an amateur, a dress manufacturer with a taste for the vaguely illicit, who thought of me as a lucky player with a hot system. Carlo knew better, or thought he did. Carlo was a pro, he was wired into the right people. His uncle was John Merlo, who ran a chunk of what once had been the DiLuca family. Uncle John gave Carlo a living—some loan-sharking, some numbers, a piece of a restaurant-supply house—enough to keep him in sharkskin suits and Guccis. With that kind of a wiseguy background he had to figure me for a cheater, and he did, but so far he hadn't been able to work out the scam. Neither of them would have believed me if I had told them the truth.

"You look tired," said Lew. "Have something to eat."

He fixed a plate of ham and eggs for me, but after the first few bites I had to put it aside. The headache was so bad that the taste of food sickened me. I managed a few sips of coffee. As I looked up I saw the girl in angora smiling at me again. Everybody smiles at a winner. At that point I should have probed, seen what she had on her mind, but I didn't. My head was beating badly and the effort would have cost me too much pain. Besides, she looked enough like Nadia that . . . well, I didn't do it. I just nodded.

Lew noticed, and said, "Very neat. You like?"

"You know her?"

He shook his head. "A hooker, maybe?"

"Not likely." Thayer made a point of keeping them out.

"So make a move. You could use the relaxation."

"I could use a hot bath and ten hours in bed by myself."

He shrugged. "Suit yourself, but at your age you ought to have priorities."

Carlo came back with the cash. He gave me my end in an envelope: twenty-five percent of the net, eighteen thousand dollars. He said, "Atlantic City next Tuesday. Allie's game. You gonna make it?"

"Depends," I told him. "Have to look at the schedule."

No argument from Carlo. That was another part of our deal. He and Lew knew that I did other work, although they didn't know what. The other work came first, the poker was a sideline, and they accepted that. If I had told them what my other work was they wouldn't have believed that either.

"Try," said Carlo. "It could be big. All kinds of money coming out of the woodwork in Philly."

"I'll let you know."

Lew walked to the door with me, his arm on my shoulder, his hand massaging the back of my neck. He would have made a great fight manager. "You were terrific tonight," he said. "There's nobody like you. You're one in a million."

He was half right and half wrong. I was one in a million, all right. That's what the statistics said. But there were hundreds of others just like me all over the world. None of them, as far as I knew, played high-stake poker with the heavy hitters. Which was just as well.

While I was waiting for the elevator to take me down I debated what to do with the eighteen large I was carrying. Into the safety-deposit box was the usual, but I was in the mood to blow it somewhere. I figured that I rated it. The date was October fifth. It was my thirtieth birthday, and according to every statistic that had ever been thrown at me there was no chance at all that I would live to be thirty-two.

I stepped out of the Devon and into the real world of nine o'clock in the morning. It was always a shock to make that switch, leaving the self-contained bubble of all-night poker. The traffic on Fifty-seventh Street was heavy and, although the day was clear, the air was already foul. The doorman had his hands full with a line of departing guests waiting for taxis. I started toward Lexington to try my luck there, and after a few steps the girl in the angora sweater fell in beside me.

"Hey there, Mister Slade," she said. She had a nice smile to go with the rest of it. "Need any help?"

Without breaking stride, I said, "Doing what?"

"Celebrating." She made a vague gesture in the air. "Party time, champagne for two, bubbles all over the place."

"Nothing to celebrate."

"Come on, you won big up there. I thought I'd help you spend it." She stopped walking, and I stopped with her. People flowed around us. She looked at my jacket critically. "You should carry it someplace else. It bulges."

"I'll take it up with my tailor." We stood facing each other at the curb. In the daylight she really did look a little like Nadia, enough to provide an illusion. I had been chasing those illusions for months. Again, I should have probed, and again I didn't.

"I can do better than your tailor," she said, and gave me the down-home smile again. She was good at it, just casual enough.

"Why don't we get rid of some of it. Then it won't bulge so much."

"It's nine o'clock in the morning."

"There are always places."

"Sorry, not interested."

"Come on, I know just the place for us." She raised her hand and a cruising cab pulled over to the curb. It pulled over much too quickly. She opened the door and tugged at my arm.

I was going to have to probe after all, and I didn't want to. I knew what it would do to my head. I pushed, and the pain went from temple to temple, then cleared. What I caught was a greedy little mind with only one idea in it. All she wanted was the money. It was nothing political. She tugged at my arm again.

"Let's go," she said, "you won't be sorry."

"I'm sorry already," I said, and I was. For her. There was still a chance to get her out of it. I shook my arm free, and moved back. "Maybe some other time."

"No, now. Look down."

I looked. The cab driver grinned up at me from his window. He was young, with a thin and pallid face. He had his cap in his hand. He moved the cap enough for me to see the snub .38 behind it. He said, "Get in."

I looked back at the girl. She had her hand in her purse. She tilted it so that I could see the glint of the pocket pistol there. She said, "Move."

"Do yourself a favor," I told her. "Get out of this. You don't know what you're into."

The driver said quietly, "Move it or I'll do you right here in the street."

"Why don't you just take the money? You don't want me."

It was a sensible suggestion, but it was too late for that. Jaspers stepped out of the crowd that flowed around us. His hand came down on the girl's wrist, and he squeezed. He had a hand like a vise. A scream started up in her throat; he had broken some bones. While he was doing that, Childress came

10

into the front of the taxi from the street side and took out the driver, one arm around his neck and the other hand plucking the pistol. Jaspers took the girl's purse away. He threw her into the back seat of the cab. She was moaning in pain, and people were looking. Jaspers got in beside her, and closed the door. He ignored the people on the sidewalk.

He said through the window, "There's a black Chevvy parked about a hundred feet back. Get into it."

I was supposed to move, but I didn't. I looked at the girl crumpled up in the back seat of the cab. In the front seat, Childress had moved behind the wheel; the driver was slumped beside him. Two hustlers in over their heads. They had been after the money, nothing more. And she had looked something like Nadia.

"Mister Slade," said Jaspers. "Move please."

Jaspers wasn't happy with me. He knew that the government spent as much to protect me as it cost to build a jet fighter. He also knew that if the jet crashed they could always build a new one, but they couldn't build another Ben Slade.

I went up the street to the black Chevvy, and got in. It was Harry Kourkalis behind the wheel. He was my control, but he had no business tagging along with my security people. I said, "What the hell are you doing here?"

"Just wanted to get some air."

"Bullshit."

He shrugged. He was short and pudgy, and he always looked sloppy no matter how carefully he dressed. He was my age, but he looked ten years older. He had been my control for almost two years, and we got along as well as could be expected. I could have probed to find out why he was there, but I was too tired to care. He was a deuce sensitive, a failed ace. He could build a block to keep me out, but not for long. No deuce could block an ace for long. But I was tired, and it was considered a point of honor not to probe your control. I had done it with Kourkalis, but not often, and not now.

He sat staring straight ahead, his fingers tapping the rim of the wheel. He said, "That was a little too close. Why didn't you probe her?"

"I did."

"Not right away. It would never have gotten that far if you had."

I told him how tired I was. I told him about the headaches. I didn't tell him that the girl looked like Nadia. He didn't know anything about Nadia, not that way. He said, "You should have probed right away. You know the routine."

I put my head back. "Screw the routine, and screw you, too." We passed the spot where the cab had been. It was gone. "It was a straight hold-up, nothing political. I was carrying a bundle and she knew it. I got that much when I probed her."

"And the cab just happened to be there?"

"It was a set-up. She's been casing me. I've seen her around before."

He accepted that with a grunt. "It doesn't make any difference. Even a holdup, if they had grabbed you. . . ." He let it dangle.

"They didn't."

"But they could have." It was one of the Ten Commandments. No one got hold of a sensitive . . . no one. We knew too much; we were prizes to be plucked.

"Harry, leave it alone, will you? My head is killing me."

He glanced over at me with a measure of concern. I was his responsibility. "You got any bombers at home?"

"A couple. I'll take one when I get there. What's going to happen to those two?"

He kept his eyes on the traffic as he made a right turn to go uptown on Park. He said, "That's a dumb question coming from a superbrain like you."

That was a typical comment from an ace to a deuce, always the needle about brain power. But the question had been dumb, indeed. We both knew what would happen to them. They would

12

be pumped, and then they would be eliminated, painlessly. Painless for them, and painless for the people who did it. The people who did it were long past that sort of pain.

"You driving me home?" I asked.

He nodded. "I've ordered backup security. They should be in place by the time we get there."

"I have a stop to make first."

We stopped at the corner of Sixty-fourth and Park, and he waited there while I went into the Transcontinental Security building where they have the twenty-four hour safe-deposit service. A uniformed guard brought me my box. Every dollar I had won through Lew and Carlo was in that box, close to four hundred thousand. I had never spent any of it; the Center paid me more than I needed. I fingered today's envelope and thought how senseless it all was. There was more money in that box than I could spend in a lifetime now that, at the age of thirty, my life expectancy had less than two years to go. The urge to spend recklessly was still on me, but I slipped the envelope into the box before I could change my mind.

I went out to the car and let Kourkalis drive me home. Home was a luxury high-rise on East Seventy-fifth Street where the average apartment rented for more each month than an Egyptian shoemaker made in a lifetime. It had all the adornments of Upper East Side living: a health club on the roof with a pool, sauna, and gym; a regiment of staff; and enough crystal, chrome, and carpeting in the lobby to redecorate Radio City Music Hall. The management frowned on children, pets, and poverty. It was a cold and sterile place, without the semblance of a soul, and it suited me just fine.

Kourkalis left the car with the doorman and went up with me. He wanted to see me safe in bed. Trouble was, the bed was occupied. Whoever she was, she was fast asleep, burrowed into the blankets. Angela something. I thought she had gone home. I poured a pony of cognac and stood at the living room window looking down at the world while Harry got her up, got her dressed, and got her out. She wasn't happy about going, and he had his hands full. I began to remember what she looked like. Just a touch like Nadia. Most of them had looked that way recently, a pale reminder of the real thing. It was a bad joke to be in love with the one woman in the world I could not be with, could not touch, could not even speak to. Nothing to laugh about, falling in love with a Russian ace.

I heard the front door close, Harry shooing Angela out. I went to the medicine cabinet in the bathroom and checked my supply of bombers. I had three left. They were jet-black pills the size of small marbles, and the Center doctors gave them out sparingly. They were only for sensitives, and only for when your headache hit eight on the Richter scale. They tasted awful, but they took effect in ten minutes and put you out cold for twelve hours.

"Take one and get into bed." Kourkalis stood in the bathroom doorway.

"Shortly, mother, shortly."

I went to the bedroom, stripped down to shorts, put on a robe, and went back inside juggling the bomber in my hand. I poured another cognac. Alcohol was contraindicated with a bomber, but I didn't know of a single ace who took them with water. I swallowed it, made a face, and said, "Okay, Harry, you can go now. It's down."

He was in no hurry to leave. He wandered about my living room examining the chrome and Lucite decor—the venetian glass tables, the grey velour upholstery, and the sausage-like sofa. The walls were hung with montages of *New Yorker* covers, with Greek prints, and with two pseudo Rothkos. None of it belonged to me. Everything was rented from a shop on Madison Avenue that turned out the ambience like cookies from a cutter. Kourkalis had seen it all before, just as he had seen the bedroom with the opulent wallpaper and the erotic statuary, the electronic kitchen, and the studio where I played at being a weekend painter. He knew the way I lived. He knew about the

14

poker action, the booze and the coke, and the constant stream of casual women that flowed in and out of my life. It was a style encouraged by the Center. Aces were supposed to live it up to the hilt, taking what they could for as long as they could. It was one of the paybacks, and it was official policy. Kourkalis knew that, but still he shook his head as he looked around the room. He lived in a split-level house in Great Neck. He had a wife, a child, two cars, and a cat. He had a mortgage. He had crabgrass. He had a home.

He said, "I don't know how you can live like this."

It was another deuce comment, typically insensitive. He would have been living the same way in my position. Who the hell is going to put down roots when you know that your statistical life expectancy is thirty-one years and four months?

"You beginning to feel it?" he asked.

I was. The bomber was buzzing me. I lay down on the couch.

"Better get into bed."

"No, I'll be all right. I sleep here half the time."

He sat down opposite me. My brain was starting to go numb, and his face looked misty to me. It was a face filled with concern, and I knew then that it wasn't because of my headache. It wasn't because of the holdup, either. It had to be something deeper than that, and I suddenly realized what it was.

"Ben," he said, "I've got some bad news for you."

"Yeah. Which one died?"

"I wanted to tell you myself."

My eyes were heavy. "Who?"

"Big John."

"When?"

"Last night. No pain, he just went. Pop was there with him."

"Good." Pop was always there when one of us went. He would be there for me, too.

"Services tomorrow at the Center. We'll go down together on the shuttle. I'll pick you up in the morning. About eight."

I closed my eyes.

"Ben, you hear me?"

"Yes. Around eight."

I felt myself slipping. So he was gone. Big John Brodski, a sensitive, an ace, and a sweetheart of a friend. He had lived thirty-one years, two months, and a couple of days, just under the average. And Harry Kourkalis, the insensitive deuce, had come to tell me himself, and had waited until I had swallowed a bomber to ease the pain for me.

"Harry?"

"Yes?"

"You're a sly son of a bitch, you know that?"

"Go to sleep."

I went.

2

OURKALIS picked me up the next morning at eight, and we flew the shuttle from LaGuardia down to Washington. My head was clear by then. The bomber I had taken the morning before had kept me under until almost midnight, and then had come a stretch in the rooftop sauna and some time on the weights in the gym. After the weights and a dose of steam I was able to sleep naturally until seven in the morning. I had not eaten in twenty-four hours. I put away a lumberjack's breakfast of bacon and beans, and was ready to roll by the time that the doorman rang up to say that Harry was waiting in the lobby.

He had a company car to take us to the airport, the usual black Chevrolet with an Agency driver. We were barely settled into the back seat when he pulled a folder from his briefcase, glanced at it, and said, "What do you know about chips?"

"Depends on the game," I said. "The other night at Thayer's place the blues were worth a thousand, the reds were five hundred, and we used the whites to tip the waiters."

"Bright eyes," he said patiently, "I mean computer chips,

microchips, the memory things. What do you know about them?"

"Why the quiz?"

"Do you know anything?"

"Just what everybody knows. They're made of silicon, they handle bundles of information in split seconds, and the way things are today we can't live without them. Why?"

"I've been ordered to brief you on the subject."

"Again, why?"

He shook his head. "All I know is that they handed me the file and said to make sure that you knew what was in it by the time we got to the Center."

So it was a business trip as well as a funeral. I was suddenly tired again. "All right, let's have it."

He gave me the file. There wasn't much to it, two sheets of paper, the cover stamped with the usual classification symbols. I said, "You call this a file?"

"That's what they gave me." He was being unusually patient. "Read it, please."

I skimmed through the opening paragraph, which told me what I already knew about computers and memory chips. Then:

The density of the computer chip is what determines how much memory it can handle. Right now the highest density chip on the market contains about four hundred and fifty thousand transistors crammed into an area four millimeters square, with a spacing between the elements of 1.5 microns. With new materials such as gallium arsenide and new techniques for etching circuits, it may ultimately be possible to produce chips four times denser, with a spacing of about. . . .

I started skimming again. Cutting through the technical talk, the gut of it seemed to be that we had just about run out of room on computer chips. The demand for more memory capacity per chip was constantly rising, and in the foreseeable future the conventional silicon chip would be unable to handle the load. The need was for something new, something radically different. Not just a denser and more efficient silicon chip, but a new material entirely. A new concept. A chip with almost infinite capacity. A chip made of . . . ? I read that part again. A chip made of protein?

. . . known as biochips. Research from the field theorizes a computer of the future in which the silicon transistors would be replaced by large organic molecules of genetically engineered proteins which would offer two distinct advantages over current devices. A vastly increased density of computing elements, and an entirely new style of data processing. Several types of biochips have been suggested, the most radical of which would produce an analog chip employing enzymes as the computing elements. Since enzymes have a large number of conformational states, they would be capable of entirely new forms of computation. The development of such a chip would radically alter not only the world of computers, but the very way in which we live our lives.

I tried to visualize a computer chip made of the same stuff as a cell in the human body, the human brain. I visualized neurons flashing electrical discharges between molecules in the brain at a speed that no computer could ever achieve. I visualized a molecular chip that would add another dimension to man-made computers, linking each circuit to an infinite number of its neighbors. I visualized a molecular computer with the potential brain power of a man. It was quite a vision.

Then came the kicker. According to the file we were decades away from this wonderland of molecular computers. It was all theoretical at this point. There was no practical application. Statements from the leading people in the field agreed that

19

researchers were just beginning to think about how molecules might be designed into functional-logic switches. There was nothing to get excited about.

I gave the file back to Harry, and said, "What else can you tell me about this?"

"Nothing. Everything I know is in the file."

"It doesn't make sense. Why brief me on something that isn't going to happen for years, if ever?" Years after I'm dead, I thought.

He pointed to a marking on the file that I had not noticed. It was designated as part one of two parts. They had given him half a file, standard procedure when the lid was on. Which meant that it was hot. He said, "They'll probably give you part two at the Center."

"Harry, do you ever get the feeling that people don't trust you?"

"Regularly," he said, unoffended. "It used to bother me, but not anymore. The less I know, the better I sleep."

I read the file over one more time, and then put it out of my head before we reached the airport. Martha Marino met us there, another ace going back to the Center for Big John's service. Martha's primary job was counterintelligence, reading the heads of high-level Agency people for signs of potential subversion, but she also worked as a hostage negotiator. We had known each other since we were twelve years old. I sat with her during the flight, and Harry took a seat down the aisle. He knew when to leave two aces alone. It was a silent flight, a time for memories, but not for mourning. Martha and I had been trained not to mourn. We stayed within our private thoughts of Big John Brodski, and I remembered how it had been half a lifetime ago when we all had been kids at the Center together. I remembered the innumerable games of chess with John, the string quartets that were his passion, and the way that he could devour an entire chicken at one sitting. I remembered debates through the night, teenage rhetoric, doubts that we shared, fears and promises. I remembered his kindness, his stubborn strength, and his firm conviction that the way we were spending our lives was not only moral, but morally appropriate for the times in which we lived. We argued a lot about that part of it.

I remembered him as best I could and, true to my training, I did my best not to mourn for him. Martha sat wrapped in thoughts of her own. She had been part of that long-ago string quartet, the cellist, and I realized that now with Big John gone she was the only one left. All the others had been senior to her. Now, at thirty, she was senior and her time was coming. As was mine. She spent the flight staring out the window, and it was only when we were about to land that she turned, a calm smile on her face, and opened her mind to me.

He was one in a million, she thought.

"Yes," I said aloud, pleased that she had used the phrase that meant so much to all of us. We were, each of us, one in a million statistically, but when we used those words they stood for more than numbers. We flew the phrase like a flag, it was our pride that we were one in a million. Pop had taught us to think that way, just as he had taught us not to mourn. The two concepts had been woven into the fabric of our lives, starting back on that day when Pop had told us for the first time how things were going to be. Just as he had told it to others before us. There were five of us that day, those who had turned seventeen during the previous year, and by the standards of the Center we were ready to come of age. We had a fair idea, by then, of what we were. We knew that we were psychic freaks with a talent beyond explanation. We knew that we were the aces; the deuces had been weeded out by then. We knew that we were something special. What we did not know was the price we would have to pay for that special talent.

It was Pop's job to tell us that part of it, explaining Rauschner's Syndrome. It was a sad job, and a delicate one. He had to tell us that Rauschner's was a neurological disorder that we had been born with, that there was no cure for it, and that the survival rate was zero. That the blessing which had given us our rare abilities eventually would kill us. Some sooner, some later, but no one with Rauschner's had ever lived past the age of thirty-two. We were all going to die young and it was Pop's job to tell us that, to destroy all hope in one breath, and in the next to rekindle it by showing us how the years we had left could be lived joyously, fruitfully, and with a satisfaction particularly our own. I don't know of anyone else in the world who could have done it except Pop Mickelson.

It was thirteen years ago, but I remembered the day clearly, the five of us sitting in Pop's shabby, paper-stacked office in a nervous semicircle, knowing only that we were about to hear something of deep importance to us. We five were brothers and sisters within the Center, bound far more closely to each other than we ever had been bound to blood brothers and sisters. Sammy Warsaw was the eldest; then Claudia Wing, whom we all called Snake; Vince Bonepart; Martha Marino; and me, Ben Slade, the youngest. And there was Pop, leaning his gangly frame against his desk, his bald head gleaming and his untidy goatee twisted in knots. He gave it to us as straight as he could, the sadness like scars on his face.

"Those are the facts," he said, "and there is nothing I can tell you that will change them. If you believe in God, then you can assume that you are the product of His divine preference. If you don't believe, then you can think of yourself as a biological accident. Either way, never forget that you are one in a million. You've been granted an extraordinary gift, but your good luck and your bad luck are tied together. That works both ways. You're going to die young, but on the other hand you're never going to grow old. You'll never know the pain of lost youth. You'll never know the frustration of middle age. You'll never know the loneliness of the elderly. You are going to live at the height of your powers, and you are going to die the same way."

22

He paused, his eyes searching for our understanding. He said, "And speaking of dying, remember this. Usually when people die there's a lot of weeping and wailing that goes on. All right, I have no quarrel with that, but the custom of mourning applies to normal people, not to you. You're beyond that sort of thing, and I want you all to promise me right now that when the time comes and one of you dies, that there won't be any grieving around here. Understand? You are not to mourn for those of you who die. Not ever."

He leaned back, his fingers combing absently through his beard. "Look at it this way. When the sun sets on a perfect day, a day that's been one in a million, only a fool regrets that it's over. The day was here, now it's gone, and the wise person remembers the joy of that day, not the sadness of the sunset. Well, that's the way it's going to be with you. You're going to have one perfect day, one that should never be mourned, and you're going to live that day in dignity, in contentment, and with pride in the knowledge that you truly are one in a million."

There was a car waiting for us at National Airport to take us down to the Center in Virginia, another black Chevrolet with an Agency driver. All of our low-level personnel came to us from the Agency, and they tended to be neat, industrious, and dull. They did not mix well with the types from the Center who could be described, charitably, as a gang of eccentrics. Even a staid deuce like Harry was a freak compared to the Agency people. This driver looked the part: tall, broad, and easily forgettable. I heard a giggle in the back of my brain, and felt Martha's delicate probe.

Ben, she said, *take a peek at this guy.*

What for?

Just do it.

I looked into his head. The entire forefront of his mind was occupied with a vision of Martha. He had stripped off her clothes and had posed her enticingly. It was quite a sight.

23

Again, that mental giggle from Martha. *My adoring public.*
What do you think?

I think he's nuts. On your best day you never looked that
good.

You're a swine, Ben Slade. No taste, no class.

I flashed her an image of an ancient crone with raddled buttocks and sagging breasts. *How's that for taste and class? Re-*
member, only your buddies will tell you the truth.

She was close enough to pinch my arm, and she did, hard. I
gave her an elbow in the ribs. Harry saw the by-play, and he
frowned. He said, "Let's get serious, we're here for a purpose."

"Never mourn," Martha said cheerfully. We climbed into the
back of the car and let Harry sit up with the driver. He muttered
something about delayed adolescence. I let it go by. It was too
close to the truth to be argued.

We drove out of Washington and south into the Virginia
countryside on Interstate 95. It was a trip I had made many
times. It wasn't my favorite part of Virginia, but any part of
Virginia felt like home. Relaxed for the first time that day, I
closed my eyes and let myself think of Nadia. Bittersweet, always that way when my thoughts were of her. Pain and pleasure
mixed in equal parts: pleasure in the knowledge of our love,
pain in the knowledge of our absolutely hopeless situation. As
I did at least once every day, I allowed myself the momentary
dream that we were ordinary people free to live the lives we
chose. Free to be with each other, to speak to each other, to
love one another. It was a dream, all right, and nothing more.
She worked for a service as demanding as mine, and if either of
us were to show the slightest interest in the other the results
would be . . . unpleasant. Probably fatal. And so we had never
spoken words to each other aloud, never touched hands, never
kissed. We had fallen in love the hard way, the way only aces
can. Head to head. It was a mess, and a sadness that burdened
both of us.

I felt a tentative probe from Martha. She asked, *Something wrong, tus?*

She startled me, using that word. It was what the Russians called their aces, but we all used it at times. I told her, *No, nothing.*

I got the saddest feeling coming off you just now. A storm of it.

Not from me.

Yes, you. It made me want to cry.

Sorry, it must have been something I ate.

If you need any help. . . ?

Give me a break, tus. Forget it.

A mental sigh is the palest blue, a breath of faint color. She sighed that way. *All right, if that's what you want.*

I kept my mind blank for the rest of the trip. We passed the Marine base at Quantico, and left the Interstate near Fredricksburg, following the state road southeast with the Rappahannock on our left and the Nathan Bedford Forrest Military Reservation on our right. We skirted the perimeter of the reservation edging southward, and then turned onto the dirt road marked by the faded sign that read: *Federal Center for the Study of Childhood Diseases—Authorized Personnel Only.*

From the turnoff we could see the first of the manned gates and the tops of the buildings, and the feeling of coming home grew stronger. It was a rolling excitement, constantly expanding. It was a childlike glee, birthday time and Christmas joined into one. Coming back to the Center was like no other feeling in the world. Martha felt it too, she gave off waves of it. She grinned at me, and squeezed my hand. I flashed her a scene of two little bluebirds winging home to the nest. She made a rude noise and flashed back an image of a pigeon dropping pellets on my head, but she couldn't stop grinning. It was always that way for all of us, coming back. The Center was the only true home we had ever had. Before the Center we had madness.

Pop found Martha in a home for retarded children in Omaha. She had been there for a year. She heard voices in her head that no one else could hear. When she heard the voices she went wild. She screamed for hours, she clawed her body, she soiled herself. When Pop found her she was under constant restraint and sedation. She was twelve years old.

Pop found Vince in a drug-abuse center in Boston. Vince also heard the voices. His parents had abandoned him when he was seven, and after that he had lived in the streets and in the odd corners of the city. He learned from his elders how to steal and how to shoot smack. The smack kept the voices quiet. When Pop found him he had been placed in a drug-withdrawal facility, and the voices were back and filling his head with their howls. He was twelve years old.

Pop found Claudia in a religious commune in Idaho. The members of the group worshiped snakes. They also worshiped Claudia. When Claudia heard the voices she went into a trance and made hissing noises. That, to the members of the commune, made her part of the godhead, a higher form of snake. They kept her in a cage and fed her what the snakes ate. When Pop found her she had not spoken a word in months, and she moved by slithering across the floor on her belly. She was twelve years old.

Pop found Sammy in an expensive sanitarium north of New York City. His parents had placed him there. He was catatonic, incapable of voluntary movement. He could not speak, and his limbs remained fixed in whatever position they were placed. His eyes stared straight ahead, unblinking. He had been that way since he first heard the voices. He was twelve years old.

Pop found me locked in the back bedroom of a shack in Freeman, Texas, just south of the Oklahoma line. The room had a bed, a chair, and a slop bucket. I was chained to the bed, and I was naked. My body was covered with old scars and fresh welts. The man I called my daddy said that the voices I heard were the tongues of the devil. He was a shade-tree mechanic and a part-time preacher, and he knew about devils. At the end of each day he whipped the devil out of me with a razor strop, and then prayed for my deliverance. When Pop found me I could not stand or sit, and my body was a festering wound. I was twelve years old.

That's what we were, my generation at the Center, when Pop found us. Other generations, before us and after, came from the same sort of background: the abused, the imprisoned, the seemingly mad. In my year, Pop found seven kids. One died before he could be gotten to the Center, and another later turned out to be a deuce. Seven was high for one year, but the accepted statistic was one sensitive for every million of population, and the overall ratio never changed.

Pop got his kids any way he could. Some he bought, some he borrowed, some he stole. I was bought, a straight cash transaction to get me away from the religious maniac who whipped me every night with a prayer on his lips. Martha, Sammy, and Vince were borrowed from their various institutions, happily turned over to the Federal Center for the Study of Childhood Diseases for experimental treatment. They were borrowed, but never returned. Claudia was literally stolen, lifted out of her community of crazies in a nighttime raid that was planned and mounted by the Agency. One way or another, Pop usually got what he wanted.

Once at the Center we were cleansed, we were nourished, we were treated, we were loved, and we were taught how to live with the voices in our heads. They were the voices of the world around us. The lust of the satyr, the sloth of the slob, the greed of the avaricious, the jealousy of the discontented, the righteousness of the fanatic, the despair of the helpless, the flaring orange delight of the arsonist, and the screaming crimson impulses of the psychopathic murderer . . . those were the voices that had howled around within our heads like winds in a cavern, and had blown us away into another world.

Were we cured? How do you cure a kid who once thought

she was a snake? It took time and care before Claudia no longer hissed and slithered. It took time to get Sammy out of his catatonic state and Vince away from his drug dependency. It took time with Martha and me. Were we cured? Of what? It was years before we were able to venture into the outside world, but we accepted that limitation cheerfully. Compared to what had gone before, the Center was Eden to us, and we had no desire to leave it. That feeling would continue for the rest of our lives, and once we were grown it would make every homecoming an occasion of joy.

"Home," murmured Martha. "Over the river and through the woods to grandmother's house we go."

"Home," I agreed. "What's a grandmother?"

The Agency car negotiated the narrow road that led to the manned gate into the Center. We left the car at the gate and were passed through on foot. The car and driver stayed behind. Only Center personnel could clear that gate; Agency people stayed on the other side of the wire. On their side were the barracks, the motor pool, and the security headquarters; all squat and functional buildings. On our side were the fieldstone and ivy-covered structures of the Center: the separate living quarters for aces and deuces, the double-winged administration building, the mess hall and lounge, the long, low block of the hospital and research complex, the athletic fields and swimming pools.

At first sight, the place looked more like a small-town college than anything else, and with good reason. No matter what the signs said, our side of the wire had only one function, the study of the talent and the disease that afflicted us. The Federal Center for the Study of Childhood Diseases was a fiction to discourage the curious, and the actual workings of the Center was classified information. Aside from our own people, only a selected few at the Agency, the State and Defense departments, and the White House, even knew of our existence. It was the same with the other countries that used sensitives: the research center was always affiliated with the intelligence branch of the government. It had to be that way. In our case the budget at the Center ran into more money than any institution in the private sector could handle. Only the government could afford to pick up our tab, and that meant the CIA. The Agency and the Center had been joined hip and thigh for over thirty years in a love-hate relationship that was often strained but never broken.

The layout of the Center showed the nature of that relationship. We were on the inside of the fence, and they were on the outside. They were very much in control. In exchange for all the money, in exchange for the Center, in exchange for our existence, we worked for them. They owned us, every single one of us. Just as the KGB owned Nadia.

3

TRIED to keep my mind on the memorial service to come as I walked up the quiet, tree-lined drive that led to the heart of the Center. It wasn't easy. My thoughts kept drifting off to Nadia, and to the card she had sent me on my thirtieth birthday. That was the evening before the poker game at Thayer's place. She had not sent it by mail; that would have been impossible. Her mail was screened, and so was mine. She had sent it the only way that she could: head to head, from ace to ace.

That evening we were both at the Hungarian Mission to the United Nations attending a reception for a trade delegation from the Soviet Union. It was the usual bash, plenty of food and booze. Nadia and I were both working, standing on opposite sides of a room filled with high- and middle-level members of the diplomatic community. I was covering an Assistant Secretary of State up from Washington for informal trade talks with his opposite number from the Soviet Union, and I had spent most of the evening inside the Russian's head. He seemed straight. From what I could read he sincerely wanted an easing off of trade restrictions and he was willing to give up points to get it. I didn't take his sincerity too seriously. Often, when they knew that a sensitive was likely to be present, they would send in a dodo, someone with only a superficial understanding of the situation, someone who was able to be sincere because he didn't know any better. So I discounted the sincerity. It was an old ploy, and our side used it, too. Besides, my job was to report, not to judge. Nadia's job was the same for her people. She was on to the man from State.

Happy birthday, darling. Her thought came to me from across the room. *I have a card for you, something special.*

You shouldn't have bothered, I told her. My back was to her as I waited at the bar for a drink. The crowd swirled around me in the aimless circles of a cocktail party. *I'm not very big on birthdays this year.*

I glanced across the room to where she was chatting with Paul Forquet, a translator with the French delegation. Her dark hair was up in a crown of glossy braids, and the severe black gown that she wore could not conceal her slender fullness. She was there to work, but she was also there with Forquet. He was a normal, and the latest in the long line of men in her life. The Russian aces were encouraged to live the same way we did. For some reason their life expectancy was even lower than ours by about a year. Thus, Nadia was a year younger than I, but according to the charts we had the same length of time left. Forquet was one of the ways that she passed the time. He wouldn't last long, they never did with her. I wasn't jealous. What she had with Forquet had nothing to do with what we had together.

Are you ready for your card? she asked. She was well trained. She was talking with Forquet, and at the same time she was tuned in on the man from State, she was sending to me, and she was sweeping the room for other sensitives. There were no others. I had done my own sweeping.

I said, *Go ahead, let's have it.*

She flashed it to me. It was a scene from her childhood, a

golden wheat field with the heads of grain bowed by a rippling wind. Off in the distance were the lines of a city masked by a purple haze, and closer by was a river that wound through the fields. The river was the Oka, and the city was Orel. It was sunset time, and a teenage Nadia sat on the riverbank, her face lifted to the sky and her eyes closed. There was a look of peace on her face, and of expectation.

It was repayment in kind. Under similar circumstances I had given her a card for her last birthday, a scene from my childhood. I had shown her the main street of Freeman, Texas, on a Saturday night: the Post Office, the Methodist Church, the Food Fair, and the Burger King; the pool hall, the movie house, three bars, and the Dairy Queen. Pickup trucks in the parking lot, low riders dragging the strip, and a boy in jeans leaning against a lamp post and trying to look as if he belonged.

Both scenes, hers and mine, were frauds. I had never stood on any such corner on a Saturday night. My childhood had gone directly from the hell of that back bedroom and razor strop to the haven of the Center. Nor had a teenage Nadia ever sat in the fields and watched the sun go down over the Oka. She had been placed in a mental institution at the age of six, and eventually had wound up in the KGB center for sensitives at Gaczyna, southeast of Kuibyshev. Still, as frauds the cards were pleasant fabrications, and for two people who could not exchange gifts, or even speak to each other, they made an acceptable substitute. I admired mine, and I told her so. I saw Forquet bend close to her and whisper in her ear.

I asked, *What does that lecher want now?*

About what you might expect at this time of the evening.

You don't sound thrilled about it.

Paul is all right. It's just that . . . you know.

Yes, I knew. It was the same for both of us. The fun and the parties were only that: mindless fun, and parties that quickly grew stale. The only satisfaction for us lay in what we could not have. If we ever were to make the slightest move toward each other, at any time or place, we would wind up dead. Her security, or mine, would see to that.

Ben? Sorry, can't talk for a while. Have to concentrate.

Which meant that she had to pay attention to the man from State. She was reading his head in English, but she could have read him in any language that he chose to use. We all could. We were not trained as linguists, but we could speak any tongue by reading it off the subject's head. It saved a lot of time.

I watched Nadia at work. There had been a time when that would have bothered me, seeing the other side tune in on one of our people, but not any more and not just because of Nadia. I had been at it long enough to realize that we were all in the same business, and that we had more in common with each other than with the people who ran us. It was all part of the game. All the aces called it a game, no matter what their nationality. The game was the work that we did to earn our keep, the services that we performed for the intelligence organizations that ran our lives. We took the assignments and we used our talents as best we could. We produced results, but we did not take it seriously. I had never known a patriotic ace, or one motivated by a particular ideology. We left that part of it to the people who ran us. They had a lifetime in which to be patriots. All we had was thirty years, just enough time to play it as a game without letting it touch us. There was too much true evil in it, and too much tragedy, to play it any other way. It was just a game.

The reception ground along the stretch from six to eight. The action at the bar thinned out as people began to make plans for the rest of the evening. The man from State and the Russian delegate wound up their conversation and agreed to meet again on a formal basis. The Russian left first and my assignment was over. The man from State went looking for his coat and I heard Nadia's call.

Ben?

Here.

Sorry, darling, time to go.

So soon?

Paul has a table booked somewhere.

I see.

Across the room, Forquet was helping her into her coat. She looked over her shoulder, smiling up at him. He grinned back. They made an attractive couple. He said something to her that I did not hear. I could have heard it, but I didn't. There were times when it paid not to peek.

Good night, Ben, she called. *And a happy birthday.*

Good night, Nadia Petrovna. Thanks for the card.

She started to leave. I had watched her do that so often, march out of a place on someone else's arm. It was a sight I had become accustomed to. You can get used to almost anything.

Nadia.

Yes? She kept on walking.

Don't go.

What's this?

Don't go just yet. Stay a little longer with me.

But I must. . . .

Get rid of Forquet. Tell him that you'll meet him later. Just stay for a while.

It was not a wise move, but she did not hesitate. She turned and said something to Forquet. He frowned, and said something back. There was a brief argument, then he nodded, turned away, and walked out. Nadia slipped out of her coat. She went to a chair against the wall and sat in it. She folded her coat in her lap. She was facing away from me. I leaned against the opposite wall. I was careful not to look at her.

I'm here, she said. *Did you want to say something?*

No, just to be with you. For as long as they'll let us.

All right.

We sat that way, doubly silent, far apart but together. The dregs of the reception swirled around us, but we did not notice that. We sat until the dregs were gone, until the bar was closed, and the waiters had taken away the last of the food. We did not move through all of that. Nadia broke the hush between us. I felt the burgeoning thought before she formed the words.

She said, *I have something to tell you.*

You're going away.

Yes. You felt it?

Yes. When?

Tomorrow. It's a temporary assignment. I don't know how long I'll be gone.

You were going to leave without telling me?

It seemed better that way. But now, sitting here like this. . . .

I did not ask where she was going. We did not ask questions like that of each other. We could not. Nor was it important. She was going away, that was all that mattered. We didn't have much together, only evenings like these. They meant a lot to me, and now she was going away.

I'm sorry, darling, she said. *Orders. No choice.*

I understand. In our crazy world it was actually understandable.

With any luck it won't be for long. She stood up. From across the room she looked directly at me, her eyes on mine. It was something she never did. She said, *I love you, Ben. Damn this. All of it. Damn it.*

She walked quickly out of the room. I gave her time to clear the building, and then went out onto the street. She was gone. Jaspers and Childress were waiting for me. They were never far away. They followed me to Thayer's suite at the Devon where I sat through the night playing cards, won eighteen thousand for myself, and twenty-four hours later flew down to the Center to attend the memorial service for Big John Brodski.

The service was held in the mess hall; services always were. There was a modern auditorium in the complex, but Pop would not use it for services. He didn't like talking down to us from a stage at a funeral. In the mess hall we were all on the same level. The coffin was up front, and it was almost always an open coffin. The final effects of Rauschner's Syndrome weren't pretty to see. The skin turned blue, and striations appeared on the face and neck. Pop wanted us to see that, to know what we had waiting for us. It was all part of that one perfect day.

The aces sat together on one side of the room. I did a quick head count. Including Martha and me, there were fifty-two of us. Sixteen were on active duty, and thirty-six were still in training. That meant that twelve other active-duty aces were absent, their stations too far away to allow for the trip. All of my gang had made it. Sammy was stationed in Washington, and Vince in London, and so it had been easy for them. Not so for Snake. She was based in Pakistan doing liaison work with the Afghan rebels, and she had traveled all day and all night to be there. Mental greetings flew as Martha and I came in, all coarse and uncomplimentary. None of this showed on their faces. Along with the other aces they sat staring straight ahead, their hands folded primly in their laps. It was a sure sign that something was going on. I took a look into their collective heads and saw that they had constructed a mental tribute to Big John, each mind contributing a detail. It was a funeral wreath in the shape of a map of the state of California. John had been big on California. He had, in fact, been tiresome about it. The aces were being careful not to mourn.

Martha and I found seats with our people, but Harry went over to the other side of the room. The few deuces around never sat with us. They stayed with the normals, most of whom were doctors and technicians at the hospital and research center. The senior doctor was old Ian Gregory. He had been at the Center almost as long as Pop had. He sat up front talking with Roger Delaney, the only outsider in the room. The rules said no outsiders, but the rules did not apply to Delaney. He owned the place. He was DD3 at the Agency, the Deputy Director for Science and Technology. He controlled our finances, our security, and our assignments. He could close us down any time he felt like it. Not easily, but he could do it. With that kind of power it was inevitable that he and Pop would be in constant conflict. The conflict was not a secret, and Delaney was not a popular person at the Center.

Pop stood up to get our attention. He seemed older every time I saw him now. The sharp blue eyes were still clear, and his jaw was firm, but everything else about him spoke of age. He was over seventy. He stood and waited for us to quiet down. The quiet came quickly, an oral hush in the room and a mental hush as well as all the aces put up blocks. It was both a tradition and a form of respect that we showed to Pop. There was no mental communication in his presence.

"Well, here we are again," he said. There was a quaver in his voice but it carried to the corners of the room. "As you know, we don't gather here to grieve but to remember a friend. Actually, I sometimes wonder why we bother with these so-called services. There's nothing religious about this organization, and we really don't have to gather like a swarm of bees to pay our respects to someone we loved. We each could do it in our own way and time, but it's a custom of the Center and I guess it serves a purpose. Gives us a chance to say hello to old friends, gets certain people away from the fleshpots of the outside world, if only for a day. So let's get on with it, no black crepe, just some recollections of John Brodski. He had his one perfect day, and now it's over. Let's remember the day, and not the sunset. Is there anyone who wants to speak about that day?"

Pop looked over at our gang. Big John had been the last survivor of the year ahead of ours. There was no one left from his year to say the words, and so the job belonged to the five of us. We looked to Sammy. Frizzy-haired, beaky-nosed, ears like the wings of a bat, he was our eldest and had always been our leader. He was also, without competition, the brightest among us. Just as Vince was the strongest, Snake the most daring, and Martha the kindest. Sammy nodded to Vince.

When I first knew Vince he had been a scrawny black street kid just off a heavy habit and sweating the fight every day. Now he had the profile of an Assyrian god and the body of an NFL linebacker. He stood up, and in a slow voice, said, "I'll make some simple statements. Big John was devoted to the life of the mind. He was wrapped up in Eastern religions. He was a good man, he loved animals. Once, when we were kids, he got lost in the woods and came back to the Center with two racoons for pets." He paused for thought, and added, "In case that sounds too sentimental, let me tell you that John wasn't above cheating at chess. Whenever I played him I had to put up a block. If I didn't, he would sneak into my head and read my moves." He sat down abruptly.

Snake stood up, and said, "I don't have much to add. I'm a better person for having known John Brodski. I'm not religious, but he was, and so I'll say God bless him and rest him. He had one hell of a perfect day. As far as cheating at chess goes, Big John could give Vince a rook and a pawn and beat him with his frontal lobes tied together. Besides, everybody around here cheats at chess."

Martha stood up and told a few stories about Big John and the string quartet. They were moving and funny. When she was finished, she added, "I'd like to mention that there was nothing cute about those racoons. They had a taste for shoes. My shoes."

She sat. Sammy said a few words, and so did I, and then it was over.

"Well done," Pop said briskly. "This service is now concluded. A lot of darn foolishness, anyway. If any of you people can come up with a better idea for a memorial, I'd welcome the suggestion. Okay, that's it. Anybody who wants to stay the night has the hospitality of the house. The bar is open and the usual blind eye will be turned."

The meeting broke into fragments. Sammy and Vince got us a couple of bottles of wine and the five of us went outside to sit on the grass. The other aces did the same, gathering in groups around the lawn. It was something that we did whenever there was a death at the Center. It was the only chance that many of us had to get together and catch up on the news. The other people, normals and deuces, stayed inside and talked about marriages and mortgages. Only Pop came out to walk from group to group, saying hello to his kids.

Sammy poured the wine. He raised his glass in a gesture that was almost furtive, and said, "Big John." We drank. It was the closest we could come to ceremony.

That was the only formal drink, and after that the conversation flowed with the wine. Everybody had a story to tell. We had killed a few of the bottles when Harry wandered out of the mess hall and onto the lawn. He looked around, spotted us, and ambled over. He had a can of beer in his hand. Three of those could sink him, and from the way he was walking that one was his fourth. He stood over us with a fond and vacant expression on his face.

"God bless you," he said. His voice was thick. "You're the senior citizens now. God bless you all."

That wasn't too bad. He had no business coming out on the lawn with the aces, but we had all known Harry for a long time and he hadn't said anything objectionable. But then he raised his beer, and said, "Here's to you, gang. Here's to the next one who dies."

He didn't mean anything by it. He said it the way those old-time fliers would toast themselves before they took off on a mission, but he was out of line. He wasn't one of us, he was a deuce. He got five chilly looks staring up at him.

He lowered his eyes, and muttered, "Yeah, well, you know

what I mean." He dropped the beer can on the grass, and walked away.

Pop saw it happen. He was standing right there. We all jumped up and crowded around him. Spending a few minutes with him was the most important part of coming home. He gave us each an individual hug, and a kiss for the girls.

He said mildly, "Why did you do that to Harry just now?"

It was up to Sammy to answer. He said, "It was nothing, Pop. You know how Harry is. He said something silly."

"I heard what he said." Pop shook his head sadly. "I don't think it was silly, not coming from Harry. You people amaze me sometimes. Have you forgotten who Harry is?"

We had. You get caught up in a world of aces with all the problems involved, and sometimes you forget about the other world. You forget that other people have problems, even deuces. You even forget about the year when you were twelve years old. That was the year when Pop found seven kids, but only the five of us turned out to be aces. One died before they could get him to the Center, and the other turned out to be a deuce. The other turned out to be Harry Kourkalis. You forget.

We looked away from Pop. He touched me lightly on the arm. He said, "Feel like taking a walk with me, son? Little stroll up the hill?"

"Sure, Pop." A stroll up the hill had been a treat when we were kids, a time for confessions, for soothings, for a new birth of hope.

We walked up a slight incline in back of the mess hall to a knoll shaded by trees. From there you could see all of the Center, the Agency area beyond the fence, and beyond that the stretch of meadows and woods. Pop lowered himself gingerly to the ground and sat with his back against a tree. I sat next to him. We were silent for a while looking out over the Center, the buildings and the roads, the pool and the tennis courts, the flagpole rising from its whitewashed base.

Pop said, "Can you imagine what this all looked like in 1955?"

I had heard what he was going to say many times before but, of course, I said, "No, Pop, I can't."

"Couple of Nissen huts, that's all there was. You wouldn't know about them, big drafty things. Those huts, and a couple of trucks and a jeep, that's all I had for myself and the technicians and eight kids. We brought the kids over from Bethesda, where I'd been working with them before I made the deal with the Agency. We bedded them down in those huts and all we had to feed them for a week was bologna sandwiches and lime Kool-Aid. Can you imagine bologna sandwiches three times a day for a week? But after that first week things started to get better."

He went on like that, talking about the early days of the Center, and even before then. Talking about those days before World War Two when he had been a graduate assistant at Duke under J. B. Rhine doing the first primitive tests for ESP. Talking about the war when he had served with the OSS. Talking about those first trips after the war when he had crisscrossed the country looking for kids who were said to hear voices. Talking about the ridicule and rebuffs he had taken from the scientific community. Talking about the deal he had made with the Agency, the founding of the Center, and the hundreds and hundreds of boys and girls who had grown into men and women over the years, all of them his children and all of them both blessed and cursed. He went on that way, talking about how the Agency called the tune these days and how he had to dance to it if he wanted to keep the Center going, the hospital functioning, the research on Rauschner's rolling forward. I began to grin. He was the least devious of men, but there were times when he simply could not spit something out and say it straight.

"Pop, hold it," I said. "Does this have anything to do with computer chips?"

He smiled. "I guess I can be pretty obvious at times. Did Harry brief you?"

"More or less. He couldn't tell me much. Is it a job?"

"It's a job, but not a very pretty one. If it were up to me I wouldn't touch it, but those people. . . ." The tone of his voice left no doubt as to who those people were. "Delaney says that you're the logical choice for the assignment. The only choice, in fact."

"And you want me to do it?"

"Ah, Ben, try to understand. I have to live with those people."

"I'm not complaining. What's it all about?"

"I'd rather that Delaney told you. I'll say only this. It's a thoroughly disgusting and immoral piece of work, and I'm ashamed to ask you to do it."

"How bad can it be? Murder? Arson? Rape?"

"Good Lord, no. All you have to do is play poker."

"That's all? Come on, Pop, there's nothing immoral about playing poker."

"There is the way you play it, son."

"I want you to imagine a world in which there is no hunger and no poverty," said Roger Delaney. "A world in which every person on this planet receives quick and efficient medical care. A world in which every child receives the same high standard of education. A world from which fear and ignorance are banished. A sane and sensible world, a world enhanced by molecular technology." He paused dramatically. "It's the world of the biochip, laddie, the world of the future, and you are going to help to create it."

That was typical Delaney. He used words like *laddie* easily. He wore plaid suits, and ties that looked like carpet samples. He was bluff and hearty, and he affected the air of a no-nonsense outdoor type. He was totally untrustworthy. We sat in Pop's cluttered and shabby office. Pop and Delaney were in deep chairs, while I sprawled all over the couch in an attitude of calculated insolence. It was childish, but it was an agreement among the aces to give Delaney the minimum of respect. It was the least we could do. It was also the most.

I got up and walked over to the window. I could see the lawn in front of the mess hall, and the aces gathered there. The bottles were still going around and some of the troops were passed out flat on the grass. I was pleased to see that my gang was still upright. Sammy was playing his guitar and the others were singing along with him. I wanted to be with them. I did not want to be where I was, listening to Delaney spout off about all the benefits that would accrue to mankind from the development of the molecular computer. I was into his head. It was against the rules and it was against tradition. You didn't do that when Pop was present, but this was one time when it didn't pay to observe traditions. When you dealt with Delaney you needed every edge you could get. So I probed him.

There was a considerable gap between what he was saying and what he was thinking. He was talking about a better way of living, but he was thinking about a better way of killing. His thoughts were filled with thunder. A molecular computer, with circuit elements a thousand times smaller than what we had now, would make the weapons of tomorrow available today. It would bring the big bang that much closer.

That didn't particularly bother me. Like any sane person, I saw the nuclear arms race as the ultimate insanity, but it was all academic to me. The chances were that I would be long dead before the big bang finally came, and so I did not feel personally threatened by a staggering escalation in weaponry. Nor was I concerned for the fate of my loved ones. They were all aces, and they, too, would soon be gone. No, what bothered me about Delaney was his arrogant assumption that he could sell me the molecular computer as a boon to society, and the equally arrogant assumption that I would not probe his head to see what he really was thinking. It was more than a little insulting.

Delaney said to my back, "Am I boring you, Slade?"

I turned to face him. "Bullshit always bores me. Let's stop the crap about benefits to mankind. What you're talking about is advanced weaponry."

There was only one way I could have known that. Delaney's face changed as he realized that I had been in his head. "You're out of line," he said tightly. "You're not allowed to do that. It's contrary to guidelines."

"Relax, I'll never say a word about that girl of yours in Chevy Chase."

He didn't know how to handle that one. He decided to laugh. "Pop, this boy of yours is quite a character."

"Well, Roger, it would help if you didn't underestimate my people," Pop said mildly. "Let's try to do this without too much of the usual razzle-dazzle." To me, he said, "Of course it's weaponry. What else did you expect?"

"A little less razzle-dazzle, I guess."

"Come back here and sit down. Please."

I went back to the couch and sat. Eighteen years of training went into that simple action, as well as eighteen years of love and loyalty. It was all part of the game. Pop looked at me warningly, and said, "You know the rules, stay out of his head."

"Sure. Who is Otto Nordquist?"

"Ben," Pop said sharply.

"Okay, I'm out and I'll stay out. I found Mister Nordquist next to that girl from Chevy Chase, so he must be important."

Delaney sighed. "I guess it makes your day to sass the boss, but can we skip that part of it and get down to business?"

"I have the feeling that Otto Nordquist is part of the business."

"He is." Delaney handed me a folder. It was part two of the biochip file. "It's all in there. Read it. And incidentally, the young lady in Chevy Chase happens to be my niece. She's been quite ill recently, and she's been on my mind."

"I like that," I told him. "Stick with it." I opened the folder, and read.

Biochip/ Part Two of Two
Ref. RJB-3749/27 daily
DD3 selected

SUBJECT: Otto Nordquist. b. 17 May 1918, Stockholm, Sweden
EDUCATION: Univ. of Göteborg, BS, MS, PhD. Honorary degrees, MIT, Harvard, Cal Tech
HONORS: Nobel Laureate, 1980; Cameron Prize, 1976; Man of the Year in Science, 1984; others
OCCUPATION: Prof. of physical sciences, Univ. of Göteborg (ret.)

Character and politics:
Subject is a man of temperate habits, good judgment and character. He is a well-known pacifist. Since young manhood he has been a member of several left-wing organizations (q.v. Appendix A.), and was signatory to the pro-Moscow Stockholm Protocol issued by the communist-front Society of Concerned Scientists.

Despite this, there is no evidence of subject's affiliation or involvement with hard-line communist apparatus. His pacifism is apparently sincere, if misguided, and he has been even-handed in his condemnation of Soviet as well as American weapons development. Since being awarded the Nobel prize in 1980, he has used his international position to call for an immediate nuclear freeze and a universal reduction in military spending and stockpiling.

Family:
Subject was married for forty-two years to Christina Nordquist, now deceased. His son and daughter-in-law also

45

died recently, in an aircraft accident. Subject's only living relative is now his grandson, Arne, age six years. Subject was known as a family man with strong attachments to wife and son. Since death of son four years ago, and wife last year, subject's affection has been concentrated on his grandson.

Work:

Subject is a theoretical biophysicist whose work in recent years has focused on the development of molecular memory chips. (Part One this file.) His work is far in advance of all others in this field. While other research is a decade away from fruition, our information indicates that subject has attained a breakthrough in the design of a workable, if elementary, biochip.

This information is difficult to confirm because of the theoretical nature of subject's work. He does not operate in a laboratory or a classroom, and thus there is no written material to be gathered and examined. Subject is involved in conceptualizing problems and working toward their solution on an intellectual basis that gives no outward indication of the state of progress. Despite this, it has been determined that subject has overcome the primary roadblocks in the field and has made the quantum jump to the realization of the first biochip.

Sources close to the subject, however, state that he categorically refuses to make this information public. As a pacifist and a "pure" scientist, he is fully aware of the military value of his work and is adamantly opposed to seeing it utilized for military purposes. This attitude extends to the Soviet Union as well as to the United States. He has been quoted as saying, "I'll sit on the chip until hell freezes over before I let those bastards use it to drop bombs."

Since the design of the Nordquist biochip exists only in the head of the subject, he is in a position to do just that.

Prognosis:

The acquisition of the Nordquist biochip on an exclusive basis is vital to the national security interests of the United States, since molecular computers would insure this country a weapons superiority that would extend past the year 2000.

Four work options present themselves:

(1) Ideological. Subject has been approached on ideological grounds by both the United States and the Soviet Union with negative results. His only ideology is his pacifism.

(2) Financial. Subject has been approached by both the United States and the Soviet Union with substantial financial offers. These offers have been refused. Subject's only apparent financial concern is his grandson, and his current estate appears to provide for the boy adequately. (Appendix B statement.)

(3) Coercion. Various scenarios based on coercion have been presented, and rejected. All such plans have involved the abduction of the subject, and the subsequent acquisition of information through physical, mental, or chemical coercion. A similar scenario involving the abduction of the subject's grandson has also been presented, and rejected. In all such cases it has been concluded that although the information could almost certainly be obtained in such a manner, the repercussions in the event of public exposure would be politically disastrous. It must be remembered at all times that the subject is a Nobel laureate and a highly respected member of the international scientific community.

(4) Under the circumstances, the only viable course of action appears to be the use of personnel from the Federal Center for the Study of Childhood Diseases.

I closed the file, and said flatly, "It won't work."

"You haven't finished reading," Delaney pointed out.

"I don't have to. This isn't a job for a sensitive."

It was something that the Agency people found difficult to understand, that we were listeners and nothing more. There were so many misconceptions about our abilities. If you listened to some of the stories that they told around the water coolers up at Langley they'd have you believing that an ace could read minds in the Kremlin from a thousand miles away, lift a two-ton truck by sheer willpower, and think himself from Kansas City to San Diego in the blink of an eye. It was all nonsense, born out of ignorance. A sensitive, because of his neurological imbalance, was highly receptive to the thoughts and emotions of others. He could hear those thoughts as if they were spoken. That was all he could do, and he could do it within the range of two hundred feet at the most. All the rest of the talk was wishful thinking. Delaney, of all people, should have known that.

"This man has formulated an abstract theory," I explained, "not some compact formula like A plus B equals C. It's not something that he carries around in his head, thinking about it all the time, and the concept isn't something I would recognize even if he did. You've got the wrong approach to the problem. Even if I could stay within range of Nordquist twenty-four hours a day for a year, I still might not get the information that you're looking for."

Delaney said calmly, "We're aware of that, Slade."

"Then why me?"

Pop said, "Ben, read the rest of the file."

Analysis:

Otto Nordquist has only one apparent weakness. He is a compulsive gambler in the pathological sense of the term. Under certain conditions his urge to gamble is uncontrollable, and at various times in his life he has lost small fortunes at the gaming tables. In the past, the only person capable of exercising control over him was his wife, Christina, who managed to limit his access to funds, and who in other ways prevented him from totally dissipating his wealth. With the death of Christina last year, this control no longer exists.

The subject has just emerged from a period of mourning, and should be considered particularly vulnerable. As in previous years, he plans to spend the winter months at Bled, in Yugoslavia, a traditional spa and resort area with a modern gambling casino. It is expected that the subject will be in attendance at the casino. His game of choice is poker.

Action:

The subject is to be broken, impoverished, and stripped of everything he owns.

The Agency will provide full financial support for the operation, with an unlimited bankroll.

Responsibility for the operation is vested in the Deputy Director for Science and Technology (DD3).

Personnel from the Center recommended for the operation: Benjamin Slade.

I closed the file, and said to Pop, "You were right. It's thoroughly disgusting and immoral."

Pop nodded sadly. Delaney said, "When did you start going to church? Those are noble sentiments coming from a card cheat."

I let that go by. I played cards only with high rollers who could afford to lose to me. Some of them actually enjoyed it. I didn't play cards with suckers who were betting the rent money. Still, I let it go by, and said, "Aside from being immoral, it isn't going to work."

Delaney frowned. "We ran the operation through CYBER. The computer gives it a seventy-six point three percent chance of success."

"Computers play lousy poker. I'd give it less than half of that, maybe thirty percent. There are too many variables. No matter how much of an edge I have, most of the time the guy with the top cards is going to take the hand, and I can't control who holds the cards. Besides, there are usually seven players in a game, more variables. Your computer is too optimistic. Thirty percent, tops."

Delaney said, "But it can be done?"

Sure it could be done. If Nordquist was really a compulsive gambler, one of the poor, sick souls with the glazed eyes and the sweaty palms who delighted in bleeding all over the card table, then it could be done. Nothing could stop those people once they had decided that it was time to lose. They couldn't win against someone like me, and they didn't know when to quit. They didn't know how.

Reluctantly, I said, "It can be done."

"How long should it take?"

I opened the file to the financial statement. Nordquist was worth something over half a million dollars in cash, brokerage accounts, and real estate. I had seen a compulsive gambler lose that much in a weekend at Vegas, but I didn't say that.

"No guarantees. If it works at all it could take a week, or a month, or more."

"Satisfactory. You'll leave for Bled after briefing."

"I haven't said that I'm going."

"Come on, laddie, let's not waste time. We both know that you're going."

I looked at Pop. I waited for him to speak, but he was silent. His eyes said it all, pleading, and I knew that Delaney was right. I was going to do it. Like everything else I had done over the past eighteen years, I was going to do it for the Center, and for Pop. I told myself it was only a game.

"All right," I said. "Who does the briefing?"

Delaney grunted his satisfaction. "Kourkalis. He'll be your control."

Sly Harry, who only had half a file. "How long for the brief?"

"Two weeks. I want you to know Nordquist inside out, and I want you prepped on biochips. Nordquist is due in Bled the middle of January. I want you there earlier, say around the first of the year."

That was all right with me. Being on the ground first would make it my turf.

"Remember, you have only one objective," said Delaney. "Strip Nordquist of everything he owns. We'll take care of the rest of it."

4

THE aces dispersed from the Center on the morning after Big John Brodski's funeral. We went reluctantly. No matter what luxuries and privileges we enjoyed on the outside, the Center was always our emotional home and we felt safest when we were within its walls. Martha and I went back to New York with Harry, Vince to London, Snake to Pakistan, and Sammy to Washington where he was involved in an in-house battle with the Agency.

There was nothing new about that. He was not only our eldest and our brightest. He was also our most cynical, the constant questioner of authority; and to a great degree the attitudes of the rest of us were shaped by his. This was not unusual at the Center: the eldest of a group tended to set the style for the rest of his year. Thus, if Martha and Snake, Vince and I, were thought of as being difficult, disagreeable, and resentful of authority, it was due only partly to the quirks of our characters. Much of it was a faithful following of Sammy's lead. He was, without trying to be, a natural leader, and nobody played the game the way he did. When I was a kid I wanted nothing more than to be like Sammy Warsaw, and when, years later, he told me that there had been attributes of mine in those days that he had envied, I found it hard to believe. I still do.

When Sammy returned to Washington he walked back into a continuing dispute with his control, Jeremy Paternoster. Sammy had his own private war with the time-servers and the bureaucrats of the Agency, a war that at times was more important to him than traditional loyalties. It was an undeclared war, one in which Sammy could not resist taking shots at the cold warriors who ran us. He took one of those shots when the Agency came up with Ipatov, the KGB defector. Sammy had Ipatov tagged as a phony from the beginning, but Paternoster wouldn't listen to him. He figured that he had a class-A Soviet defector and, no matter what Sammy said, he wouldn't let go of the idea.

Vladimir Ipatov was attached to the Soviet embassy in London when he defected to us. He received preliminary debriefing at the Agency way-house outside St. Austell in Cornwall, and deep debriefing in New York and at The Hospital. After they were finished with him at The Hospital he was settled into a safe house near Fredricksburg, Virginia, for a period of transition. Sammy got his first crack at Ipatov in St. Austell and he got him again in Fredricksburg. By then he was convinced that the Russian wasn't kosher, but by then the Agency was ready to advise the White House that they had on hand a high-ranking defector, a serving KGB officer with the rank of candidate-general who, within his recent career, had been in charge of operational networks in Italy, Holland, and Scandinavia. That was what Ipatov told them, and they believed it. They wanted to believe. They saw his defection as the intelligence coup of the decade.

Jeremy Paternoster was in charge of the Ipatov defection. Close to sixty, tall and elegant, Paternoster was an Agency saint *sans peur et sans reproche*. His knowledge was encyclopedic and his commitment total. He saw Ipatov as his final step up the ladder that led to a corner suite at Langley, and he was less than happy when Sammy told him that his defector was a phony. People like Sammy disturbed him under the best of circumstances. He had never felt at ease with sensitives, and he dealt with them as little as possible. They were unorganized, unreliable, and, he suspected, unsanitary. Sammy, in particular, with his frizzy hair, bat-wing ears, and inquisitive nose, offended him.

"Your man is a fraud," Sammy told him. That was after the first debriefing at St. Austell.

Paternoster sighed, and said, "Would you care to define that term for me?"

"He isn't what he claims to be."

"Then what exactly is he?"

"I don't know yet."

"Then perhaps you will tell me what reasons you have to suspect his sincerity."

"I can't. Not yet."

"Then, pray tell me, why are you wasting my time with an unfounded supposition?"

"Because I sense something. That's what I get paid for. That's why I'm called a sensitive."

"Yes, no doubt," Paternoster said with a sniff, and that was the end of it as far as he was concerned.

It wasn't the end for Sammy. After the St. Austell debriefing, he made an intensive study of the Ipatov file. On the surface the man fit the pattern of a defector. He was at a turning point in his life, mid-forties, and disillusioned with the communist system. He was a childless widower with no apparent vices, not a womanizer, not a drug user, not a drunk. He enjoyed good food, wine in moderation, and a competitive game of chess. His single passion in life was jade. He was knowledgeable in the field, had written monographs on the subject, and owned a small but select collection that he kept in his Moscow apartment. According to his dossier, his greatest source of pleasure was to stay home at nights and contemplate the smooth perfection of his figurines and bowls, some of which dated back to the Han dynasty. Nothing in the file suggested duplicity, save the very act of defection, but Sammy sensed that it was there. It was nothing that he could put his finger on, but, because he trusted his senses, Sammy decided that the Russians had thrown him a dodo.

By definition, a dodo was someone whose thought processes were so simple and unsophisticated that he could be trained to present a false façade. They were not easy to find. A true simpleton was useless, and anyone with mental abilities much above that level could not be programmed into believing his own deception. The grey area in between was the land of the dodo, and although they were rare, the Russians were expert at finding and training them. Supplied with a verifiable story, they could fool the sharpest ace. At least for a while.

Once Sammy was convinced that he was dealing with a dodo, he began to spend more time with the Russian. This was during the Fredricksburg phase of Ipatov's debriefing and he was being allowed a considerable amount of personal freedom. He asked for, and received, permission to dine out on occasion, to go to theatres and concerts, and to visit the jade collections in the Washington galleries and museums. He was always accompanied, and Sammy was one of those who went along with him. It was during this time that Sammy learned about jade. Ipatov, given free rein, could talk for hours on the subject, and so Sammy learned the difference between jadeite, nephrite, and chloromelanite. He learned about *Pi Yü* and *Fei-Ts'ui*; about the translucent vases of the Ch'ien Lung period, the recumbent horses of the T'ang Dynasty, and the *Fo* dogs of the late Ming. Ipatov described in detail the Chinese gallery of animals carved in jade, some from the zodiac, some from mythology, some from the personal need of the artist who had done the carving. Of all the animals, he confessed, his particular favorite was the turtle.

"The Chinese call him *shen kuei,* the divine tortoise," he said shyly. "He is the River God in their folklore. Somehow I feel more at home with the *shen kuei* than with any of the others. I could never be at ease with an elephant or a tiger. I am content to be *shen kuei,* slow and plodding, safe and divine. All of life, you see, is represented in the jade."

"This divine tortoise," Sammy asked, "do you own one?"

"A small example from the Sung Dynasty. Not very valuable, but priceless to me." He sighed. "I will never see it again."

Sammy made sympathetic noises, but he was smiling inside. He had listened carefully to Ipatov's words, and with equal care he had probed his thoughts. Now, comparing the two, he had the key to his dodo's defection.

"Ipatov is a plant," he told Paternoster. "You've been set up and you're about to be screwed."

Paternoster was in a genial mood that day. He was ready to send off the report that eventually would reach the White House, the report announcing the defection of Candidate-General Ipatov, and he was counting the kudos that would be coming his way. Thus, he received Sammy's statement with amusement rather than his usual sarcasm. "Ipatov has already supplied us with a wealth of information about Soviet assets," he said. "I wish I had ten more like him."

"I don't think so. What has he given you? Low-level stuff, nothing that they can't afford to lose."

"That's standard. Every defector starts off giving you junk, it's part of his guilt complex. Once the guilt wears off he gives you the gold."

"Not in this case. He was programmed to give you nothing but junk. He has a different mission. His job is to defect, spend some time here, and then redefect back to the Soviet Union."

Paternoster continued to be amused. "Now why in the world would Vladimir want to do something like that? He seems to be enjoying our hospitality."

"The short-term goal is to milk you on debriefing techniques.

The long-term goal is to embarrass you internationally. A public redefection will make the Agency a laughingstock. You'll never live it down."

"Is this another one of your sensitive guesses?"

"It isn't a guess, I'm sure of it. He's going back."

"Name your proof. What has he done?"

"It isn't what he's done, it's what he hasn't done." Sammy paused for effect. "He doesn't miss his jade."

Paternoster stared at him blankly. "He doesn't do what?"

Sammy explained patiently. "Ipatov's most important possession is his collection of jade. It's the center of his life and he left it behind when he defected. To anyone else it would be like leaving behind a wife and a child. He should be mourning the loss of that jade, he should be in despair, and he isn't. He says that he is, but he isn't. It doesn't bother him at all. I've been in his head, and I know." Sammy paused again. "There's only one reason why he could play it so cool. It's because he knows that he's going to see that jade again. He knows that he's going back."

Paternoster yawned and stretched. Totally unimpressed, he said, "And that's what you call proof? What in the world do they pay you people for?"

Sammy stood up. "I figured you'd see it that way. I'll be making my official report in writing. My opinion will be in it."

"Yes, you do that." Paternoster's mind was already elsewhere, his eyes flitting to the papers on his desk.

Sammy put his hands on that desk and leaned across it. "Look, I don't much like you," he said, "but we're supposed to be playing on the same team. Take some friendly advice. Don't send in that report just yet. Wait a while. You're liable to make yourself look foolish."

Paternoster picked up the nearest file on his desk, and stared at it. Then he looked at Sammy, and said, "I'm busy, Warsaw. Why don't you go read some tea leaves?"

Paternoster's report went in, and was forwarded to the White

House with predictable results. The news that a major KGB figure had defected to the United States was made public at a presidential news conference, and created an immediate sensation. The defection was hailed as a triumph for the CIA, and within the Agency, Paternoster received all the credit he had hoped for. Eventually the furor died down and Sammy settled in to wait for Ipatov's redefection. He wanted to see Paternoster's face when it happened. More, he wanted to see him slapped down badly. With a little luck he might even be forced to take early retirement. The trouble was that nothing happened. A week went by, then a month, and Ipatov remained in place in the Fredricksburg safe house. He continued to dine out several times each week, go to theatre, and visit the museums. He seemed content to live out the rest of his life as a defector. Finally, one night Sammy drove out to the Fredricksburg house and cornered the Russian.

"What the hell is going on, Vladimir?" he said bluntly. "And don't bother blowing any smoke at me. You were supposed to redefect, and you didn't. How come?"

Ipatov beamed at him jovially. "You're a clever boy, Sammy. How did you figure it out?"

Sammy told him about the jades. Ipatov's smile grew broader. "Amazing," he said. "A little thing like that."

"Then you admit it?"

"To you, yes, but not to anybody else. If you say that I said it, I'll deny it."

"What made you change your mind? I was sure you were going back."

"Don't blame yourself for that. I *was* going back until I realized something. Nobody yells at me here. Everybody treats me kindly. You have no idea how they used to yell at me back home. They called me a dodo, you know. Well, maybe I am, but here they don't yell at dodos. It may not seem like much to you, but because of that I decided to stay."

"But what about your jades? What about the divine tortoise?"

A look of sadness came over the Russian's face. "That's the bad part, but who knows. America is the land of opportunity. Maybe some day I'll make enough money to start a new collection."

Sammy saw his plans for Paternoster slipping away. His voice rising, he said, "Damn it, you can't do it. You're going back."

Ipatov stared at him, hurt. "Are you going to start yelling at me, too? Why would you want me to go back?"

Sammy swallowed his anger and lowered his voice. "Sorry, Vladimir, it's just that you surprised me. I thought you were a good communist and a patriot."

"I used to be. Now I'm a defector."

"But not a real one."

"Real enough. I've made my decision, Sammy. I'm not going back."

It was an unkind twist of fate. Paternoster was going to wind up a hero for the wrong reasons, but Sammy was not the sort to take those twists philosophically. Paternoster had to be slapped down, which meant that Ipatov had to go back to the Soviet Union whether he wanted to or not. That night Sammy stopped by the Hell's Bells in Georgetown. The bar was a hangout for embassy people. One of them was Yuri Muzalev, a Russian ace working for the KGB, and Sammy's opposite number in the area. Yuri was at the Hell's Bells every weekday evening between six and eight, and during those hours it was his custom to drink exactly ten iced Stolys with metronomic precision. He called it showing the flag. When Sammy came in he was halfway through his run, surrounded by people who knew him only as a second secretary at the embassy. Sammy stayed away from the group. He cased the room for other sensitives, and found none. From the far end of the bar, he called, *Hey, tus, got a minute?*

Who's that? Yuri's eyes moved around and made contact. *Oh, Sammy. How's it going?*

Not so good. I need a favor.

How much?

Not money. I've got a problem with my control.

Who doesn't? You think Paternoster is tough, you should try working with Mishustin for a while. What's the problem?

Vladimir Ipatov.

There was a pause while Yuri downed another iced vodka and laughed at a joke that someone in his crowd had told. *Sorry, Sammy, too much noise in here. Can't hear a word you're saying.*

This is serious, Yuri.

That's what I'm afraid of. Well, what about him?

He isn't going to redefect.

That means you broke him. How?

Nobody broke him, he gave it away. Sammy told him about the jades.

Aren't you the wily one. Well, don't think that you're giving me any news. He was due back two weeks ago. The theory around my house is that your boys have him under lock and key.

No, it isn't like that. He really wants to stay here.

So, what's your problem? You've got yourself a triumph.

Not me. Paternoster has the triumph, the lucky bastard. I'd like to see him stub his toe on this one.

Yuri gave the mental equivalent of an appreciative chuckle. *I see your point. Where do I come in?*

I want you to snatch Ipatov. I can set it up for you one night when he goes out to dinner. That way we both win. You get your defector back and Paternoster gets what he deserves.

Yuri laughed out loud. The people around him laughed, too. They thought they had missed a punch line. Yuri said, *That's cute, except for one thing. I don't want him back.*

Why the hell not?

Because if he doesn't come back my boss is in a heap of trouble. I like it better that way.

Yuri had the same problems with Aleksandr Mishustin that

Sammy had with Paternoster. They were the problems that were built into the relationship between the ace and his control, the sensitive opposed to the insensitive. Yuri had been against the Ipatov defection from its inception. He had considered the mission poorly conceived and Ipatov the wrong man for the job. He had argued his case forcefully with Mishustin and, as Sammy had done with Paternoster, had recorded his objections in a formal memorandum. In a very real sense he had staked his reputation on the failure of the mission, and when Ipatov had not redefected as expected, his in-house stock had risen appreciably. Mishustin, on the other hand, now faced a reprimand and a transfer. Yuri was riding high, and he had no interest at all in bringing his dodo back home.

He told this to Sammy, and said gleefully, *Sorry, tus, you're stuck with him.*

No, I'm not. He's got to go back, one way or another.

I don't see how you're going to do it. I won't help you, that's for sure. You can't expect me to.

No, Sammy admitted, *I'd do the same in your shoes.*

You could always go to Mishustin. He'd be glad to work out something with you.

The suggestion was not meant seriously, and Sammy did not take it that way. It was one thing to cut a deal with a fellow sensitive. It was quite another to suggest such an arrangement to an officer in a hostile service. One was business, the other was treason.

There's got to be a way, said Sammy.

Have another drink and forget about it. Yuri had a fresh Stoly in his hand. *You win some and you lose some. It's all part of the game.*

Not this time, it isn't.

Sammy threw a bill on the bar, and walked out. He took a taxi over to Mulcahey's. He had a couple of sad drinks at the bar, sat at a table and ate Mulcahey's corned beef and cabbage, and went back to the bar for coffee and a cognac. After two of those he was deep into a brooding mood. He knew that Yuri was right, that it was time to let go of the idea. There was no way in which he, by himself, could get Ipatov to redefect. Through sheer luck, Paternoster had his triumph, and now he would be more insufferable than ever. It was the breaks of the game, but it was difficult to accept. He had been right all along, and now, damn it, he was wrong.

He ordered another cognac, raised it to his lips, and heard a voice in his head say, *Hey, tus, good to see you.*

Who's that? He looked around the room and saw Theodore Kwan sitting at a table with an attractive young woman, staring at a menu. Theodore was listed in the directories as the number-three man at Pacific Consultants. He was, in fact, the Washington ace for the People's Republic of China. *Hi, Theodore, how's it going?*

The usual. Tough day today.

She doesn't look that tough.

Oh, no, not her. Just the usual hassle with my control.

Don't tell me your troubles. If you think Mister Li is tough you should try working with Paternoster for a while.

Mister Li is in a class by himself. What's good here?

Try the corned beef and cabbage. He saw Theodore murmur to the woman, and then give his order to the waiter. *Li is a pussycat compared to my boy.*

Some pussycat, more like a dragon, Theodore protested. *In my outfit there's nothing worse than a party man who really believes in the old ideology.*

A closet Maoist?

Believe it. He still has a copy of The Little Red Book, keeps it in a plain brown wrapper. The man really thinks that the People's Republic is the Garden of Eden. I mean, you wouldn't believe what he said to me today. What kind of wine goes with corned beef and cabbage?

Budweiser. What did he say?

I'm embarrassed to repeat it. He actually said that he

couldn't understand why politicals never defect to the People's Republic. We have everything, he said, so why don't they come to us? They go to the Americans, they go to the Russians, but never to us. Can you believe it?

Sammy could believe it. He believed it just as he believed in the glorious sunburst that he knew was forming just over his head. He took a deep breath, took the tiniest sip of his cognac, and said, *Theodore, I have something to discuss with you. Something important.*

Hey, check it out, man. Can't you see I'm busy?

I said important, tus. Something that will do us both some good.

One week later, Vladimir Ipatov informed his Agency hosts that he wished to dine that night at Le Petit Auberge in Fredricksburg. It was a Thursday, and usually on Thursdays his choice was a roadhouse for spare ribs and home fries, but Le Petit Auberge was known to have one of the finest kitchens between Washington and Savannah, and his request was understandable. Ipatov and his two security men arrived at the restaurant at seven-fifteen, drank sherry at the bar, and were seated at seven-thirty. Ipatov ordered the gallantine of pheasant, and then the braised lamb with carrots. He ordered a strawberry tart for dessert, but before the pastry cart arrived he excused himself from the table and went to the men's room. He did not return to the table. He walked outside and slipped into a Lincoln Continental parked at the curb. The car drove slowly down William Street, turned left onto Sophia, and left again to go up Amelia to the Confederate Cemetary on Washington Avenue. There, on that darkened, solemn street, the car eased to a halt.

Theodore Kwan, seated in back with Ipatov, turned on the overhead light. The window shades were drawn. Kwan handed a velvet-covered box to the Russian. Ipatov hesitated.

"Go ahead," Kwan said. "Open it."

Ipatov removed the cover, looked inside, and drew in his

breath. He lifted out an intricately carved jade bowl. The high relief carving on the side of the bowl was that of *shen kuei*, the divine tortoise, resting on a pattern of crested waves. The color was emerald, and it dated from the K'ang-Hsi period. Ipatov rotated the bowl in his hands and the *shen kuei* appeared again and again. Moisture collected at the corners of Ipatov's eyes, and after a while a tear rolled down one cheek.

Kwan said gently, "Flown here from the People's Museum in Peiking. For your eyes only."

Ipatov nodded.

"I have something else to show you. A spill vase carved with a cat and a Fêng Huang. From the Chia-ching period, as you might expect."

Ipatov shook his head, his eyes still on the bowl. "Not right now."

"I understand." Long moments went by. Kwan broke the silence. "Need I describe the jade that exists in my country?"

Ipatov shook his head.

"Then I will say only this. All of it awaits your eyes and your touch."

Ipatov nodded.

"Do you wish to return to the restaurant? There is still time."

Ipatov closed his eyes and put back his head. "No, certainly not. Drive on."

Ipatov surfaced in the People's Republic of China at a press conference in Peiking organized by the Ministry of State Security. He appeared to be well rested and in good spirits. He was introduced to the representatives of the international press as the same Vladimir Ipatov whose defection to the United States had been recently announced in Washington. Speaking slowly, but firmly, he said:

"Not long ago I left the Soviet Union and sought refuge in the West because I could no longer subscribe to a totalitarian regime that denied the fundamental rights of its citizens. I was quickly disillusioned by what I saw in the United States of

America. I saw licentiousness, corruption, and a materialistic philosophy that cripples the spirit. Now I have arrived in the People's Republic of China to take my place alongside my proletarian brothers and sisters in the long march down the road to a truly socialist society. In a way, I have come home, for this land possesses that which I cherish most."

Jeremy Paternoster retired three days after the Peking press conference. The following day, Aleksandr Mishustin was transferred home to Moscow. That afternoon, Sammy and Yuri had a celebratory drink together at the Hell's Bells. They stood at opposite ends of the bar, but they were together. After the drink, Sammy wandered through a downtown curio shop, picking over the cheaper bits and pieces on the counter. He finally chose a tiny turtle carved out of inexpensive soapstone.

"*Shen kuei,*" he murmured. "Divine tortoise."

It cost him seven dollars, and he put it on his key chain.

5

NORDQUIST said, "Let me tell you something about my grandson."

"You already have," I said, laughing. "That's all you've been talking about."

He laughed with me, and at himself. He was a man built for laughing, round, and jolly, and ruddy. "You'll have to excuse me, but I get a little silly when I talk about Arne. He's all I have now."

"He's a fine-looking boy." He had shown me a photograph.

"Just past six, and bright." Nordquist sipped his wine. "Too bright for me sometimes. At my age, to be the father as well as the grandfather. . . ." He shrugged. "Not so easy. Let me tell you what I just gave him for Christmas. Or am I boring you with all this?"

"No, please, go on." The second-floor bar of the casino was almost empty and our voices, even in murmurs, echoed.

"This was back in Sweden, of course, just before I came down here. Well, I knew that he wanted a bicycle, he'd made that clear enough. And he knew that I'd be leaving just after Christmas. He was really looking forward to that bicycle. So what did I get him? Some shirts and some socks. You should have seen the look on his face, so disappointed. But he handled it well, he never complained."

"I don't get it. Was he being punished?"

"Not at all. I arranged for the bicycle to be delivered the day after I left. I didn't want to be there when it arrived."

"I still don't get it."

"I don't want him associating me with gifts. Good old Gramps, the man who makes the dreams come true. I said before that he's all that I have now. Well, I'm all that he has, too, and I'm sixty-eight years old. I won't be around forever, and once I'm gone he'll have to handle those dreams by himself. It's time for him to understand the difference between good old Gramps and Father Christmas."

"But he got his bike?"

"Oh, yes, I made sure of that. But not directly from my hands. Am I making any sense?"

"Plenty."

"Do you have any children?"

"No, not married."

"Well, I've always been a family man. It suits me. My wife is gone now, and my son, and his wife. All I've got left is Arne, but it still suits me."

"Why isn't he with you?"

"School time now, he's with the governess. I wouldn't have left him, but . . . my wife and I came to Bled every year at this time. I still come, even though she's gone. Habit? Sentiment? Who knows?"

He lightened the words with a grin, and I grinned back. He was an easy man to talk to, and an easy man to like. I had been in his head. He was an honest man with a healthy dose of greed in his system.

That greed, it was something we were trained to look for. Any sensitive knows that our lives are laced with it. You learn that quickly, reading heads. Greed is what pushes us, not love, or

67

hate, or lust, or fear. Just greed, coupled in our western society with an ever-present anxiety: one the horse, and the other the rider. Greed pervades our thoughts, it controls our lives, it alters our souls. It creates an atmosphere that is unmistakeable to the sensitive, yet it is so common that we rarely notice it. After all, how often do we consciously notice the air that we breathe? What we do notice is the absence of air, and in the same way a sensitive is at once aware when the atmosphere of greed is missing. It's like a slap in the face, demanding your attention, and in our training at the Center we were warned about it.

"When that single ingredient is missing," they told us, "you know that you're in trouble, because the absence of greed most often means the presence of the obsessed. The people who have gone beyond greed. The people who have learned to live without the feelings that are common to the rest of us. The people, in short, who are highly prized for certain occupations by the clandestine organizations of the world. The kind of people who would harm us for a higher purpose."

So you learned to check the greed factor, and Nordquist checked out just fine. A healthy, acquisitive nature set within the limits of an honest man. He wanted as much as he could get, not so much for himself as for his grandson. He was determined to leave that boy well fixed. It made me like him even more, which did not make my job any easier.

I had spent two weeks in New York being briefed on Nordquist and his biochips, and they had been two weeks of misapplied energy. By the end of the briefing, I knew as much as any layman about the properties of the protein memory cell, but all I really had to know was the difference between a king and a jack. Still, I spent the weeks with Harry working on the details of the operation. It was arranged that I would enter Yugoslavia as Brian Patterson, a Canadian bound for some winter fun at the gaming tables and in the mountains of Slovenia. Jaspers and Childress would provide security for me under similar covers, while Harry, as control, would set up shop across the border in the Austrian town of Klangenfurt. Harry was in charge of the bankroll. He would forward funds to me as the need arose. There was no limit to what was available; I had the U.S. Treasury backing me. I couldn't lose, but, personally, I couldn't win, either. All profits would go back to the bankroll. There was no way for me to cut a piece. That was all I was told of the operation. Once I had done my job, broken Nordquist and made him vulnerable, somebody else would move in and make the deal with him.

I came into Bled just after the first of January, flying into Ljubljana and then driving a rental car up into the beginnings of the Julian Alps. The town, situated beside a moraine lake, lay just south of the Austrian border, and in the days of the Austro-Hungarian Empire it had been a watering hole for the aristocracy. Even now, after decades under a communist government, Bled retained many of the aspects of a *fin de siècle* middle-European spa. The best hotels—the Toplice and the Golf—still were supplied with mineral water from the hot springs on the shore of the lake, the lilt of waltzes still echoed in the night, and on Sunday afternoons the families still strolled along the lakeshore and stopped in the cafés for lemonade and tea. In the old days it had been strictly a summer resort, but now there was a skiing area five miles out at Zatrnik, and the more serious sportsmen could go further into the mountains to the competition runs at Kranjska Gora. The top hats, the frock coats, and the parasols were gone, but the spirit of *The Merry Widow* lived on in Bled.

I checked into the Toplice; Jaspers and Childress stayed at the local Kompas. The casino was directly across from my hotel on the Ljubljanska, a massive building that looked like a black marble bank. Once I was settled I paid a call on the casino manager and explained the sort of action I was looking for. He said that there was a high-stake poker game in a private room almost every night, and that a seat could be found for me.

69

He gave me the arrangements. It was standard American poker with no limit; you could bet your socks. The house supplied the room and the dealer, and cut one and three-quarters percent of the pot. The dealer dealt for everyone, moving a button around the table after each hand to show whose turn it was next. Having a dealer was supposed to save time and keep the game straight. It certainly saved time.

I spent the next few days getting to know the town and the game. Bled was popular with those Yugoslavians who could afford the prices, but the hard-currency visitors were the Austrians, Germans, and Italians, who were attracted by the exchange rate and the traditions of the spa. The poker at the casino was five-card stud or draw, the language at the table was French, and the currency was Swiss francs. I played every night for a few hours while I waited for my pigeon to appear. The players were all men and all foreigners; the locals were barred from the casino. Some of the faces changed every night, but there were several regulars. The action was heavy enough, but erratic: a string of quiet hands, and then a flurry. I checked each head in the game. No one seemed to be out for a killing. They were all men of substance, on vacation and looking for a flutter, nothing more. I played the same sort of game, fitting in, losing a bit one night and winning it back the next.

During the day I played the role that my cover called for. I visited the Church of St. Mary on the circular island in the middle of the lake; I toured Castle Bled high on a crag above the water; I admired the seventeenth-century frescoes in the chapel and the Turkish walls in the Church of St. Martin; and I drove up to Kranjska Gora for the skiing. Childress went with me. He had skied for Dartmouth, and he kept me on the lower levels of the mountain, away from the steeper slopes at the top. I wanted to go higher, it was embarrassing to ski with the kiddies and the snow bunnies, but he was responsible for my safety and he wouldn't allow it.

"We stay down here," he said. "Anything happens to you and it's my ass that gets busted along with yours."

Nordquist arrived on the seventeenth of January. I had expected him to stay at either the Toplice or the Golf, but he rented a villa just out of town on the road to Bohinj. He came into the casino that first night and played for several hours. He played a conservative game, winning a few hundred francs. He drank one glass of wine during the evening, and left before midnight. His displayed none of the characteristics usually associated with the compulsive gambler: no signs of stress, no urge to bet on every hand, no rush toward destruction. I was not surprised. They came in all shapes and sizes, and some of them could cruise along under what appeared to be full control until something happened to throw them off course. Anything could do it, a disappointment or a triumph, a big win or an unexpected loss. Once it had happened it was rare to see them regain the control they had abandoned.

I probed his head that first night. The surface was all poker, and I had to dig for what was underneath. There were random thoughts of his grandson, of his work, and of a woman named Clara, but there was nothing of substance. The man had the ability to concentrate exclusively on one subject at a time. It was the sign of a first-class mind, but I had expected that.

What I had not expected to find was this warm and amiable man who opened himself up to me about his family and himself. Nor had I expected to find myself on a friendly basis with him, but it happened that way. On the first night that he played, we quit the table at the same time and he invited me to a glass of wine at the casino bar. It happened again the next night. That was when he told me about Arne's bicycle, and after that we grew closer in an easy progression of friendship. I probed his head to see why he was taken with me, and was not surprised to find that I reminded him of his son. We fell into a routine of effortless conversation, and several nights later he told me about the woman named Clara. He spoke about her hesitantly, but he wanted to talk. She was something new in his life.

"To tell you the truth, I'm embarrassed," he said. "She's a lot younger than I am, and at my age . . . well, you don't want to look like a fool. It isn't the usual situation, you see. She's a fine young woman."

He looked at me sharply to see if I accepted that. I didn't know what to say. He was almost forty years my senior and he was looking for my approval. All I could do was nod for him to continue.

Her name was Clara Johansen and she was Danish, a secondary-school biology teacher. They had met the month before at a seminar in Copenhagen where he had lectured, and it had happened quickly. He was the aging genius, she was the eager apprentice, and the result had been storybook. She would be joining him shortly in Bled, which was why he had rented a villa instead of staying at a hotel.

"She'll be here next week," he explained. "I wanted some time by myself, because of my wife. This place used to mean so much to us. And Clara, she understood. You go ahead, she said. Roll around in your memories, get finished with it, and I'll come down later. She is an unusual woman, believe me."

"She sounds like it."

"And what do I sound like? An old dog howling at the moon, I guess. A foolish old dog."

"There's nothing foolish about grabbing for a little happiness. You take it where you can get it, no matter how old you are."

"Thank you for putting it that way."

"I mean it."

And I did. I wished him well. I truly liked the man. It was all wrong, of course, the fox getting chummy with the chicken, but I hated the idea of breaking him. All I had done so far was play country-club poker, not pressing him at all, but I knew that I couldn't keep that up much longer. Harry was pushing me. He called each day from Klangenfurt, using a simple weather code to find out what was happening. Nothing was happening, and he wasn't happy about it. He wanted progress and there was none to report. It was time for me to go to work, time to play the game.

What I needed was a hand that would change Nordquist's style, something that would shake him loose from his conservative routine and onto the downhill tumble of the compulsive gambler. He knew all about that tumble, he had fallen before. All I had to do was remind him of it. It was a job comparable to waving an open whisky bottle in front of a reformed drunk.

It happened on a Tuesday, midway through the evening. The game was stud and we were head to head; the others had dropped. After four cards dealt I was holding a pair of eights wired, a trey, and a third eight. Nordquist had a jack in the hole, a deuce, a second jack, and a second deuce. On the last card, I bought my fourth eight; Nordquist got his third jack. With three eights showing, I chipped a thousand Swiss francs, about five hundred dollars.

Nordquist studied the cards. He could figure me for the three eights that were showing, or the fourth eight that I actually had, or a full house. If I had the fourth eight I was a winner. Any other way I was beat. He tested the water by calling my thousand and raising the same.

I called his thousand, and raised him ten thousand more.

He smiled at me gently. There was a dreamy look in his eyes. He was hearing the call of long-ago trumpets, remembering the songs that the sirens sang along the road that was lined with the graves of the losers. That was his road, and he was ready to ride it. He shoved twenty blues into the center of the table. I called and raised, he did the same, and by the time the dust had settled there were over a hundred thousand francs in the pot.

I made the last call. He showed his hand: jacks full. It didn't make much difference if I won or lost. The job was done.

Losing was marginally better than winning. I scooped my cards and tossed them face down in the deadwood.

"That beats three eights," I said, and sat back trying to look unhappy.

He raked in the chips. His eyes were bright, and a fine film of sweat had formed on his face. I went into his head. The wheels were spinning. The finely controlled mind that I had admired was gone. He was on his way.

Before the night was out he had given back the hundred thousand, and the same again. The slide was on. The next night, Wednesday, he dropped another hundred thousand and wired Stockholm for funds. On Thursday he dug into his account at Lombard Odier et Cie in Geneva, and on Friday he closed it out. He lost the Geneva money over the weekend, and on Monday he instructed Hasslebeck, his brokers in Zurich, to start selling securities. It took him two days to clean out his brokerage account. In just over a week he went through more than four hundred thousand dollars. During that time I saw a capable and intelligent man decline into a senseless wreck intent on self-destruction. He played every hand, called every bet, and raised whenever the circumstances allowed it. He could not have gotten rid of the money faster if he had used a shovel.

I missed the man he had been. There were no more glasses of wine late at night, no more chats about Arne's future, or Clara Johansen, or the ways of the world. We saw each other only at the card table where, oddly enough, he bore me no ill will. He saw me not as the author of his misfortune, but as a participant in it. In truth, he was so far gone that he could not tell the difference.

We were close to breaking him. At that point I wanted to get the job over with as quickly as possible, but on Wednesday night Harry called a meeting for the next day in Klangenfurt on his side of the border. Jaspers and I made the trip together, driving up into the mountains to the tunnel at Loibl Pass that connected Yugoslavia and Austria. The tunnel allowed the pass to stay open during the winter months. The Germans had built it in World War Two. They had built it with slave labor, a life for every tile in the walls. It was a clean and efficient tunnel. Once we were through it we drove down onto the Austrian plain to Klangenfurt. The meeting was in Harry's hotel room. The room was a mess of unmade beds and trays of unfinished meals. Harry cleared a space on one of the beds and motioned for me to sit there. Jaspers leaned against the door.

Harry dug around in the bedclothes and came up with his file on Nordquist. He had been monitoring the Swede's assets through Agency connections in the financial community, watching the money melt away. He adjusted his glasses and peered at the papers.

"We're close," he said. "All he's got left is some property in Sweden. It's on the island of Gotland, the family estate. We've got it valued at two and a half million krona, but there's a heavy mortgage on it. The equity looks like about a million and a quarter, which makes it in dollars. . . ." He scribbled figures. "Call it a hundred and fifty thousand. How much could he raise on that? A hundred?"

"That's what he's been trying to get. He's been on the phone with Stockholm."

"Once he gets it, will he blow it?"

"Of course. Those people just keep on going."

"Once that's gone he's finished."

"What happens then?"

"Then it becomes Agency business. They'll send somebody in to make the deal with him."

"Just so long as I don't have to do it."

"You won't," he promised.

"You're sure of that?"

"Positive. How long will it take you to finish him off?"

"The way he's playing, he could do it by himself in a couple of days. Even quicker if I push him some more."

"Are you going to push him?"

"I suppose so."

"You're not happy about this, are you?"

"I like the man. I don't feel good about hurting him."

"You took the job."

"That was before I met him. He's a fine man. He shouldn't have to be put through something like this. Actually, neither should I."

Harry shook his head sadly. "Don't tell me about it. I'm not some Agency ass-hole. I'm Center just like you. None of us should have to do things like this, but we do them because we have to. What choice do we have?"

I did not try to answer that one. I went over to the window and looked out. There was a park across the street and children were playing there, young children. Nordquist had told me about the Gotland property. The land and the house had been in the family for seven generations. Arne lived there now. It was only a game.

Harry said to my back, "You want out of this, don't you?"

I nodded. There was no way out, but that's what I wanted.

"All right, you've got it. You're out."

"What's that?" I turned around.

"You're out. You're off the job. I'll advise Delaney back-channel."

"Why?"

"You asked for it, didn't you?"

It was hard to believe. Things didn't work that way. I looked at him closely. It was the same old Harry, he needed a shave and there were food stains on his shirt, but he was grinning. He was holding something back. I went into his head. He was blocked. It was the kind of block that a deuce would throw up, the kind that couldn't hold me for long. I leaned on it.

"Cut it out," he said sharply. He knew me, and he knew I was there. I eased off. He said to Jaspers, "Get out. Wait downstairs."

"I'm supposed to stay with him."

"He's with me. That's good enough."

Jaspers stared at him stolidly, and left. Harry went to the door and locked it. He sighed, shook his head, and said, "I shouldn't have said that about Agency ass-holes in front of him."

"He's heard it before. Harry, what the hell is going on? Are you really taking me off it?"

"If you want me to. Take a look at these. You may change your mind." He dug under the bedclothes and came up with a large manila envelope. He tossed it over to me. "Photos," he said. "Nordquist and his girlfriend, Clara Johansen. Taken at that conference where they met."

The prints were eight-by-ten, grainy and taken from a distance. Nordquist looked relaxed and happy. So did Clara. They could have been shots of a young woman and her proud grandfather, but they weren't. The woman was Nadia. Her hair was blonde and cut short, which changed her appearance, but it was she. I wondered how long it had taken her to brush up on her Swedish and learn about microchips.

"Know her?" asked Harry.

There was a screaming temptation to lie, but I stepped on it. "Sure. She's a Russian ace named Nadia something-or-other. We work the same route in New York."

"Looks like she's got a new route. She spent the last ten days at Gaczyna Center, and she arrived in Belgrade yesterday. According to our information she should be in Bled tomorrow."

"How good is your source?"

"The best."

Which meant that it came from the Yugoslavs themselves, probably from within the Ministry for State Security. They had a reputation as a Mickey Mouse outfit, but they were strong on their own turf and they had as little love for the Russians as they had for us.

"This sort of changes things," I said.

"I thought it might. Still want out?"

"No, not now."

"I figured that, too." He knew nothing about Nadia and me, but he knew that I would never pass up the chance to play the game against a Russian *tus*. "How do you figure her angle?"

"Bedroom. What else could it be?"

"What are her chances?"

"Long odds. You can't read something like that head to head. I told that to Delaney."

"Can she hurt your play?" He was into it, as if he were playing the game himself.

"I don't see how. She can't keep him away from the card table. Only his wife could do that, and she's dead. No, she can't stop me, but she can make it interesting."

"Maybe too interesting. I'm doubling your security. I'm not taking any chances with a Russian ace in the game."

"No need. Jaspers and Childress are enough." Actually, they were too much. There would be no way for Nadia and me to actually meet in Bled, any more than in New York, but with only Jaspers and Childress on my tail there at least would be chances for us to speak head to head. Doubling the security would halve those chances.

"No," said Harry, "we'll do it my way."

"What's the matter with you? Do you think she's going to pull out a pistol and shoot me? She's an ace, not an agent. I've got too much security as it is."

"Ben . . ."

"No, definitely not."

"Damn it, you're being stubborn."

"Just sensible."

"No, stubborn. Mule-headed, that's what. You were always that way, you and the others. Sammy and Snake, Martha and Vince. Just plain stubborn."

"Were we? I don't remember." I wanted to get out of there. I wanted to get back to Bled.

"All five of you when we were kids." His voice rose. "If I said the sky was blue, then one of you said it was green. If I said it was Tuesday, then one of you said it was Thursday. Just to be stubborn."

"It wasn't that bad."

"Yes, it was, and now you're doing it again."

"Harry, don't whine. Your face gets all red when you whine."

I got out of there and went back to Bled. Nadia arrived the next day and moved into Nordquist's villa. The old man was so excited that he took a night off from the casino. He insisted that I do the same, and he invited me to the house for dinner. He had to show off Clara Johansen. When he introduced her to me she kept a calm façade, but her mind was churning.

"So good to meet you," she said cordially, but head to head, she said, *What is this? What are you doing here?*

"A pleasure, I've heard so much about you." I smiled. *A little vacation, babe. A little skiing, a little poker.*

But why here?

I go where the action is.

There was sudden understanding. *You're the one he's losing all the money to.*

Right, and you're the one . . . well, we both know what you've been doing, don't we?

Ben . . .

That's all right. What weary old whores we've both turned into.

We have to talk.

Not now. It wouldn't be fair to your lover.

Stop that. He's not my lover.

Tomorrow morning at eleven, the Café France, on the Kidriceva.

Nordquist was beaming at us. He was so damn proud of her.

At eleven, I'll be there, she said. "Would you care for a drink before dinner?"

6

H ARRY was right about the streak of stubbornness. I had always been that way. So had Sammy and Vince, Martha and Snake. We all were willfully stubborn, and I don't know why we should have shared the trait. We were not, after all, related by blood, but we were a mule-headed bunch. Snake was the worst, she could really dig in her heels. She was only a touch over five feet tall, less than a hundred pounds, and built like a boyish whip. So small, but so stubborn. While the business in Bled was going on she was back in Pakistan on the Northwest Frontier working with the Afghani rebels. Along the frontier, and in Afghanistan proper, to say that someone was as stubborn as a Pathan was to concede the ultimate. Snake was as stubborn as a Pathan, and she proved it when the rebels hijacked the shipment of Stingers.

The Stingers were American hand-held antiaircraft missiles, and they hadn't been meant for the Afghani rebels in the first place. We were shipping plenty of arms into the *mujahideen*— the holy warriors fighting the Russians—but nothing as sophisticated as Stingers. The missiles were meant for the Pakistani army, which had a particular use for them. At that stage of the war one-fourth of the entire population of Afghanistan had been driven into exile, most of them living in refugee camps across the border in Pakistan. That was as if 60 million Americans were huddled in camps on the wrong side of the Rio Grande. The camps were the training centers and resupply depots for the *mujahideen,* and late in that year the Russians decided to forget about diplomatic niceties and began to raid the camps on the Pakistani side of the line. It was an undeclared war. During the last four months of that year, the Russians made more than fifty air incursions into Pakistani territory, attacking the camps, and the Paks needed something to throw back at them. That was when we started supplying them with Stingers.

The deal was that the Stingers were strictly for the Pakistanis, not for the rebels, but that was a State Department concept. The Agency people in the field had ideas of their own. They figured that they had a responsibility to their clients, the *mujahideen,* who needed the Stingers just as badly as the Pakistanis did. The rural rebels were getting badly beat up by the Mi-24 Hind choppers that the Soviets were using in their search-and-destroy missions. They had no ground-to-air weaponry, the Stingers were the obvious answer to their problem, and the Agency people went to work to get some for them. Shipments to the Paks were diverted, lost, and eventually found their way into Afghanistan. They were meant for specific groups of the *mujahideen,* but sometimes they went astray.

At that point there were over forty resistance groups operating against the Russians, and in true Afghani fashion they often fought with each other as vigorously as they did with the nominal enemy. Two of the larger groups bore the same name. The Hezb-i-Islami, led by Gulbuddin Hekmatyar, had ties with the Ayatollah Khomeini and received financial support from Iran. A breakaway faction, also known as the Hezb, was led by Younis Khalis, and had similar connections. Their goals were the same, to throw out the Russians and then establish an orthodox Islamic state, but they were divided by tribal loyalties. We were supporting both groups, Islamic fundamentalists who were joined hip and thigh with the Ayatollah, thus once again proving the maxim that the enemy of my enemy is my friend.

Our shipment of Stingers had been intended for the larger Hezb group, but had been hijacked by the smaller. That, in itself, would have been enough to spark off a civil war within the war, but the situation was further complicated by the fact that both groups were made up of Pathans. The Pathans were superb mountain fighters who lived by the Koran, the rifle, and by a social ethic that often pitted tribe against tribe, village against village, brother against brother. Under the Pakhtunwali, the Code of the Pathans, death was the only acceptable punishment for offenses against honor, and honor, to a Pathan, was a constant companion. Both sides were poised for a blood bath over those Stingers when the Agency stepped in and got them to agree to a peace conference at Baraki, a caravan stopover south of Kabul. They sent Gerald Haymond in to be the moderator. Haymond was the Agency man on the Pakistani side of the border, working in the refugee camps there, and Snake was attached to him as a translator. She was reading heads, of course, but she was also there because she spoke Pashto and Persian. When Haymond told her that he was going into Afghanistan, she said that she was going with him.

"The hell you are," he told her. "The Pathans wouldn't stand for a woman at the meeting. It would be an insult to them. They'd walk out."

"Depends on the woman," she said. "Wait here, I'll be right back." Ten minutes later she returned to Haymond's tent wearing the knee-length shirt, the baggy trousers, and the turban of a Pathan tribesman. She had a dagger in her belt and a Kalashnikov slung over her shoulder. She knew how to use both.

"What do you think?" she asked. "Can I pass for a teenage boy?"

Haymond inspected her critically. "It might work. Actually, you look like a boy even without the costume."

"Thank you," she said dryly..

"Sorry, I didn't mean it quite that way. I meant, you know . . . slim."

"Slim. I see."

Haymond was a heavy man in his forties. Snake liked him and wished that he were not quite so heavy and not quite so bureaucratic in his thinking. She had known him for two months and for most of that time she had been waiting for him to suggest something romantic. She had probed his head, and knew that he liked her, too, but so far he had not made a move. Now she knew why. She looked like a boy to him.

Haymond tried to lighten the mood. "Listen, this might present a different problem," he said. "You keep a Pathan out in the hills long enough and a young boy begins to look mighty good to him."

Snake said quietly, "That won't be a problem, Gerald." Her hand dropped casually to her belt. Her knife sped past his ear and chunked into the tent pole. "Really, it won't."

That didn't end the discussion, it only began it, but Snake had her heels dug in, and in the end she went along. They left from the border town of Teri Mangal, traveling for protection with a group of rebels heading for the northern provinces. There were five of them: Haymond, Snake, and three armed guards. They were all well mounted and they had two pack horses trailing. The journey took three days of hard riding. The trail that they followed was the main rebel supply route and it was well known to the Soviets and to their Afghan Army allies. Some of the route could be traveled only by night, and even then it was subject to regular air attacks and ground ambushes. It was spotted with the graves of men and the bones of horses and camels killed on the way. Green pennons of the faithful hung limply over the graves, and the animal bones glistened in the moonlight.

They crossed the border just after sunset and bypassed the two Afghan Army posts at Zazi in the mountains that formed the frontier. An hour past Zazi they heard the explosions of howitzers and mortars behind them and, looking back, they saw the streaks of tracers in the night. The party behind them had run into the posts and now would have to fight its way down the gullies, or turn back. They went on. There was nothing they could do for those behind them. Just before sunrise they stopped to rest, and late in the morning they started off again. They followed the bed of a river up a narrow valley, the horses slipping on scree and shale. They traveled high along the side of the hogback ridge, partly because the Pathans, for tactical reasons, always took the high ground, and partly because it was the rainy season and a flash flood could fill the valley within minutes. Below them the river was a twisted silver wire, and saw-toothed mountains rose all around them. They spent the night in the mountains, and as the sun came up they rode into the old fort of Dubandi and rested there. Haymond slept through the day, exhausted. The traveling was hard on him; he was years away from active duty in the field. Snake lay down beside him on the ground. She slept for two hours, and then got up to wander about the fort.

Dubandi was a strategic stopping point on the ancient trail across Afghanistan, and it was filled with men and animals gathered for the next step in the journey northward, a nighttime dash across the desert to Baraki. Snake counted over two hundred men in a rainbow of turbans, and as many horses and camels. She squatted beside fires playing the part of a youth far from home, chatting with the travelers, sometimes in Pashto, sometimes in Persian, sometimes in Tajik and Hazara. She heard the gossip of the desert and the hills.

She heard that a caravan to the north had been caught in the open on the Kabul road and destroyed to the last man.

She heard that the poppy crop that year would exceed expectations.

She heard that the city of Baghlan had been virtually destroyed by the Russians, and that the city of New Baghlan had sprung up to the south of the old site.

She heard that some enterprising *mujahideen* had shot down a Russian helicopter with an antitank missile by firing down at it from a hilltop.

She heard that the two branches of the Hezb-i-Islami were still feuding over the shipment of American missiles and would meet soon in Baraki to settle the matter; that Ahsen Gul would represent the major faction in the negotiations, that Amir Rasool would represent the minor faction, and that men were gambling horses and camels on which side would get to keep the arms.

She heard tales of honor outraged and honor avenged. She heard of how a commander in the north had executed his own brother for dealing with the Russians. She heard of how Babrak Tarqus, after seven years of patience, had finally slain the killer of his cousin. She heard of how Nur Amin had discovered that his younger sister was with child, but still had not discovered the name of the man who had dishonored her. This was the same Nur who would be at the Baraki meeting as second-in-command to Amir Rasool, and who was slowly becoming a figure of ridicule among the Pathans because he had not yet enforced the code of Pakhtunwali.

She heard all this and more while sitting at fires, reading heads, and sipping tea. Late in the afternoon she slept again for an hour, and at sunset rode out with Haymond and the guards for the dash across the desert. They traversed the flat wasteland without incident and the next morning came into Baraki. The city was an example of the discriminating nature of the war in Afghanistan. Baraki had never been bombed or shelled, even though it was a major stop-off station on the rebel supply trail.

"The place is like a little Switzerland," Haymond explained as they came riding in. "The *mujahideen* don't keep any bases here, they just pass through. The Russians have spies in town and they report on the traffic. That way there's no need to bomb the town and everybody gets to use it. Convenient, isn't it?"

"Civilized," Snake agreed.

"No, that's going too far. You can't call anything in this God-forsaken country civilized, but it certainly is convenient."

They found a tea house where they could rest and care for the animals. The guards unpacked the horses, watered and fed them, while Haymond slept again. Snake knew that she should also sleep, but she shook herself awake and went into the marketplace to wander, to talk, and to spend a few coins. It was just past dawn, but the market was busy. She bought some shriveled oranges for an outrageous price, some cans of fruit juice made in Bulgaria, a slab of bread, and another of cheese. Again she listened to the gossip, and again heard a recounting of the feud between the Hezb factions, the gambling on the outcome of the meeting, and the fun that was being poked at Nur Amin, who still had not discovered the name of the man who had dishonored his sister.

"Nur had better find someone to kill," one wizened merchant told her gleefully, "or one day he will look behind him and see camel tracks, but no camels."

Snake nodded the agreement proper for a Pathan youth. The code of Pakhtunwali demanded immediate blood retribution when family honor was offended. As second-in-command to the minor faction of Hezb-i-Islami, Nur was losing face daily because of his failure to take action and the time was near when he no longer would be able to lead his men. Their camels would take them away from him.

"Can he not find the one who did it?" Snake asked. For a verb she used the grossest word she knew in Pashto. "Surely the slut of a sister will tell."

"Surely not," cackled the merchant. "I have heard that they beat the soles of her feet with rods and keep her confined to her tent, but she spits in their faces and will not reveal the name of her lover. What a great whore she must be." He cackled again, and added perversely, "Now there is a Pathan woman for you."

The meeting with the rebels was scheduled for noon. Snake went back to the tea house and found Haymond awake, sitting against a wall with a tin mug in his hand. He looked rested. The three guards slept nearby in the shade of the wall. She sat down next to Haymond and gave him one of the shriveled oranges.

"Thanks," he said. He looked at the orange doubtfully, and put it in his pocket. "Where have you been?"

"Scouting."

"How does it look?"

"Rotten. These people will bet on anything, and the odds are five to one that Rasool gets to keep the Stingers."

He nodded. "That's about right. I never figured that Rasool would give them all back. The best I can hope to get is a fifty-fifty split. Ahsen Gul has to get half."

"They're betting on that, too. Three to one against a split. And they're saying that if he doesn't get half there'll be blood on the ground. Even money on that one."

He caught something in her voice. "What else?"

She hesitated. "They're laying three to two in camels that you don't get out of here alive."

He looked at her, startled. "Me? Why me?"

"You're the one who made the deal. If it comes to blood, you have to go too. That's what they're saying."

"They don't love us very much," he said thoughtfully. "No reason why they should. They belong to the Ayatollah, not to us. We give them guns, but he gives them eternity. Are they really laying three to two against me?"

"In camels. That makes it heavy action."

He smiled. "Which way did you bet?"

"I'm waiting for better odds." She liked him very much in that moment.

He nodded toward the sleeping guards. "What about them?"

"Worthless in a situation like this. They won't go up against another Pathan, not for us."

"Yes, I was afraid it would be that way." He looked at his watch. "Let's not keep them waiting."

The meeting was in the courtyard of a tea house on the other side of town. The two factions were already there when Haymond and Snake arrived, seated on opposite sides of the yard. Each faction had sent six men, but a crowd of supporters milled around outside. Ahsen Gul, leader of the major faction, sat cross-legged on the ground, his arms folded stiffly. His beard was grey, and his face was set in stern lines. Amir Rasool, the minor faction leader, was younger and fleshier. He lolled on an elbow, and he smiled often. His second-in-command, Nur Amin, sat farther down the wall. His eyes were never still, darting rapidly from face to face as if he were still looking for the man who had dishonored his name. His fingers drummed nervously on the stock of the rifle that lay in his lap. All of the men in the courtyard were armed. The idea of a weaponless meeting would have seemed ludicrous to them.

Haymond greeted the leaders by name and seated himself against the third wall. Snake sat beside him. He said to her, "Get it rolling."

She said in a high, clear voice, her Pashto carefully enunciated, "In the name of God, the merciful, the compassionate. We meet to decide a question of ownership. My master asks that Ahsen Gul speak first."

Gul unfolded his arms. Staring straight ahead, his expression unbending, he said, "There is no question of ownership. Certain weapons were promised to us. They were sent to us. Before they could reach us they were stolen by the man in front of my eyes. The weapons must be returned to us, or new weapons given to us. There is nothing more to say."

Snake started to translate, but Haymond shook her off. He

could understand more Pashto than he could speak. "I've got it," he said. "The son of a bitch knows God damn well that we can't get any more Stingers right now. Tell the other guy to speak."

Amir Rasool did not bother to pull himself erect. He yawned, as if bored, and said, "I agree that there is no question of ownership. Ownership resides with the possessor. We possess these weapons, therefore we own them. There is nothing more to say."

Haymond muttered, "Arrogant bastard. Keep it going."

Snake said, "My master reminds you that the way of Allah is the middle way. Let us seek a compromise to this question."

"The way of Allah is the way of truth," said Ahsen Gul. "And the truth is with me."

Rasool pointed out, "And the weapons are with me."

"Observe the boasting of a thief."

"This calling of names accomplishes nothing."

"Stubborn idiots," murmured Haymond. "Blockheads."

"Brothers," said Snake. "My master says that we all fight a common enemy. We must work together for victory."

Gul said darkly, "Victory will come when the last thief is hanged." The men behind him fingered the knives in their belts.

"And who will be the hangman?" Rasool asked politely. He turned to his followers. "These people speak of hanging. Did anyone bring a rope?"

Nur Amin, his eyes still darting about, said, "Who needs a rope when bullets are cheap?"

From the other side, someone called, "A knife is even cheaper. Where is your knife these days, Nur Amin? Have you lost it, or did you leave it at home for your sister to sharpen?"

There was laughter from that side of the courtyard. Nur Amin started to his feet, but one of his companions pulled him down. Haymond leaned close to Snake, and said, "Go for the split before they start shooting."

Snake held up her hands. "Brothers, my master reminds you of the words of the Prophet. It is a blessing to share with a neighbor. Can you not divide these weapons between you?"

"Never," said Rasool.

Gul said, "They belong to us, all of them."

"Shall we reward them for thievery?" cried one of his men. "They must return every one."

"Try to take even one," called Nur Amin. "You will see your blood."

Voices rose in the courtyard as insults were flung back and forth. Haymond said to Snake, "It isn't going to work. Pig-headed bastards."

"Don't try to force it. Let the pot boil for a while."

Haymond glanced at his three guards. They were staring intently at the ground, doing their best to remove themselves from the scene. He said to Snake, "Get ready to bail out. We're not going to stay for the fireworks."

While the pot was boiling, Snake reached out to probe some heads. It was like reaching into a sandstorm, a whirling mixture of fury and bloodlust, weariness, frustration, and dark religious fervor. Underneath that she caught friendlier thoughts of fires and homes, women cooking and children playing. But the surface of the sandstorm raged with the passions of angry men, with the fierceness of the Pathan, with his unbending stubbornness, his uncommon bravery, and . . . something else. Something that did not belong in such company. It was shame. In a Pathan?

She probed again, looking around her at the contorted faces, the open, screaming mouths like black holes buried in beards. She chased the strange thread of thought and it brought her over to Rasool's side of the courtyard. She focused on Rasool, himself. No, not there. She let her mind run down the line, and stopped at Nur Amin. Yes, there it was. She opened her mind to it.

She felt the darkness of a night, and the confines of a tent. She felt the warmth of desire and the icy thrust of passion. She felt the male urgings, the female reluctance, and then the liquid submission. She felt the gasps and the moans of accomplishment, and then the long sigh that signaled the end. She felt the contentment of completion. And she felt the shame. Not from the two in the tent. The shame came from a solitary figure high in the rocks, observing. A cloak-wrapped figure filled with shame, and lacking the will to do what had to be done.

Snake smiled.

"Get ready to move," Haymond whispered. "We're getting out of here."

"No, I think I can work this out."

"Not a chance, this place is ready to explode." He got to his feet. "You first. Work your way toward the door."

She stood up next to him. There it was, that pig-headed pride. "Not me. I'm not going to run from a bunch of clowns in pajamas."

"Those clowns are ready to start shooting."

"No, it's still just words."

"You'll get us killed."

"Not if you let me handle it. Just back my play."

Before he could say any more she unslung the Kalashnikov and strode to the center of the courtyard. The angry words swirled around her. She pointed the weapon at the sky and loosed off a volley. There was sudden silence.

"Brothers, my master wishes to speak," she called out. She looked over at Haymond, and said, "Say something to me. Make it sound as if I'm translating. Say anything."

He looked at her intently for a moment. He said loudly, "Actually, you don't look anything like a boy. Quite the opposite."

"Thanks. Say something else."

"You're a damned attractive female, that's what you are."

"Nice of you to notice. Took you long enough."

"I'm sorry. You see, people like you . . . sensitives . . . you sort of scare me."

"I know. It happens all the time. Don't be scared. Please."

"I'll try. Have we said enough?"

"Enough for now," she said happily. "Here we go."

She walked over to where Amir Rasool sat lounging, his rifle on the ground beside him. He looked up at her with an easy insolence. She said, "My master says that this meeting is over. He says that only a fool negotiates with a dead man."

"Indeed," said Rasool. "And who is this dead man?"

"You are."

The men behind Rasool muttered angrily. He quieted them with a glance. The easy smile was still on his face. He asked, "Who is going to kill me, boy? You?"

"No, someone else has the right to do it, not me. He is going to kill you, and then he is going to hand over half of those weapons. And then this meeting will truly be over."

She turned her back on him and walked down the line. She stopped in front of Nur Amin. There was no smile on Nur's face, and no insolence. His rifle lay across his lap, his finger on the trigger guard. It was pointed toward Rasool.

"You cannot wait any longer," she told him. "He is the man who dishonored your sister, and you must kill him. Pakhtunwali demands it."

Heavy silence in the courtyard. Nur Amin's eyes locked on hers. He said nothing.

"Pull yourself together, man, you have to do it," she said. "He is your chief and you respect him, and so you have waited. But you cannot protect him any longer. You cannot wait any longer. If you wait, then you will live in shame for the rest of your life."

Eyes in the courtyard turned to Rasool. He was good. He kept his pose of ease and insolence. He said, laughing, "Sit down, boy. You are speaking foolishness and everyone here knows it."

"You should not speak," Snake told him. "Dead men do not speak."

Rasool's weapon was only a reach away from his hand. It was a short reach, but the slightest shift of that hand would have been both a commitment and an admission of guilt. The hand stayed still. Snake turned back to Nur.

"Do it," she said. "Do it now."

Nur looked from her to Rasool, and back. Only his head moved.

Haymond called in English, "He can't do it. He can't shoot his chief."

"He'll do it," she said without taking her eyes off Nur. And then, in Pashto, "What are you waiting for? Everybody knows it now. You have to do it."

"Nur Amin." Rasool's voice was steady. "It would be better if you left this meeting."

Nur's mouth opened, then closed.

Snake spat on the ground in front of him. "What kind of a man are you? What do you have between your legs?"

"Nur Amin," said Rasool. "Go now."

Nur looked up at Snake pleadingly.

"You faggot," she said. "You camel-fucker. If you won't kill him, then I will. Is that what you want? Shall a woman kill him for you?"

She reached up and pulled off her turban. Her hair fell free. Nur's head jerked back as if he had been slapped. Rasool grabbed for his weapon. Nur saw the move; his rifle came up, and he fired. The bullet caught Rasool full in the chest, and he went over backward. Snake swiveled, the Kalashnikov covering Ahsen Gul and his party.

"*Allah akhbar*," she said. "This is not your fight."

Gul nodded gravely. "It is not our fight," he agreed. He looked at her uneasily, not sure how to treat her.

Snake laughed at his look; her blood was pumping. She went over to where Rasool lay. He was dead. Nur stood over him, staring down. He was lost somewhere, his face sweaty and his eyes blank. The other men in his party had their hands visible and empty. They, too, were out of it.

Snake said in Pashto, "Honor is satisfied." Nur nodded dumbly. "You are now in command. Let your first command be a wise one. The weapons must be divided."

Nur turned to her slowly. He was coming out of it. He frowned, and said, "This is no place for you. I take no orders from a woman."

Snake called to Haymond, "This dinosaur wants to hear it from the male member of the firm. Say something."

Haymond walked over to them, and said loudly, "You've got a real cute little ass, you know that?"

Snake translated that as, "My master suggests that the weapons be divided."

Nur nodded. "Tell your master that it will be done."

Snake said to Haymond, "Say something else."

"You've got a nasty temper, you're as stubborn as a Jefferson County mule, and I think that I love you."

Snake turned and announced to the courtyard, "My master says that this meeting is now concluded." To Haymond, she said, "If you think I'm stubborn, you should meet some of my friends. Compared to them, I'm a pushover."

7

HAT last week in Bled was a happy time for me. I was playing the game and I was winning, but far more important than that, I was able to see Nadia every day. We saw each other in our own particular way, meeting every morning for coffee at the Café France overlooking the lake. We sat at separate tables, on opposite sides of the room, and with our backs to each other. I could see her head reflected dimly in a mirror on the wall. It was the closest together that we could be, and be safe. Although we had formally met at Nordquist's house, we still could not be seen together in public, and Jaspers and Childress were always close by. Still, we were together in our own way and nothing could spoil that for me, not even her blonde hair.

You don't like it, do you? she said. *I'm just getting used to it myself.*

It looks awful.

You bastard, I was hoping you'd like it.

Why? You didn't do it for me.

No, but it would have been nice if you liked it.

I had admired her black and glossy hair, but now it was the

color of cornsilk. Nordquist's wife had been blonde, and Gaczyna Center had decided that Clara Johansen had to be one, too. I asked her how the old man was holding up. I knew that he was miserable as he slid down the chute of despair, unable to break his fall. Not even the presence of his adored Clara could ease it for him. He was in the process of losing everything he owned, everything he had assembled so carefully for his grandson's future, and there was nothing he could do to stop himself. Each night he lost a little more, each morning he swore that he would never touch another card, but every evening at eight he was back in the casino convinced that this was the night when his luck would change. It never did.

He's unbelievable, said Nadia. *He's an incurable optimist. He really thinks that he's going to win back everything he's lost.*

That's the way they are, right down to the last dollar. He has about fifty thousand left. The way he plays, one long session could wipe him out.

And then Ben Slade wins again.

That's the name of the game.

Yes. She was touchy about that part of it. Her assignment was the same as mine, the biochip, but she was trying to read it out of the Swede's head. All she could get that way were dribs and drabs about triple-folding enzymes and quantum-mechanical tunneling; nothing that could be translated into progress. It could never work that way, and I could have told her that before she started. It was exactly what I had told Delaney.

What happens once he's broke? she asked.

We'll make him an offer for the chip. It won't be anything blatant. My people will put it into the form of a university grant, or a prize, but it will cover all his losses.

What makes you think that he'll take it?

He'll have to.

I'm not so sure. He's a pacifist and an idealist, a real one. He means everything he says. He's determined not to see the chip used in armaments.

He'll take the deal. Who the hell does he think he is, trying to live with principles in an age like this? If nothing else, there's his grandson to think about.

It's a shame. He's such a sweet person.

You don't have to tell me that. I like him, too.

You like him so much that you're trying to ruin him.

Of course I am. So are you.

No, there's a difference. I'm just after some information.

And you're not getting it.

No, I'm not. You'll get yours before I get mine. If I get it at all.

Right, so don't kid yourself, we're after the same thing. You're using the bedroom and I'm using the cardroom. That's the only difference.

That bothers you, doesn't it? The part about the bedroom.

Yes.

It never did before.

That was your private life. This is business.

And who are you to pass judgment? You're cheating a helpless old man.

I'm not going to argue the point. Neither of us has much to be proud of.

We're just playing the game. Do you really care who gets the chip?

No, a plague on both their houses. I just want to spend some time with you while I can. Do you ski?

Are you serious? I'm Russian. You mean go skiing together?

Why not? Nobody would know. We could be a hundred feet apart on the mountain.

When?

Tomorrow? The next day?

It's a tempting idea. I saw her smile in the mirror. *All right, yes. This isn't going to last forever. A week from now you'll be back in New York bowling over the ladies in the Third Avenue saloons.*

And you'll be back with Forquet, or somebody like him.

We had gone a touch too far, over the line from casual banter. My eyes were on the mirror and I could see her head bowed down. She was staring at her hands. I caught what was coming. She said, *Ben, I know you don't like me to say this. . . .*

Then don't. You know it's impossible.

We have so little time left. If we could find some way to spend it together . . . really together, not like this.

Babe, you're dreaming, you know it can't be done. Leave it alone. Every time we talk about it we wind up feeling rotten.

I know. I'm sorry. It's just that . . . I'm sorry. She stood up. *Same time tomorrow?*

I'll be here. Skiing the next day?

Yes. She walked to the door, her hair bobbing in rhythm to her step. It might have been the way that it swayed back and forth, but I didn't much mind it being blonde anymore.

I waited a while, and then left. Jaspers and Childress were outside and they walked with me down the Kidriceva toward the hotel. Two men leaned against a building up ahead of us. They were wearing ski clothes. I went into their heads at fifty feet. They were from the Ministry for Internal Security, the local version of the KGB. They straightened up as we drew closer, and moved to block the sidewalk.

Jaspers saw the move and took a step to get out in front of me. Childress edged toward the curb. He said, "Get back to that café and wait there."

"No," I said, "it's the local law."

"Son of a buck. Do we make a fuss?"

"No, you can't fight a badge, not here. Stay out of it. Tag along behind and see where they take me."

"Notify daddy?"

"Once you've got me located."

That was as much as we had time for. The two men stepped forward, and one of them flashed a card case at me. "Security," he said. "Your papers, please."

We handed over passports. Mine was the Canadian one in the name of Brian Patterson. The examination was quick. Jaspers and Childress got theirs back. The taller of the two men checked mine, shook his head, and said, "This passport is out of order. You will have to come with us."

"No, I'll go only to the Canadian consulate," I said.

"Please, there is no need. This is only a formality." He put his hand on my arm.

I felt Jaspers stiffen beside me, but that was just habit. I muttered, "Like I said." He nodded.

There was a Fiat parked at the curb. They put me into the back seat, one of them beside me and the other driving. At first I thought that they were taking me to the local shop up behind the zoo, but they kept going on the Ljubljanska and we were headed for the city. The trip into Ljubljana took over an hour on the snow-covered roads. I stayed in their heads for a while, but learned nothing. They were cops doing a job, bringing a man in. That's all they knew. The one beside me had his mind on his lunch, and the driver was busy handling the road.

We came into Ljubljana from the west, and up into the city proper. They took me to a building in back of Liberation Square, beyond the park where the trees are planted in the shape of a star. It was an old building, grey and sheathed with grey ice. I did not want to go into it. They hustled me inside and down a corridor to a room with only a long table and some chairs. The room smelled of disinfectant and wet concrete.

The driver said, "Empty your pockets, put everything on the table."

I said, "I thought this was just a formality."

He hit me across the mouth. My hand came up. He grinned. I lowered it. He said, "That was like a kiss from your sister. You want the real thing?"

I put wallet, keys, and change on the table. They already had my passport. They took me down another hallway to a room with a holding cell in it. It looked like a drunk tank on a

Saturday night. The smell was overpowering, and so was the noise. There were about twenty men in the cell, and they looked and smelled like garbage. They were gutter dregs in greasy rags. The noise fell off when they saw me. They pressed to the front of the cage and looked at me silently, curiously, through the bars.

"What is this?" I asked the driver.

"Sewer rats. We round them up every day. This is the latest collection. Charming, aren't they?"

"You putting me in there?"

"Just for a while."

"Another formality?"

"That's it."

They put me into the tank and the door clanged shut behind me. I stood with my back to the bars. The nearest rats backed off, still staring at me. One of them took a step toward me and stopped, his nose up and sniffing. He actually looked like a rat, with a pointed face and small eyes. One of those eyes was gone, the socket red and leaking. He took another step toward me. I raised an arm and he backed off.

"Don't be afraid," said the driver from outside the bars. "He just wants to be friendly."

"He likes the way you smell," said the other one. "He's not used to people who smell like you."

I said over my shoulder, "If somebody is trying to prove something to me, tell him that he's made his point, whatever it is. We don't have to go any further with this."

They thought that was funny. "What's your hurry?" asked one of them. "You just got here. The rats are all right once you get to know them."

The other one said, "I think they like you. They want to be friends."

The men in the tank moved forward into a semicircle around me, with One-Eye the closest. They were silent and staring. There was only the shuffle of their feet on the slimy concrete, and the rustle of their rags. One-Eye got too close and I kicked out at him. I missed, and he scrambled back and then edged in again. The others moved with him. They made a tight ring around me.

"Listen," I called, "what does it take to get out of here?"

"Patience, just patience, my friend," said one.

"Take my advice," said the other. "Give them whatever they want. They'll leave you alone if you give them what they want."

"What the hell do they want?"

"Your clothes, of course. You don't have anything else that they need."

A door slammed. They were gone. One-Eye took the slam for a signal. He jumped forward, reaching for my arm. I backhanded him across the face and he fell. He got up and scuttered away. The others moved back a step, and then another, and then, suddenly disinterested, they turned away and moved aimlessly about the tank. The back of my hand felt wet. There were two red lines where One-Eye's teeth had grazed flesh. I found a corner to hunker in, back to the wall, and waited. I did not know what I was waiting for, but the clock on the wall outside the tank read three in the afternoon.

Food was brought at six: metal mugs of tea and slabs of white bread slathered with margarine. Orderlies pushed the food into the tank and left it on the floor. There was a scramble for it. I did not try for mine; I stayed crouched in my corner. I watched as the others drank their tea and ate the centers of their slices of bread. With a strange fastidiousness, they did not eat the crusts. They threw them in the single, open toilet in the far corner. They drank all of the tea, some of them holding the mugs over their mouths for the last drops. None of them looked at me.

The lights went out at six-thirty; evening outside but midnight in the tank. The place was totally dark. I stood up, and stretched; I had been squatting too long. I heard the rustling sounds as they moved about in the darkness. I waited for them to come, and as I waited I probed some heads. There wasn't much to read. The greed was there in its simplest form. They wanted my clothing and they were going to get it. That was all.

I don't know what time it was when they came. I was asleep. I had tried to stay awake, but I had slumped in my corner. I felt the first one tug at my boots, and that brought me up. I kicked and connected, heard a squeal, and then they were all over me. I lay on my back, kicking and punching. The stink of them sickened me, and the slither of their bodies. They tore at my clothes, ripping and pulling. They tore flesh, as well. They weren't men to me anymore, they were rats. I had had my fill of rats in that Texas shack in the years before Pop found me. They had often come in the night when I was tied to my bed, and I had screamed. I heard a voice screaming now, and I knew that it was mine. After a while the voice stopped, and after a while it was morning. When the lights came on I was still in my corner, my legs drawn up and my head on my knees. They had taken all my clothing . . . everything. I was bitten and clawed, and sometime during the night I had been sick. My eyes were shut. I did not want to open them.

Someone pulled me out of the tank. Someone stood me against a wall and turned a hose on me. The water was icy. I kept my eyes shut as it pounded into me. Someone told me to open my eyes, but I wouldn't. Someone shoved a rough towel into my hands and told me to dry myself. When I was dry, someone slapped an oily salve all over me. It smelled like the disinfectant that clung to the walls, and it stung.

"I told you to give them what they wanted. Open your eyes, it's all over."

I opened them. It was the driver. The rats were pressed against the bars of the cage, staring at me silently just as they had the day before. I saw pieces of my clothing on them. One-Eye was wearing most of my shirt. My feet were cold on the wet concrete. I looked down at myself. The salve was purple and thick, but through it I could see the marks of nails and teeth.

"Wrap this around you," said the driver. He handed me a blanket. It was old and faded, but it looked reasonably clean. I let it drop on the wet floor.

"Keep it for your mother," I said. "It gets cold on the streets at night."

He liked that. He nodded appreciatively. "That's good," he said, "but you'd better take it."

I let it lie on the floor.

"You can't just walk around naked."

I didn't move.

He shook his head. "All right, but the major isn't going to like it."

We walked down another long corridor. It was much longer than the one I had walked the day before, so long that I began to wonder if we were still in the same building. The walls were of the same unfinished concrete and bore the same chemical smell. The floor was gritty under my bare feet. I was conscious of my nakedness as I walked. I had never been that way before. Nakedness was for lovemaking, and medical checkups, and nothing else. Walking that way I was aware of how undisturbed a life I led, and had led since the Texas days. Nothing I had learned at the Center, or in almost ten years in the field, had prepared me for the simple act of walking naked down a long, dank corridor in the center of the capital of Slovenia. I was aware of the slight roundness of my belly that I had sworn to lose, of the pectorals that needed building, and the buttocks that were not quite tight enough. For all of that, I tried to walk jauntily. It wasn't easy.

"In here," said the driver.

It was just another door in the corridor. We had walked a long way. The room inside was brightly lit, and warm. I was grateful for the warmth. There was a table, and a chair that looked comfortable. On the table were a television camera that was pointed at the chair, and a television monitor. That was all.

"You sit in the chair," said the driver.

"What's it all about?"

He shrugged. "Gadgets. The major loves gadgets." He added, "You're shivering."

"No, that's nothing."

"And you're sweating."

"Why the sudden concern?"

"You're not supposed to die. If you die I catch all kinds of hell."

The business with the blanket had gotten to him. I said, "Don't worry, I'm not going to die. I always sweat and shiver first thing in the morning. It's good for the liver."

He gave me a long look, then said, "I'm glad it's good for something." He went out the door and closed it behind him.

I sat in the chair. It was coated with a plastic that was cold against my skin. My eyes felt hot. The red light on the camera glowed, and the screen lit up. The picture of a man appeared. He was dressed in uniform, and seated at a desk. His face was long and thin, less Slavic than Hapsburg, and he looked to be in his fifties. His voice came out of speakers attached to the monitor.

"Good morning, Mister Slade," he said. "My name is Mihevc, and I hold the rank of major in the Ministry for Internal Security. I have some questions to ask you."

He had called me Slade, and so the Canadian cover was finished. I could have gone through the routine, insisted that I was Brian Patterson, and demanded to see the Canadian consul, but that seemed useless now. I said nothing. I reached out and probed all around me. I found nothing. I probed again, and harder. Still nothing. There was no one near enough to reach.

He said, "Do you admit that your name is Benjamin Slade?"

I said nothing.

"You're wasting my time, Mister Slade. You are not Canadian, you are American and you are attached to the so-called Federal

Center for Childhood Diseases. We both know what that means, so let's not fence with each other. Agreed?"

I did not answer. I kept probing, and getting nothing. The television hookup told the story. He had placed himself out of my range. He was sitting in a room at least two hundred feet away from me. It was not a new ploy, but it was effective. My head was dizzy and the sweat was pouring off me. I shook myself, and took deep breaths. It didn't help.

"You seem uncomfortable, Slade."

Silence.

"Is there anything you wish? Clothing? A cup of tea? Something to eat?"

Silence.

"Would you like to go back to the holding cell? Is that what you want?"

The stick, soon to be followed by the carrot.

"That doesn't seem to bother you. Perhaps that was a mistake last night. I admit it, it was meant to soften you up, but you don't soften very easily, do you? You're a lot tougher than I thought you would be."

The carrot. I was having a hard time sitting straight in the chair. I kept falling forward, and catching myself.

"Are you going to say anything at all, Slade?"

I forced myself up in the chair. I wondered what Sammy would have done in this position. Or any of the others.

"Aren't you at all curious? Don't you want to know why you are here?"

By this time, Sammy would have sold him the Brooklyn Bridge, the Washington Monument, and a half interest in the Chicago Bears.

"You're in Yugoslavia on a false passport. That's good for five years inside if that's the way I want to handle it."

By this time, Snake would have decided exactly what sort of fatal accident the major was going to have some day soon.

"Or we can have a little chat now, you can answer a few questions, and I can forget about the business with the passport."

By this time, Vince would have twisted the camera off its mounting and kicked in the monitor screen.

"Which will it be?"

By this time, Martha would have convinced the son of a bitch that his karma was out of kilter and that all his problems would be solved if he'd only stop eating red meat.

"Look here, Slade, try to see this my way. After all, I'm a policeman. A glorified policeman, but that's what I am, and policemen are curious. So here comes Mister Brian Patterson wandering into my cabbage patch with a Canadian passport in his pocket. He plays poker at the casino, he skis, he spends money in the shops, and he does nothing to arouse my suspicions. He seems like a legitimate tourist, the kind we like to see here. But then we run him through the machine and he comes up Benjamin Slade, an American sensitive. Does this bother me? Not terribly. Everybody is entitled to take a vacation, but why the false passport? Obviously, he's on a job. Does this bother me? Again, not terribly. We all have our work to do. But this is my cabbage patch, and I have to ask a few questions. Essentially, I have to know if my national interests are involved. Not that I expect any truthful answers, but I have to observe the quality of the lies. If I decide that my national interests are not threatened, I might stand back and let you play out your game. If I decide that you are a potential threat, then I might boot you over the border. But before anything else I have to ask some questions and I have to hear some answers. Sitting there silently gets you nowhere, and you surely must know that. If you push me hard enough I'll have to find out exactly how tough you really are. I'd rather not. I'd rather do this the easy way. Now, what do you say?"

I said, "Turn off the cameras and come in here. Let's talk face to face."

He smiled. "Do you really think I would do that?"

"I'm suggesting it as a course of action. You're asking for some open talk from me. I'm asking the same from you. I'm not looking to pick any state secrets out of your head, but before I say anything else I have to see how straight your offer is, and I can only do that face to face. If you can't go along with that, then you'll just have to do it the hard way."

It took him about thirty seconds to make up his mind, his lips pressed into a thin line. Then the screen went blank and the light on the camera went off. A few minutes later he came into the room. He was shorter than he had looked on the screen. He walked around the table and stood in front of me. His body was tensed, his shoulders squared.

"Go ahead," he said.

I took a quick look around. He knew nothing about Nordquist or biochips. Nothing about my operation. He was straight.

I said, "All right, I'm out."

The tenseness went out of him. He slid a hip over the table, and rested there. "Well?"

"This is as much as I can tell you. As you assumed, I'm operational. My subject is a foreign national temporarily in Yugoslavia. My assignment is the collection of information, nothing more. It is in no way prejudicial to the interests of your country, and it does not involve overt action of any kind. You wouldn't be hurting yourself if you winked at this one."

"What is the name of your subject?"

"Sorry."

"What is the nature of your collection?"

"No, I've gone as far as I can. You'd have to get that the hard way."

He looked thoughtful. "It might be best if I did."

"That's up to you, but I'll tell you one thing more. You've been around this business long enough to know that favors sometimes get returned. Now, either let me go, or throw me back in the tank. That's all I'm going to say."

He stared at me stonily. I was back in his head. He was going to let me go, but he wasn't being generous. He was going to let me run and see what I brought him. He stood up and walked out of the room. He left the door open behind him.

After a while the driver came in. He had an armful of clothing, and an envelope with my passport, wallet, and keys. He laid it all on the table. The trousers and shirt were made of thick, rough wool, the shoes were tan and pointy, and the coat was a navy pea jacket. There was a woolen cap as well. I stared at the pile, trying to think of something to say about his mother. Nothing came to me.

"Put them on," he said, "and don't even think of saying no this time. It's snowing out."

He helped me into the clothing. I had trouble standing straight, and with the salve all over me it was like trying to squeeze toothpaste back into the tube. We finally got it done and he took me down the hallway to a door that led to the street. It was not the same way I had come in. He was right about the snow, it was falling thickly. I stepped outside and felt the flakes on my face. I licked them from my lips. I turned back to look at the driver.

"Give my regards to your mother," I said. "She's probably a lovely lady."

"She's been dead twenty years and she was a nasty old bitch," he said. "How did you know she was a whore?"

"I didn't. It was just something to say."

He nodded, and closed the door.

Jaspers and Childress were parked across the street. Their car was a mound of snow with a plume of vapor curling from the exhaust. They saw me, and came running. Jaspers swore when he saw my face. They got me across the street and into the back of the car. The heater was blasting away and the air was thick with cigaret smoke. Harry Kourkalis was in the front seat. He wanted to give me his parka, but I told him that I was warm enough.

"How bad is it?" he asked.

"Looks worse than it is, but I'll need a shot of antibiotics. What the hell are you doing here?"

"We'll get you a doctor in Bled," he said. Jaspers had the car going, driving slowly down the street toward Liberation Square. "What was it all about?"

"Standard intimidation. I'm blown." That was all I was saying right then. He could get the rest of it later on. I was too angry to talk to him. He had no business being there. It was like the morning after Big John Brodski died. If Harry was there, he was bringing bad news. He stared over the front seat at me, his eyes heavy and sorrowful. Finally, I said, "Stop looking at me that way. What is it? What happened?"

"Your pigeon is ready to be plucked. He walked into the casino last night and lost fifty thousand in less than an hour. He's broke. Finished."

So it wasn't bad news, at least not the kind I had expected. I was sorry for Nordquist, but it meant that my part of the job was over. I managed a grin, and said, "That's fine with me. He's the Agency's pigeon now."

I was wrong. It was bad news after all. Harry shook his head. "The Agency wants you to make the deal."

I exploded. I said some wild things. Harry listened patiently. When I had run out of steam, he said, "That's the way it is. My instructions are to give you the details of the offer. Your instructions are to make the offer and close the deal."

"That wasn't the agreement. I was supposed to break the guy, that's all. After that it was an Agency job."

"That's been changed. The thinking now is that you're the logical one to make the offer. Nordquist knows you and he trusts you. It makes sense, Ben."

It made sense from their point of view, but not mine. The old man knew me and trusted me, and now they wanted me to stick it to him. It put me out in the open, not the place to be after what I had done.

I said, "It was always going to be this way, wasn't it? They planned it this way from the beginning."

He looked away.

"They did, didn't they?"

He nodded. "I didn't know it. I'm sorry. It's a hell of a thing to ask you to do."

"Nobody's asking, they're telling."

He nodded again. He still couldn't look at me.

8

D ENNIS Costello was shaving when he first heard the news
of the hijacking of Pan American flight 204. It was six-
fifteen in the morning, and the radio was turned low. He stopped
shaving, razor poised as he listened. The flight, en route from
Athens to Cairo, had been seized over the Mediterranean and
forced to land in Tunis. The hijackers had not yet announced
their demands. Several Americans were believed to be on board.

Costello said to himself, "Anybody who flies out of Athens
ought to have his head examined."

He knew something about airport security. At the age of forty-
four he had been a New York City cop for twenty years and
now, with the rank of captain, he was head of the department's
hostage-negotiating team. He had been in charge of dozens of
hostage situations, had served a training tour with the FBI, and
he knew that when it came to terrorist penetration, Athens had
the least secure airport in Europe. Despite the pious protests of
the Papandreou government, the Greeks were careful not to
offend any Arab interest including those of the Libyan- and
Syrian-trained terrorist groups, and on those rare occasions when
airport security was enforced because of world opinion, it could

always be breached by bribery. Costello would sooner have played Russian roulette with his service revolver than have boarded a plane in Athens airport.

He heard a follow-up to the story with his breakfast. The hijacked aircraft had been surrounded on the ground by Tunisian troops. A breakaway faction of the PLO, the Lions of the Sand, had claimed responsibility, and the mainline PLO had denied any involvement. The hijackers were demanding the release of seventeen of their comrades being held in Kuwaiti jails, and were threatening to kill one hostage every hour until their demands were met. Despite a series of hijackings and hostage-takings over the past year, the Kuwaitis had steadily refused to release those same seventeen prisoners. Their response this time would no doubt be the same.

"Sons of bitches," Costello muttered into his coffee cup.

It was an unchanging script. Every hostage situation eventually boiled down to how far the terrorists were willing to go. Would they spend their lives, or not? They all claimed to be martyrs to the bone. It was, after all, the essence of the hostage scenario that the terrorist must be willing to die but, in fact, there were those who lacked that final inch of determination. So you never knew, and whoever was in charge of the negotiations always had to assume the worst-case possibility unless. . . .

"Unless." He said the word aloud, lost in thought. Unless you had a negotiator who knew what they were thinking. One of the federal negotiators from that place in Virginia. The Center. He had seen them at work during his training tour with the FBI, and as hostage negotiators they could not be beat.

Which led him to thoughts of Martha Marino. She had been his instructor during that tour, and after a while she had been something more than that. He remembered a cap of curly chestnut hair, a heart-shaped face, and a smooth and rounded body that put a catch in his throat even now as he thought of it. By the end of the tour they had been spending their nights together as well as their days, and for Costello, a bachelor by conviction,

112

it had been the one time in his life when he would have been willing to cast those convictions aside. But not Martha. After a month or so she had been ready to move on to something new, and at the end of his tour Costello had been left with a handsome set of memories, and nothing more. Except a profound respect for the sensitives who formed the core of the federal hostage-negotiating teams. Although two years had gone by, the memories still were strong and the respect had never faded.

He threw the memories aside, and finished his coffee. There was no profit in looking backward. The business with Martha was long finished, and as a city cop he had nothing to do with the federal teams. But the memories returned later that morning as he sat in his office and heard the latest reports from Tunis. By then the Pan Am hijackers had started to kill their hostages, and Costello had a problem of his own.

Michael Ali Rachman heard about Pan Am 204 on the seven-thirty news, listening to the radio as he stacked leaflets in the clubhouse of the Palestine-American Friendship Society in the Jackson Heights section of Queens. Rachman was the president of the society, an organization of local shopkeepers and small businessmen of Middle Eastern origin. Few of the members were actually Palestinian. Most were Syrian, Lebanese, Egyptian, Lybian: representatives of a broad range of the Arab world who, nevertheless, considered the Palestinian cause so much their own that they were willing to march under that single banner. Their clubhouse was a simple place, the back room of a warehouse on Roosevelt Avenue, the walls stacked high with sacks of chick-peas, and cartons of figs and dates.

On this particular morning there were twenty-seven members of the society in the small room—men, women, and teenagers—all preparing for the day's demonstration in front of the Israeli government offices on Fifth Avenue in Manhattan. Today's demonstration was against the West Bank settlements, but the society demonstrated so often that the banners that they carried seldom changed. *Down with the Imperialist Zionists* was always prominent, followed by all the other slogans they had been repeating over the years. Demonstration was the lifeblood of the Palestine-American Friendship Society. It was a peaceful organization, dedicated to lecturing the American public on the evils of Zionism, and its leaders knew the value of a low profile in a city that had more Jews than Tel Aviv. They marched, they picketed, they chanted slogans, always within the limits of the law. Only Rachman and his two closest associates knew about the case of Armalite submachine guns and the carton of Mark VI grenades under triple lock in the storeroom of the warehouse. The weapons were not for now. They existed for a day that might never come, but if it ever did, the weapons would be there and would be ready.

But today, Rachman was concerned not with weapons but with the everyday logistics of moving his twenty-seven demonstrators from Jackson Heights to mid-Manhattan without incident, and without losing any of them to the whims of the New York City Transit System. He was not concerned about the women. They always sat quietly on the subway, did not wander, and gave out their leaflets cheerfully on the picket line. Some of the men did the same, but others, with the headstrong independence of the male Arab, found the leaflets burdensome and the trashcans convenient. More, when the emotions ran high, they tended to shout the sort of inflammatory slogans that were more appropriate to a demonstration in East Beirut than to one in the shadow of the Empire State Building. The teenagers were the worst of all. They were uncontrollable and constantly in trouble with the police. Given his choice, Rachman would have done without them, but most were there at the insistence of their fathers and uncles. When teenagers were being formed into suicide squads in Syria and Lybia, it was difficult to keep your own children away from the safety of a demonstration.

The most difficult of the young ones were Abu Hassani and

Jimmy Abdul Farag. Abu was a fanatical supporter of the Palestinian cause, which was to be applauded in one so young, but there was a bubbling violence in the boy that was unpredictable, and thus frightening. He had twice been arrested for fighting with the tough young Jews who heckled the picket lines, and he fought with a vicious savagery. He was only seventeen, but there was a darkness in his soul that Rachman both feared and respected. It was the darkness of destruction. Abu Hassani properly belonged in the front lines of the struggle for the liberation of Palestine, and not in the pale New York world of leaflets and slogans. In the Middle East he would have been well on his way by now to an honorable martyrdom. Here he was only a nuisance.

Jimmy Abdul was another sort of nuisance. The other kids called him The Dummy. Slow, gentle, hulking, and dim-witted, he was helpless at handing out leaflets, he never remembered the slogans, and he broke into trills of idiotic laughter without warning. Only Abu Hassani could control him, and he did that with the delicacy and understanding of an elder brother. He treated Jimmy gently, and with a genuine affection that was like no other facet of his character; and Jimmy repaid that affection with a devotion that was close to being slavish. They were always together, often causing Rachman more trouble than they were worth, but he continued to use them. Like the other young ones, they were entitled to participate in the struggle.

Jimmy Abdul, at that moment, sat in a corner of the room and watched as the others stacked leaflets and rolled banners. He wanted to help, but the pain in his head was too strong. It was a screaming, shouting pain, knife-edges of voices shrilling round in his skull. It was always there to some degree, and he was accustomed to living with it, but sometimes it filled his head to bursting and whenever that happened he was good for nothing at all. His eyes misted over and his hands would not work right, and sometimes he did crazy things just to make the pain go away. Nobody knew about the pain except Abu. Nobody else would have understood how bad it could get, even if the words had been there to explain it. And Jimmy did not have the words. Words, like the pain, stayed bottled in his head. But, somehow, Abu knew. He didn't need words with Abu; a nod or a look was enough. Like now, as Abu tied up a bundle of leaflets and flipped them onto the table, he looked over at Jimmy, and winked. He knew, without words, how bad the pain was, and so he winked to show his sympathy. Jimmy winked back, but even that caused pain. He covered his ears with his hands, trying in vain to shut out the keening voices.

Up at the front of the room, Rachman looked at his watch and saw that it was time to go if they were going to be at the picket line promptly at nine. He was about to give the order to leave when the news came over the radio about the hijacking of Pan Am 204. There was a momentary silence, and then the room exploded in a roar of approval.

David Krulewich stood in the doorway of the Congregation Beth Hillel synagogue and looked up and down East Thirty-second Street. At eight-thirty on a weekday morning there were plenty of people on the street, but not the people he wanted to see. He wanted to see someone named Leonard Greenspan. He wanted to see Carl Berman, or Jack Kaufman, or any other member of the Beth Hillel congregation. He looked at his watch and wondered how much longer he was going to have to wait for someone to show up. Which reminded him of a story. Nothing new about that, everything reminded Krulewich of a story these days. He even began most of his sentences with, "That reminds me of the time when. . . ." Well, why not? It was a habit, a figure of speech, and quite understandable in a seventy-four-year-old man. He had lots to remember.

So he was reminded of the story about the poor Jew who came to America, and decided to go out west. A hundred years ago this was, or at least seventy-five, and there's this poor Jew, let's call him Chaim, bumping along on a railroad train through the wilds of Texas, or Arizona, or one of those places that's full of cactus, and Indians, and *antisemiten*; and it's the last of those that's making Chaim nervous. He doesn't speak much English, he's a long way from home, and he's been filled full of stories about what they do to Jews once you get across the Mississippi River. But Chaim is making the best of it, humming a little tune to keep up his nerve, when all of a sudden there's a scream of the brakes and the train stops smack in the middle of the desert. Chaim looks out the window and he begins to shake. There's a tough bunch of hombres on horses out there. They've stopped the train, and now two of them get off their horses, hitch up their gun belts, and come clumping onto the train right into the car where he's sitting. *Gevalt*, just look at them. Big, and broad, and mean, they look like everything that he had been warned about before he headed west. Cowboys, roughnecks, *antisemiten* who would hang a Jew from the nearest tree just for the fun of it. Chaim is really shivering now, his bones are out of control, because sure enough these two thugs are walking down the aisle of the train, stopping at every seat and asking every man only one question.

"Hey, you. Are you a Jew?"

So there it is, his fate. He should never have left the *shtetl*, and after that he should never have left the congenial streets of New York. But he did and now he's finished because these two cowboys are looking for a Jew to hang from the nearest cotton-wood tree. They're going to ask him if he's a Jew, and what is he going to say? No, I'm not? Is that what he's going to say with the *payes* hanging down over his ears and his gaberdine buttoned up tight around his neck? He scrunches down in his seat, hoping that they'll walk right by him, but no such luck. They stop and look down with those cold, hard eyes, and one of them asks the question.

"Hey, you. Are you a Jew?"

"Who, me?" he manages to say. "No, no, not me."

The cowboy looks surprised. "Are you sure you're not a Jew?"

117

"Definitely not, I'm telling you."

One cowboy looks at the other, and says, "Whadda ya think, Chuck? He looks like a Jew, don't he?"

"You bet he does," says Chuck. He leans over to look Chaim dead in the eye. "Look here, you sure you're not a Jew?"

"I'm not, I'm not. I just told you."

The other cowboy bends over too, and now Chaim has both their faces up close to his. The other one says, "I don't know, fella. Are you plumb sure you ain't some kind of a Jew?"

That's as much as Chaim can take. He snaps. If he's going to be hanged, he'll be hanged like a *mensch*. He throws up his hands, and says, "All right, all right, leave me alone. I admit it. I'm a Jew." He sits back to await his fate.

"*Denks Gott*," says the cowboy in Yiddish. "We've been looking all over. We only have nine men and we need you for a *minyan*."

Which was exactly what David Krulewich had, nine men inside the synagogue, including himself. Nine, one short of the necessary ten to form the *minyan* that Jews must have when they pray. One short. It was the same story every morning at the synagogue when he came to *dovon minecha*, waiting around for an eighth, a ninth, and a tenth to show up. Any Jewish man would do, and sometimes it was necessary to go out in the street and search for someone to make up the group, just like the cowboys in the story. Borrow a body, so to speak. It was sad, but time had passed the congregation by. Years before . . . but that was something else. Now Beth Hillel was only a narrow storefront of a synagogue on a commercial street in midtown Manhattan, an inconvenient place for a temple. With no residential base on which to draw for its members the congregation dwindled further each year, and now there were only the old men like David Krulewich who still came every morning to say their prayers. Sometimes with a *minyan*, and sometimes without. Sometimes there was no choice but to go ahead with less than ten, which was what was going to happen today unless some-

118

body showed up within the next few minutes. After all, how long can you wait to say morning prayers? Pretty soon it gets to be time for lunch.

Krulewich stepped out onto the street, prayer shawl around his shoulders and skullcap on his head, craning his neck to look up toward Fifth Avenue. No Greenspan, no Berman, no Kaufman. Enough, he would have to ask some stranger to join the *minyan*. He looked around for a likely candidate and saw a group of people approaching, going west on Thirty-second Street. They were handing out leaflets to pedestrians, and some of them were carrying banners. He peered at the signs. *Stop Zionist Murders. Israel Out of the West Bank. Halt Jewish Terrorism.* Oh, my God, *those* crazies. He took a quick step back into the shelter of the doorway, and let the parade pass by. He watched them go down the street, and smiled. Krulewich, he told himself, you used to be a pretty good salesman, but do you really think you could sell a *minyan* to a bunch of Arabs? Still smiling, he looked down toward Madison and saw two men hurrying up the street. Young men, but that didn't matter. Past the age of *bar mitzvah* was enough to qualify for a *minyan*. He stepped out onto the sidewalk again, and held out a hand.

"Excuse me," he said, "but would either of you happen to be Jewish?"

They stared at him, uncomprehending for the moment. They were very young, teenagers. One of them was short and wiry, with an intense look around his eyes. The other was taller, awkward looking, and his eyes were empty.

"I'm sorry," said Krulewich. "Maybe you didn't hear. I asked if you were maybe a Jew."

"Me?" asked the intense one. "You mean me?"

"You're not? Sorry, I made a mistake."

"You sure did. My name is Abu Hassani. Does that sound like a Jew name?" He reached out and poked at Krulewich's prayer shawl. "You're the Jew, not me. That's what Jews wear."

"Yes, well, sorry to bother you." Too late, Krulewich realized that these two belonged to the group that just had passed by. He started to turn away, but Abu's hand clamped on his arm and held him.

"Why did you call me a Jew?" he asked. He turned to his friend. "Did you hear that, Jimmy? He thought I was a Jew." The hulking one nodded slowly.

"Listen, forget it," said Krulewich. "I didn't mean it that way."

"Who the hell do you think you are, calling me a Jew? Jews kill people."

"Let go of my arm."

"They killed the babies at Sabra and Shatila."

"Let go or I'll call a cop."

"They stole the homeland."

"What is this? Get away from me."

"They bomb our cities, they murder our people. Why do you murder our people?"

"I never murdered anyone in my life."

"You did. You and all the other Jews."

Abu's voice was riding high, and Krulewich knew that he had a problem. This one was a *mashuganah*, a real nut case. He pulled away and his arm came free. He darted for the doorway of the synagogue. It was a momentary freedom. Abu came after him, caught him, and they both went crashing through the door. Krulewich fell to the floor inside. He landed on his elbow, and he felt pain shoot along his arm. He looked up. Abu stood over him, staring open-mouthed at the simple storelike temple: the wooden benches, the stacks of prayer books, the eight startled men in prayer shawls and skullcaps gathered near the ark.

"Jews," said Abu. He breathed the word, almost reverently. "Hey, Jimmy, get in here."

"Go away," screamed Krulewich. "Get out of here."

"Jews," Abu repeated. "Lots of Jews." Over his shoulder, he called, "Jimmy, get your ass in here, you hear me?"

The awkward one appeared in the doorway.

"Look at this," said Abu. "Look what we got here. This is it, man."

Jimmy looked at him questioningly.

"This is our chance," Abu said excitedly. "This is what I've been waiting for. I'll never get a chance like this again."

Jimmy shook his head, confused.

"The plane, don't you get it? The hijackers on the radio. This is where we make our stand with our brothers."

Troubles, thought Krulewich. Big troubles.

Then Abu's coat fell open, and he saw the stubby submachinegun and the grenades hanging in loops, and he knew how big the trouble really was.

Martha Marino did not hear about Pan Am 204 until after eight o'clock. She awoke at seven, and as she always did when coming up from sleep, she rolled from her mattress to the floor, assumed the lotus position, and snapped herself into meditation. For the next seventeen minutes she reviewed her actions of the day before, contemplated the day to come, and thought lovingly of Pop, and of Snake, Ben, Sammy, and Vince.

Particularly of Vince. From her position on the floor she could see him lying on the bed, still sleeping soundly. He had tossed off the covers, and now he stretched in his sleep, mahogany skin stretched over a smooth musculature. The sight of him warmed her in more ways than one. There was the warmth of excitement in the pit of her belly, but there was also the warmth of embarrassment on her cheeks. The second warmth annoyed her. She had nothing to feel guilty about, but . . . Vince? Vince, of all people.

They were the newest of lovers, but lovers nonetheless in the fashion of oh-my-God-how-did-this-ever-happen-to-us? It had taken them both by surprise, blindsided by Eros. It was not all that unusual for two sensitives to be lovers, but it was a rarity, if not unheard of, for two aces of the same year. They were, after all, brother and sister in a fashion deeper than any blood tie, and from the age of twelve onward they had thought of themselves only in that way. Bratty sister. Big-shot, know-it-all brother. He had taught her how to dance, she had taught him how to fish. She had giggled at his clothes, and he had laughed at her braces. They had shared all the secrets of the young and the growing, and after they were grown they had shared some sadness, too. That's the way it had always been with them, not just the two of them, but all five.

And then Vince had flown into New York four nights ago, and everything had changed. On his way back to the Center from an assignment in London, he had stopped by to say hello. Hello, indeed. A pair of steaks, three bottles of wine, and what in the world are we doing in bed together? Oh yes, they knew what they were doing, and they had kept on doing it for the next four days. Delightful. Sinful, but delightful, and she still could not understand how it had happened.

Her meditation broken, she dressed in jogging clothes and stood over the bed again looking down at him. That body, strength piled on grace. She reached down and pressed her palm against his bare belly. His eyes opened at once.

You, he said. I still can't believe it.

I know, me too. Sleep well?

Flat out. You off running?

Come on along. Do you good.

Not me. You see this magnificent physical specimen in front of you? I aim to keep it that way, not run it into the ground.

Slob.

He reached for her lazily. *Hey, there's more than one way to exercise.*

She danced away, and said aloud, "I'll be back soon. Bagels for breakfast?"

"Gotta be. No sense being in New York if you can't have bagels for breakfast."

"That stuff will kill you," she said as she went out the door.

She ran her usual twenty city blocks north on Second Avenue, and twenty blocks south back to Tenth Street. Her home was a third-floor studio apartment off St. Mark's Place, and she lived there easily among the artists, the hustlers, and the dealers, as well as the working people of the area. The East Village neighborhood wasn't quite a jungle, but it wasn't a conservatory, either. Trotting down Second Avenue on the homestretch, she turned into Calucci's Deli and, jogging in place, plucked a banana from a stalk, a container of yogurt from the cold case, and two bagels from a wire basket on the counter. The bagels felt hard.

"Are they fresh?" she asked Calucci.

"Came in on the truck this morning," he assured her.

She went into his head. Ah, Calucci, you devil. The bagels were two days old. She sighed for all the tiny evils in the world, but took them anyway. She bounded up the two flights of stairs to her apartment and found Vince up and around. And up and ready.

"Are you winded?" he asked solicitously. "Are you exhausted?"

"Both," she said, "and hungry. I want my breakfast."

"Coming right up." He scooped her up in his arms, carried her over to the bed, and for the next half hour the paper bag from Calucci's lay undisturbed on the kitchen table.

Later, she said, "Can you imagine what Sammy would say if he could see us now?"

"Something witty."

"And Snake?"

"She'd just laugh."

"And Ben?"

"Ben, he's something else again. I don't think our Ben would be very happy about this." He propped himself up on his elbows. "Did you get bagels?"

"Two, but they're stale. You'll have to toast them."

She popped a thousand milligrams of vitamin C and a thousand of calcium phosphate, chopped the banana into the yogurt, turned on the radio, and as they sat down to breakfast they heard for the first time about Pan Am 204. The hijackers had just killed their second hostage.

Martha closed her eyes and said a prayer for the souls of the hostages, and another for the souls of the terrorists. She had been inside the heads of terrorists as a hostage negotiator. She had seen their minds launched into orbit as martyrs, glowing with the incandescent gasses of the trip. She considered them equally in need of her prayers. Vince caught her thought.

Chewing on his bagel, he asked, "How many hostage jobs have you done?"

"There was the one in Munich that we did together, and two others."

"Akron?"

"No, Sammy did Akron. You?"

"Five of them. Five big fat mothers, and I hated every one. The heads on those people." He pretended to shiver. "Scary."

"The worst," she agreed. "I'd rather do anything else than a hostage job. Anything."

"You know who's the best at it?"

"Snake," she said promptly.

"And you know why? Because she doesn't care. She goes in there like she's ice. She's just as cold as the opposition. I love that girl, but she can be like ice when she wants to."

"This business in Tunis. Do you think . . . ?"

"No, it's too late for us. You would have heard by now. And as for me . . ." He grinned broadly. "Nobody knows where I am."

He lived with that thought until breakfast was almost over, and the telephone rang. Martha answered. It was Pop, calling from the Center. That was the way the bad news came. She closed her eyes.

She said, "Pop. don't tell me anything that I don't want to hear."

"No, it's nothing like that," he told her. "Somebody wants a favor from us."

She opened her eyes and breathed again. "What sort of favor?"

"Hostage negotiation."

She sighed. "I was hoping that wouldn't happen. Tunis?"

"No, something local in New York. I can't say much over an open line. Do you recall a police officer named Dennis Costello? He did the training course with you."

"Yes, I remember him."

"He just called and asked if he could borrow you. I said yes. He still has all of his security clearances, so you can speak to him freely."

"What's involved?"

"Costello will tell you. He's sending a police car to pick you up."

"I thought we only did federal work."

"As I said, it's a favor."

"All right, Pop."

"One more thing. Tell Vince that he was due back here two days ago."

"Ahh . . . yes, Pop."

"And as long as he's there, take him along with you. He just might be helpful."

She hung up, and gave Vince a sour look. "Sure, nobody knows where you are."

Vince shrugged it off. "I should have figured. Pop knows everything. You still got the guilts?"

"Of course. Don't you?"

"Maybe a tad," he admitted. "What's happening?" Without waiting for an answer he went into her head and got the picture. "Yeah, Costello, you told me about him. There was a touch of romance, as I recall."

"That was years ago," she said, irritated.

"And as I also recall, he didn't want to say bye-bye. There was a scene, was there not? Some shredded emotions? Some moaning in the night?"

"I never should have told you that."

"It was funny at the time."

"But not now. We'd better get dressed if he's sending a car. What do you wear to do a cop a favor?"

"Depends on the favor," he said, and moments later they both found out what the favor would be when the radio gave them the latest news about Pan Am 204. The hijackers had just killed their third victim. And then:

"In an associated development, the police have just announced that two unknown men claiming to be sympathizers with the terrorists in Tunis are holding nine hostages in a synagogue on East Thirty-second Street in Manhattan. Their demands are the same as those of the Pan Am hijackers. Unless the Kuwaiti prisoners are released, they will shoot one hostage every hour."

9

H E Agency's offer to Nordquist was generous. He would be offered a grant-in-aid from a major American university. From another university would come the title of Distinguished Scholar, a nonworking position bearing a distinguished stipend. From the philanthropic sector would come the annual Cumberland Prize. Taken together, all three would more than equal the amount of money he had lost, and as a final sweetener a private fund would be established for his grandson's education. Even Nordquist agreed that the offer was generous.

"I'm impressed," he said. "It must give you a feeling of power to control such large sums of money."

"I don't control it," I told him, "and I'm not very happy about what I'm doing."

"Still, you were in it from the beginning, weren't you?"

"Yes."

"You set out to break me so that this offer could be made."

"Yes."

"Putting it bluntly, you cheated me."

"You cheated yourself, Otto. You could have quit any time you pleased."

He looked at me levelly, silently.

I looked away. I said, "Yes, I cheated you."

It was the confessional. Perhaps I hoped that by being so open with him I might rekindle the affection he once had had for me. Hoped that he would understand. Hoped that he would forgive. I was hoping for too much.

He said, "You're not much of a man, are you?"

We were standing on the lakefront not far from the casino. It was a cold and cloudy day, and the water was the color of slate. Jaspers and Childress were close by: one in front of a café and the other on a bus-stop bench. I looked out over the lake to the circular island and the Church of St. Mary perched there. I could have used a little forgiveness right then. Still, it was the game, and I had to play it.

"My people want an answer today," I said.

But he wasn't ready to let me off the hook. "They must pay you well," he said. "You're good at what you do. You have a pleasing appearance, you're reasonably intelligent, you project a warm sincerity, and you're an accomplished card sharp. It makes for quite a package. It certainly fooled me."

"Otto, I know what you think of me, you've made it clear enough. Can we get down to business now?"

"Business, of course. Business must always come first." He shook his head. "I'm afraid that I can't give you an immediate answer. I'm going to have to think about this. Half an hour ago I thought I was ruined. Now, it seems, I'm not. It takes getting used to."

I had expected that. It was impossible for him to refuse the offer, but he needed time to square it with his conscience. "How long do you want?"

"This evening?"

"Shall I stop by your house about eight?"

"Very well."

It was time for me to say that I was sorry, but I could not say the words. I nodded, and said, "At eight."

I watched him go along the esplanade, then I turned and went into the casino. The second-floor bar was empty at that hour of the morning. I ordered a cognac and waited for either Jaspers or Childress to show up. It was Jaspers. He slid onto the stool next to me.

"I have to call home," he said. "What do I tell daddy?"

Poor Harry, sweating it out in Klangenfurt. He had nothing to sweat about. "Tell him that I'll have an answer tonight. Eight o'clock at the villa." I put the cognac down in one piece and wiggled the glass for another.

"Is the Swede going to go for it?"

"Of course he is. He has no choice."

"There's always a choice. He's an honest man."

That surprised me. I had never heard him express that sort of an opinion before. He did what he was paid to do and he didn't get involved with personalities.

I said, "You like him, don't you?"

"He's straight arrow. My old man was that way. There aren't too many of them left."

"It's gone out of style."

"You're the gambling man. I'll bet you ten bucks he says no."

"You've got it. It'll be the first money I get to keep on this job." I signaled the barman for another cognac.

"Maybe." He looked at my glass. "You gonna do that all day?"

"I'm thinking about it."

He shook his head and went off to call Klangenfurt. He needn't have worried. I finished the drink and went over to the Café France to wait for Nadia. I waited until noon, but she never showed up. I figured that she had heard the news from Nordquist. The job was as good as over, and so was our interlude. No more café meetings, and we never had gotten to ski together. It was just as well. Seeing her in Bled brought too much pain along with the pleasure. It had been easier to handle in New York.

I went back to the hotel, ate too much lunch, and napped through most of the afternoon. I was still building up after the night with the rats. I went down to the hotel bar at six and nursed a couple of vodka-tonics until it was time to go out to the villa. Jaspers and Childress were already there. Jaspers was waiting for me about a hundred yards from the driveway.

"The place is clean," he said through my car window. "Nobody in and nobody out all afternoon."

"Where are you parked?"

"Up the road behind a stand of birch trees on the right."

"Wait for me there."

I drove up to the front door, left the car in the driveway, and knocked. Nordquist, himself, let me in. I followed him through the tiled foyer and into the salon. Nadia was waiting there. When we came in she got up and stood next to Nordquist. Her face was set in solemn lines, but there was the hint of a smile in her eyes. Nordquist took her hand.

"I wanted Clara to hear this," he said. "Your offer is refused. Now, get out of my house."

I couldn't believe it. I said, "Are you sure about this, Otto?"

"You don't call me by my Christian name anymore. Yes, I'm sure. I was never so sure of anything in my life."

I went into his head. And bumped my nose. I couldn't get in, he was blocked. Only another ace could have done that.

Don't bother trying, said Nadia. *I've got him locked up tight. What's happening here?*

Go home, darling. You made your play and you lost.

I tried her head. She had blocked herself as well. I asked, *How much did you offer?*

I mean it, Ben. There's nothing here for you anymore.

I said, "Mister Nordquist, if you've received another offer I'm sure that my people will match it and beat it. Just tell me what it is."

"Get out."

Win some, lose some, said Nadia. *See you back in New York.* She was laughing, playing the game.

Nobody saw me out. I got my car and drove up to where Jaspers and Childress were parked. I put my car where it couldn't be seen, and got into the back seat of theirs. As usual, the air was thick with cigaret smoke. Jaspers turned around and held out his hand.

"Give," he said.

"How did you know?" I found ten dollars and gave it to him.

"He reminded me too much of my old man. What now?"

"It isn't as clean as it looks. We wait."

We didn't have long to wait. Twenty minutes later Nordquist's car came down the driveway and turned up the road toward town. They were both in the front seat, and Nadia was driving. Their tires whirred on the snow. There was luggage on the roof rack.

"Moonlight flit," said Childress. "Do we follow?"

"Gently."

Following them into town, and after that on the road to Ljubljana, was a simple tail. It was still early, the section of the road was well-traveled, and we were able to stay a half-dozen cars in back of them. I thought at first that they were headed for the city or the airport, but north of Ljubljana they turned onto the E93 that went to Maribor. It was a two-hour drive to Maribor, part of it on an autobahn, and the snow started then. It snowed every night in those mountains during the season, but we weren't high enough to get the really heavy stuff. It drifted down lightly, just enough to slow traffic and to mask our tail.

"Why Maribor?" asked Childress. "It's just another resort like Bled."

"They could be going into Austria," I said. "Graz, or even Vienna."

"They could head down to Zagreb," said Jaspers.

"Long way around to Zagreb. Doesn't make sense."

Childress said, "If they turned east at Maribor. . . ."

He left it hanging. We all knew what lay east of Maribor. Three countries came together there: Austria, Yugoslavia, and Hungary. An hour's drive east of Maribor was the Hungarian border.

The snow grew heavier as we came up into the mountains around Maribor, bullets of white whipping out of the darkness at us. There were still other cars on the road. I had not eaten since midday and I was hungry. Childress produced a bag of peanuts and a couple of candy bars from the glove compartment. The candy had melted but I ate the peanuts. There was nothing to drink.

"Turning east," said Childress.

The autobahn ended at Maribor, and there were three ways to go after that: north into Austria, west into Austria, or east toward the Hungarian border. They made the right-hand turn, east on the road to Ptuj, and then Varazdin, and then the border. Childress made the turn with them, laying back as far as he could.

I tapped Jaspers on the shoulder. "I may want that ten bucks back."

"How come?"

"It looks like he isn't as straight as you thought he was."

"Hungary?"

"First stop on the Soviet express."

"Maybe." He was still thinking of his father.

The road beyond Ptuj was narrow and dark. It was farming country, and every so often there was the single, far-off glint of a lamp in a window. There were trees on both sides of the road, tall pines that leaned in toward each other above us. The snow was thick on the road, and the fall was heavy through the beams of our lights. We kept about a half mile behind Nordquist's car, and by now we were the only ones on the road. It was close to midnight when we went through Varazdin, and the town was closed up tight. After that the road dropped down to a single lane and I knew that we were running out of time. We were less than fifteen minutes from the border, and it was a border that we could not cross.

"Have to make a move," I said. "Can you get up there and cut them off?"

"Sure," said Childress. "What happens then?"

"I want to talk to Nordquist alone. Away from the woman, far away. She stays in the car and you keep her there. I don't want her touched. Just make sure that she stays in the car."

"Right."

"Just that, nothing else. I don't want her bothered, understand?"

He looked at me strangely. "I understood it the first time. What the hell did you think I was going to do to her?"

"Sorry. Let's go."

Childress did it smoothly, a long acceleration that brought us close up on their tail, and then a rapid move outside that forced them onto the verge of the road. Nadia tried to run back in on him, but he crushed a fender and forced her to stop. We were out of the car quickly and had their doors open. Their faces looked up at us. Nordquist's was pale, Nadia's defiant.

What is this, the wild west? she asked. *When did you join the Agency?*

All part of the game.

Not the way I play it. Her eyes were dark, reproaching me. *I didn't think you'd try something like this. At least, not with me.*

Maybe it isn't a game anymore. Maybe it never was. I tried for Nordquist's head. She had him blocked again. *I'm going to borrow our friend for a while. Not for long, and he won't be hurt. You stay in the car. These men will make sure that you do.*

My God, it is the wild west.

I went around to Nordquist's side and motioned for him to get out. He straightened up and leaned against the car. He said, "What is going to happen?"

"You're in no danger. We're going to take a walk."

133

I took his arm and got him moving. I walked him down the edge of the road away from the car. The snow had drifted and we had to kick through it. Nordquist stumbled, and I pulled him on. The block in his head grew weaker as we moved away from the car. At about two hundred feet the block disappeared. I turned him around to see his face. The wind around us was high and cold. He looked older than he had a few hours before.

"Doctor Nordquist," I said formally, "I'm going to ask you the same question that I did earlier. Has anyone tried to beat my offer to you?"

His lips tightened; he did not answer. He did not have to. I was into his head and I read it there. He had told his Clara everything. She knew what he had lost, she knew about the biochip, and she knew how strongly he felt about having it used as the centerpiece of a weapons system that someday might destroy the world. She knew about my offer and all that it could mean to him. She had been as shocked and as angry as he had been, but unlike him she had been able to produce a middle road between ruin and dishonor. She had concocted a story about an uncle, the Danish financier Karl Jorstadt, who was presently in Budapest on business. I caught the stray thoughts whipping through Nordquist's mind.

Large loan, interest-free . . . no questions asked . . . no quid pro quo, no moral mortgage.

Personal favor to a distinguished scientist . . . biochip never to be mentioned . . . an agreement between gentlemen.

Urgent . . . see him now . . . solution to all the problems.

It was so full of holes that only a desperate man would have bought it. He was on a one-way trip to Moscow. I checked him again. He thoroughly believed it. He had to. He had to believe in his Clara. Nothing I could have said would have changed his mind.

Discarding the formality, I said, "Otto, after this is all over I have a bridge that I want to sell you. It's in a place called Brooklyn and I can let you have it cheap."

He stared at me, uncomprehending. I took his arm and turned him around. We slogged through the snow back to his car. He got in and sat there, confused. As far as he knew, nothing had happened. Nadia looked at me expectantly.

Well, she asked, *what do you think of it?*

Not bad. A touch obvious, but not bad.

I had to put it together in a hurry.

I liked the part about Karl Jorstadt. He really is in Budapest. I saw it in the papers.

Thank you. It never hurts to add a fact or two.

You realize what you're doing to him, don't you? Once he goes over that border he's finished. Your people will squeeze him dry and bury him someplace. He'll never see daylight again.

I can't let myself think of things like that. Any more than you can. Did you stop to worry about what was going to happen to him after you did your part of the job?

No, I admitted. *That isn't part of the game.*

Exactly. I take it that you're not going to try to stop us?

If I thought I could talk him out of it, I'd try. But I can't, you've got him sold. No, I won't try to stop you. No more wild west.

So bedroom wins over cardroom.

This time.

The three cars came down on us so quickly that they must have been coordinated by a radio link. Headlights bright, two of them came racing from the direction of the border, and the other one from the west. They slammed to a stop, blocking both our cars. Armed men tumbled out of them. Jaspers and Childress made moves, and then stopped. They stood very still, hands well away from their bodies. Major Mihevc got out of one of the cars. I shivered when I saw him, and not from the cold. Just the sight of him reminded me of rats. He crunched through the snow and touched a finger to his fur hat.

"Mister Slade, Miss Petrovna," he said. "It's a bad night for wandering about the countryside. We will go back to Ljubljana and talk there."

I shrugged. Nadia nodded. She knew at once who he was. To me, she said, *You bastard, you led him to me.*

I smiled. I didn't try to deny it. I was surprised that he had let us get that close to the border. It was all part of the game.

Mihevc leaned over and said to Nordquist, "I must ask that you come along as well."

Nordquist looked at him stiffly. "You've made a mistake. You have nothing to talk to me about. I am a tourist. My fiancée and I are on our way to Budapest."

Mihevc looked at him at if he were a small child. "You are not going anywhere even close to Budapest tonight."

"My fiancée and I. . . ."

"Doctor Nordquist, please. Your fiancée, as you call her, is a known agent of the KGB. Mister Slade here is an agent of the CIA. Finding you in their company, don't you think that we have something to talk about?"

Nordquist said slowly, "The KGB?"

"Yes. The Soviet intelligence service."

Nordquist turned his head to look at Nadia. She looked back at him coolly. He opened his mouth to say something, then closed it. He waited for her to speak. She was silent. He looked away. I took a quick scoop of his head. He was breaking up inside.

They divided us up and took us back to Ljubljana. They brought us to the same building near Liberation Square where I had spent the night with the rats. This time I was given a cell to myself and, after a careful search, was allowed to keep my own clothing. It was all very civilized. I was there for three days, and during that time I was interrogated twice daily. The interrogations were carried out by remote television cameras, and they followed an unvarying routine. Mihevc wanted to know every detail of my operation against Nordquist from the time I entered Yugoslavia until the time we were collected near the border. I told them everything. There was no reason not to. I had not been operating against Yugoslav interests, and it was standard procedure to cooperate in such situations. I emptied the bag for them, and on the afternoon of the third day I asked Mihevc how much longer the interrogations would continue.

"This is the last of it," he said. He was happy with me. By playing me loose and letting me run he had spotted and picked up a KGB agent and spoiled one of their operations. He had gained nothing for himself, but the rivalry between the two services was emotional and intense, and he had made points in his own particular game. "You will be released this evening. Released and deported, of course."

"That's too bad. I was hoping to do some more skiing here."

He laughed. "There's always Austria. Miss Petrovna and Doctor Nordquist will be released at the same time."

I was surprised that they were still holding the old man. "You squeezed him, too?"

"Very gently, hardly a squeeze. After all, I don't often get a chance at a man like that. A most unusual person. So brilliant in his own field, but so innocent in the ways of the world." He shook his head. "That story she fed him, amazing. And he believed every word of it."

"He loves her."

"Obviously. He was most reluctant to believe that she was a Soviet agent. I had to show him her dossier before he would accept the fact."

"It's the world he lives in. It's a good world. I wish it were mine."

After the last interrogation I was allowed to shave and shower for the first time in three days, and by the time I was done my clothes had been sponge-cleaned and pressed. A warder took me to Mihevc's office on the eighth floor of the building. It was a modern, well-appointed room. The chairs and the carpeting were deep, and a floor-to-ceiling window provided a panoramic view of the city. Nadia and Nordquist were already there, and Mihevc

137

had given them tiny glasses of plum brandy. Nadia sat in one of the comfortable chairs and sipped her brandy calmly. Nordquist would not sit, and he would not touch his drink. He would not look at either of us. He stood with his back to the room, staring out through the broad expanse of glass at the lights going on all over the city.

Nadia smiled when she saw me, and said, *Hello, you louse. I should be angry with you, but I'm not. Not anymore.*

How did it go? Any bumps or bruises?

Nothing like that. I've had worse interrogations in training sessions. How about you?

The same. He just wanted to show that he could make the eagle scream and the bear roar. To Mihevc, I said, "What's this all about? I thought I was being released."

He beamed at me from behind his desk. "A touch of civilization between colleagues. Your release papers are ready for you downstairs, together with your deportation orders and air tickets to Vienna. From there you each can make your own arrangements. Doctor Nordquist is not being deported. He may do as he wishes."

"What about my two men?"

"They were released yesterday."

I took a sip of the plum brandy. It tasted like gasoline. I asked Nadia, *Where will you be going after Vienna?*

Gaczyna Center. Reassignment, I suppose.

Back to New York?

I hope so.

I'll be waiting for you. I tried the brandy again. It didn't taste any better. I must have made a face because Mihevc laughed.

"It's an acquired taste," he said.

"Thanks, but I think I'll skip the cocktail party." I put down the glass. "I'd just as soon get going now."

Nadia stood up. "I, too, should leave."

"Not very gracious," said Mihevc, but he did not look perturbed. "Actually, there is another reason for this little occasion.

Doctor Nordquist requested it. He wanted to see the two of you one last time. Perhaps he thought you might care to extend your apologies to him. That would be appropriate under the circumstances, don't you think?"

There was silence in the room. Nadia and I looked at each other. I knew that she could not do it, and neither could I. Not for doing what we had been trained to do, for playing the game we had been taught to play. To apologize for that would be to apologize for a lifetime. The silence deepened.

Nordquist turned to face us. He had lost weight in the three days. His cheekbones jutted and his clothes hung loosely. He stood framed by the picture window and the lights of the city. I did not want to know what was going on in his head, yet even without trying I could feel the depth of the sadness within him.

"Major Mihevc is quite wrong," he said. "I did not ask for this meeting to hear your apologies." He looked at me directly for the first time. "You can't return the money you stole from me. It is probably sitting in Washington now." He looked at Nadia. "And you can't return what you stole from me, either. It isn't transportable. So, no apologies."

He put his hands behind his back and half-turned to look out the window again. "I wanted to see you both to tell you something that I've learned over the past three days. I've had a great deal of time to think about what has happened, and about what might have happened if I had not been stopped at the border. I've also had some interesting talks with Major Mihevc, sitting right here in this pleasant room. He has explained to me about the sort of work you both do, things I never knew existed. He has shown me the world as it exists today, and having seen it I now know that I could never be a part of it.

"I could never be part of a world that could take my work and turn it into a killing machine. I have always known that. Now I also know that I could never be part of a world in which a man I trusted would feel free to cheat and steal from me. I could never be part of a world in which my love for a woman could be used as a political tool. I'm too old for such a world. It's all yours, and you are welcome to it."

He shook his head, as if searching for words. After a moment, he went on. "It seems I've been confused. I was confused by losing the savings of a lifetime. I was confused by a love that I thought was real. I was confused by the fear that I had betrayed my grandson and condemned him to a penniless future. I was so confused that I couldn't think straight, couldn't see the simple solution to a simple problem. But I'm not confused anymore, and that's why I wanted you here. I wanted to show you the simple solution to the problem you created. I wanted you both to see this."

He smiled faintly. "You see, in all my confusion I forgot about the insurance. There's a great deal of it. More than enough."

I jumped to stop him. Nadia moved too, but he was far away from us. He was a world away.

He turned and walked through the window. It was simple plate glass and he walked right through it. Out into the cold evening air and down eight stories to the street.

It stopped being a game then, and it never was a game again.

10

MARTHA and Vince sat with Dennis Costello in a back booth of a luncheonette on East Thirty-second Street, diagonally across from the Beth Hillel Synagogue. The street had been cordoned off between Fifth and Madison, stores and offices had been commandeered, and police sharpshooters placed in windows. The luncheonette had been cleared out and turned into a command post with a telephone link to the synagogue. The place was filled with uniforms, with suits, and with flak jackets topped by baseball caps. Costello had made the rear booth his operations area.

"We'll stay back here away from the others," he told Martha and Vince, "and we'll keep our voices down. As far as I know, I'm the only one in the department who knows about you people, and that's only because of my FBI clearance." He looked directly at Martha. "It's good to see you again."

"And you," she said politely. "What's your situation here?"

"I didn't expect two of you."

Oh, Lord, she thought, it's going to be like that. She said smoothly, "Vince and I often work together. He happened to be in town and I was able to get in touch with him."

And I'll bet you didn't have to reach very far to find him, thought Costello. Just the other side of the pillow. You've got that look on your face, fresh out of bed. It's been two long years, but I still remember that look.

Vince said, "Would you like to fill us in, Captain?"

"Yeah, sure." And it has to be a black guy who looks like he could eat Rambo for breakfast and spit out the bones. Jesus, what a world we live in.

"Dennis?" It was Martha, prompting.

"Right," he said, forcing concentration. "What we have are two crazies across the street holed up with nine old men as hostages. It's a copycat operation, tied in with the Pan Am thing, and it was apparently done on the spur of the moment. They saw their chance and they grabbed it. Now they're making the same demands as the Pan Am hijackers." He paused. "I'm sure I don't have to tell you that those demands are impossible to meet."

Martha said, "The Kuwaitis aren't going to move from their position."

"Not for the passengers on the Pan Am plane," said Costello, "and certainly not for a bunch of elderly New York Jews. So our crazies are in a no-win situation, which makes them that much more dangerous."

"What can you tell us about them?" asked Vince.

"From what we've learned, they're both about seventeen, both members of an outfit called the Palestine-American Friendship Society, and they both were born here in New York. That's where the similarities end. Abu Hassani comes from a Palestinian family that emigrated here about twenty years ago. He's short, wiry, tough, and he's the one with the brains. He's known to be fanatical, and he's known to be violent. The other one is Jimmy Abdul Farag, both parents dead, lives with an uncle who came here from Cairo. Jimmy Abdul is apparently the pawn in this piece. He's been described to us as mentally retarded and physically awkward. Thirty years ago he would have been called a moron. Today they'd call him a ree-tard. The thing to remember is that Jimmy Abdul is totally dependent on the other boy. Abu whistles and Jimmy jumps. Hold it a second."

"Captain?" A man with a baseball cap over his eyes stood next to the table.

"Go ahead," said Costello.

"I'm on the phone with them. The Abu kid insists on sticking to the schedule. He says that he's going to shoot the first one in thirty minutes."

"Jerry, this is Miss Marino and Mister Bonepart, the federal people. This is Sergeant DiLuca."

DiLuca stared at them coldly. He did not offer his hand. There was an awkward silence. Costello broke it. "Jerry, keep him talking. We'll be ready to make a move in a few minutes."

DiLuca nodded, and went back to the telephone. Costello said, "Don't take that the wrong way. He's one of my best men and he doesn't understand why you people are in on this."

Vince said, "Make sure that he never does know why."

Costello said stiffly, "The FBI seems to think that I know how to keep my mouth shut."

"Just a reminder."

Costello decided that he didn't like Mister Bonepart. Aside from the guy being black and beautiful, this wasn't the way he had thought it would be. He had figured on Martha alone, and maybe later. . . ? But they both had shown up looking like two fresh loaves of bread, hot and crisp from the oven. . . .

Martha said, "What about weapons?"

Again, Costello pulled his thoughts together. "We've seen Abu with a piece that looks like an Armalite, and he claims to have grenades as well. We have to believe him. It's an awkward situation. Some of these small societies have weapons stashed away. Nothing we can prove, but we know that they have them. These kids were probably trained on the stuff."

"One thing more," said Vince. "Have they asked for safe conduct once this is over?"

"The usual. A flight out to Damascus or Tripoli. You're authorized to agree to that."

Vince looked at him narrowly. "But they won't get it, right?"

Costello shrugged. "You can agree to it."

Slowly, patiently, Vince said, "Captain, I'm aware that standard procedure calls for interdiction of the perpetrators at the point of departure, in this case an airport. Now I don't give a fat rat's ass how you handle it. If you figure to knock those two suckers off as they get on a plane, that's fine with me. But tell me about it. You've got to level with me. If you don't, then I can't do my job right."

Vince, cut it out, said Martha. *Don't ride him.*

Why not? Did you catch that bit about the two hot loaves of bread?

I thought that was touching.

Two loaves, one white and one pumpernickel. Your friend doesn't like me. He's still hurting.

Don't let it get in your way. To Costello, she said mildly, "It's important, Dennis. We really do have to know."

Costello said, "It is possible that interdiction will be attempted at that time. If it is, you will be told about it in advance."

"Fair enough," said Vince. He stood up, and said to Martha, "Let's get to work."

Jimmy Abdul sat on the synagogue bench and stretched out his legs. The bench was hard, but it was better than standing. He knew that he should be standing. Abu had told him to stand guard over the old men, and even a dummy knew that standing guard meant that you stood up. But the pain in his head was bad, and he had to sit down. Besides, Abu could not see him. Abu was up at the front near the door, yelling out to the cops in the street. Yelling to stay back or the old men would get killed. Yelling about the brothers in Kuwait. Yelling about the Zionist imperialists. So Abu could not see him, and he could stand guard just as well sitting down. There wasn't much to do. The Jews were all lying on the floor, face down, and they weren't supposed to move. Abu had said, if anyone moves you give him a kick in the head and make him lie still. That was easy, but nobody had moved yet. They just lay there. And Abu had said something else. The Armalite. He said wait for the word. If I give you the word, then you use the gun. You click the safety and you pull the trigger. You use it like a water hose, you spray it on the Jews. But only if I give you the word.

The old men lay without moving, without making a sound, but Jimmy could hear them screaming in his head. Screams of fear. He wanted them to stop. He could feel their screams like knives behind his eyes. He knew that if he kicked them hard enough they would stop, but he could not do that. Abu had said to kick them only if they moved, but they weren't moving and so he had to listen to the screams.

Amazing grace, how sweet the sound, that saved a wretch like me. He hummed the music without forming the words. That sometimes helped. The screams grew fainter. Not much, but some. They were such old men. Like the old men in the neighborhood who sat every night in the candy store and drank mint tea and ate little chunks of *halvah* with toothpicks. Some of them were very old like the Jews on the floor, but they were good men. They were the fathers and the uncles of the people, good men, not like the Jews. He knew what Jews were. They were the ones who stole the homeland and killed the babies. Everybody knew that. They were bad people, and that's what the struggle was all about. Abu had explained it all to him. He had tried to understand, but sometimes the words got mixed up and he couldn't say them back the right way when Abu asked him. But that didn't matter, Abu didn't care. Abu didn't yell at him when he got things mixed up. Everybody else did, but not Abu.

Amazing grace, how sweet the sound. He ran his hands over the stock of the Armalite, and wiggled the safety with a finger.

145

Not hard enough to click it, but enough to get the feel. He had to be ready if Abu gave him the word. Because Abu was going to kill these old men. He knew that. Maybe not all of them, but some. Never mind what he said to the police about the brothers in Kuwait. Abu was going to kill somebody, no matter what happened. Jimmy knew that. He always knew what Abu was going to do.

Abu left his spot near the door and came to the back of the synagogue. Jimmy stood up quickly. Abu had one of the grenades in his hand. He had pulled the ring and was holding the pin down with his thumb. If somebody shot him, or tried to take the grenade away, it would go off. That was the way the freedom fighters did it. Abu looked the part. He had tied one of the prayer shawls around the lower part of his face and he looked like the pictures of the freedom fighters in the magazines. Jimmy wondered if he should tie one of those things around his face. He decided to wait until Abu told him to.

Abu put a hand on his shoulder, and asked, "How you doing, kid?"

Jimmy liked it when Abu called him kid. He nodded to show that he was doing all right.

Abu looked at the old men on the floor. "They giving you any trouble?"

Jimmy shook his head. *I once was lost, but now I'm found, was blind but now I see.* There was no way he could explain to Abu about the screaming.

"You scared?"

Jimmy shook his head.

Abu gripped his shoulder. "Good, there's nothing to be scared about. Fear is the enemy of action, remember?"

Jimmy nodded. He had heard that from Abu many times.

"Fear is for the Jews, not for us."

Jimmy nodded.

"We're part of the movement now. No more demonstrations, we're fighters. Our demands are the same as the brothers in

Tunis. Let our people go, or we kill these people one by one. Right?"

Jimmy nodded.

"So don't worry about anything, just do what I tell you. Remember, what happens to us doesn't matter. We're part of the struggle now. That's what's important, the struggle and the liberation of the homeland. Right?"

Jimmy nodded.

"Individuals don't count, just the struggle." Abu looked at his watch. "Twenty minutes to go, and then the executions start. On the dot. It's important to be on the dot. That way they know you mean business." He looked at Jimmy sharply. "You ready to do that, kid? You ready to kill?"

Jimmy nodded.

Abu punched his shoulder. It felt good. "That's the way. It's all part of the struggle. Do what I tell you, don't screw up, and we'll get out of this okay. I got you in and I'll get you out. Right?"

Jimmy did not nod. He looked at Abu directly, their eyes locking. He knew that Abu was lying. He always knew.

Abu knew it, too. He grinned, and put his head close to Jimmy's. "Yeah, sure you know, don't you. You're not such a dummy. Maybe we get out of this, and maybe we don't. I figure we don't."

Jimmy nodded.

"Is that all right with you?"

He nodded again. It was all right if Abu said it was.

"We're doing something for our people, something that's gotta happen. What happens after that . . . is it important?"

Jimmy shook his head.

"Then that's it. We'll do what we have to do, and the hell with the rest of it."

Jimmy nodded. The hell with the rest of it. He smiled to show Abu that he really didn't care what happened. He felt good, except for his head. If only the Jews would stop screaming.

When we've been there ten thousand years, amazing grace, how sweet the sound.

The telephone rang, and Abu picked it up. He spoke into it for a moment, then put it down. He turned to Jimmy with a look of satisfaction on his face.

"They're sending over a negotiating team," he said. "How do you like that? Just like on television."

Martha and Vince stepped through the broken door of the synagogue and into a world of white. The place looked like a snow-covered cornfield with a flock of crows perched on the drifts. Then they saw that the snow was paper, dozens of prayer books ripped into shreds, and that the crows were the thick black covers from which the pages had been torn. The nine old men huddled under the paper storm, their faces to the floor. Martha and Vince heard their silent voices all saying the same words: *Shema yisroel adonai eloheinu adonai echaud. Hear, oh Israel, the Lord our God, the Lord is one.* Martha and Vince both understood the Hebrew, but neither of them realized that those were the words that an orthodox Jew wants to have on his lips at the moment of his death.

Jimmy Abdul stood over the men, his weapon trained on them. He was a hulking boy with a head too small by several sizes. His eyes were empty, and a fraction of a smile seemed pasted to his face. He looked relaxed compared to Abu, who stood half crouched behind a bench. He had the grenade in his left hand, thumb pressed on the pin, and a pistol in his right. The lower part of his face was covered with the white, tassled shawl, and his eyes jumped from point to point, never still. The four people stood in tableau for a moment, and then Vince spoke. His voice was warm and friendly.

"Abu, let's take it real easy with that grenade."

"Make you nervous?" Abu grinned. He looked at his watch. "In ten minutes I'm going to execute my first hostage, so let's get down to business."

"Sure thing. My name is Vince, and this is Martha. Let's see if we can settle this thing without anybody getting hurt."

Standard opening, followed by the standard questions to be asked and the standard answers to be given. It was the routine known to both the negotiator and the hostage-taker, learned by one from textbooks and by the other from the exploits of shadowy veterans. It was what both sides did to establish the framework of the situation. It had to be done. It was the one commonsense action in a scenario that was essentially nonsensical.

Abu started it off. "What about the demands? What about the prisoners in Kuwait?"

"Right," said Vince, "let's deal with that first. Now you realize that your brothers in Tunis have made the same demands that you have, so there's bound to be some confusion, but we've forwarded your statement to the Kuwaiti government. You understand how that works? We notified the State Department in Washington and they're making the official request. That's going to take some time but we're working on it. Considering that, I'm going to ask you to move your schedule up an hour. How about it?"

"Not a chance. The schedule doesn't change. What about the plane? You got the plane ready?"

"That's in the works. We've cabled Damascus and Tripoli to see if they'll let you come in there."

"Let us in? Are you kidding? Jimmy and me, we're fighting for the cause."

"They know that, Abu. It's just routine."

"They have to take us in."

"They will, I'm sure of it."

"Then why did you say something stupid like that? You've got nine minutes to go and you're talking stupid."

Abu was shaking with anger, and the hand that held the grenade was shaking, too. Vince went into his head, scooped him, and came out sobered. To Martha, he said, *This kid is for*

*real. He's a stone killer. He's going to take some lives today if he
can. What about Jimmy?*

Just going in.

Vince went to work calming Abu down while Martha went
to work on Jimmy Abdul. It was not the sort of work she had
expected. Getting into Jimmy's head was like approaching an
alien planet, coming in on a space probe to circle around it
cautiously, checking the atmosphere. She found that the upper
level of that atmosphere was calm and passive, a superficial
place filled with primary sensations, the strongest of which was
an unswerving devotion to Abu Hassani. It was the simple-
minded world of a simple-minded boy. Martha cruised through
it to the level below.

At the same time, Vince worked Abu with words, stroking.
"The whole Arab world will be watching you today," he said.
"Don't spoil that, Abu. Give the system a chance to work. Move
your schedule up an hour."

"No changes in the schedule," screamed Abu. "Tell me about
the plane."

"It's on the line out at Kennedy. It's a DC-10, and you know
how long it takes to get one of those big babies gassed up and
ready. That's something else you have to be patient about."

"You keep talking patient. In a few minutes I'm gonna do
my first execution and then you'll see how patient I am."

The second level of Jimmy's head was a zone of storms.
Martha cruised into it, and at once was rocked by an emotional
turbulence that stopped just short of uncontrolled madness. It
was a place of black clouds and lightning bolts, purple haze and
high winds that screamed as they whipped around the brain.
Martha fought her way through it and pressed further into
Jimmy's head.

Vince was saying, "Let me make a suggestion that might do
you some good. Would you consider releasing some of the
hostages? Let's say the two oldest men."

"Bullshit. They stay, all of them."

"Think about it. It would make you look like a humanitarian, and you'd still have seven of them."

"Forget it. These old bastards are like gold to me. I want them all."

"Then let me announce that you're moving the schedule back an hour. What do you say? No killing for an hour. It's the smart move to make, Abu."

"I'm not smart. If I was smart I wouldn't be here." He looked at his watch. "Six minutes."

"Half an hour."

"No. No compromises."

Martha entered the third level of Jimmy's head, and ran into a wall of ice. It stopped her cold. It was solid and thick, a protective coating that seemed to surround this alien planet she was probing. She pushed against it, but it would not give. She skimmed over it, searching for cracks, but there were none. She chipped at the surface, made a slight dent, chipped again and made another, and settled down to bore her way through.

Vince's technique called for diversion. He said, "Look, what about sanitary facilities? These people are going to have to relieve themselves. What are you going to do about that?"

Abu did not answer. He was staring at his watch.

"What about food?" Vince asked. "You're going to get hungry pretty soon. We can bring in some hamburgers and cokes. How does that sound?"

"Like a diversion." Abu looked at him contemptuously. "That isn't going to work, I know the routine. Five minutes to go."

"But why? Be sensible. You're not going to get an answer from Kuwait in the next five minutes."

"Once you make a schedule you stick to it," Abu quoted. He moved to stand over one of the old men. It was David Krulewich. "Anything else is a sign of weakness."

Jesus, he's going to do it, Vince said to Martha. *Is that the way you read it?*

Martha did not answer at once. Then she said, *I haven't been into Abu yet. I'm busy with Jimmy.*

Take my word for it, he's going all the way.

Silence from Martha.

You hear me?

I hear you, I'm sorry, but I've got something strange going on here with Jimmy.

Vince shot a glance at Jimmy. He seemed no different, still with his weapon ready. *I don't get it. What's happening?*

Can't say now. Busy.

I don't see how I can stop Abu. Any ideas?

I can't concentrate on that. I have to work with Jimmy.

The work that she was doing was the final chipping away at the shell of ice in Jimmy's head. Almost through it, she chipped again, pushed hard, and fell, like Alice down the rabbit hole, into the center of Jimmy's world. She tumbled through and landed there. It was a warm world, and soft, the warmth of a summer's day of buttercups and butterflies, of garden grass and droning bees, and of a voice singing sweetly. The voice of a young girl. Singing.

> "Amazing grace, how sweet the sound
> That saved a wretch like me.
> I once was lost, but now I'm found,
> Was blind, but now I see."

Martha said in wonderment, *Amazing grace?*

That's me, said the voice. *Amazing Grace. Who in the world are you, and how did you get in here?*

Oh my God, said Martha. *Vince?*

What?

I think we've got ourselves an ace.

What I don't understand, said Martha, *is what a young girl named Grace is doing buried down here inside of a boy named Jimmy Abdul Farag.*

152

What I don't understand, said Grace, *is where you've been all my life. Do you realize that you are the first person who has ever spoken to me like this?*

You answer first.

Doing here? Where else should I be? Up there with stupid Jimmy Abdul and his obnoxious friend? Do you have any idea of what it was like before I came down here? All those voices screaming at me all day long, and people staring at me as if I were some sort of freak? All the ugliness, all the ugly people and the ugly things that they do to each other. I had to get away. Can you understand that?

I can, said Martha, who had done something quite similar as a young girl. It had landed her in the mental institution where Pop had found her. *I certainly can, but why a girl if Jimmy is a boy?*

Amazing Grace, that's me. I can be anything I want to be. I certainly don't want to be anything like Mister Peanut-Brain Jimmy, or Abu, that creep. Would you?

No.

So there you are. I stay down here, I tend to my garden, I sing to myself, and nobody bothers me. That is, until now.

Am I bothering you?

Oh no, I didn't mean it that way. Actually, it's lovely to have a visitor. One gets a touch weary of gardening and singing all day. Of course, I really don't grow anything, but it's the thought that counts, don't you think?

Of course. What songs do you sing?

You just heard me. "Amazing Grace."

Yes, but what else?

A pause, and then, *I'm embarrassed. You mean there are other songs?*

Why, yes.

Totally mortified. I had the feeling that there had to be others, but I wasn't sure. Trust that dimwit Jimmy to know only one.

Do you talk to Jimmy often?

You must be joking. What would I talk to him about? I have absolutely nothing in common with that person. Or with that friend of his, either. What are the other songs?

I wouldn't know where to start. There are so many.

I'm in pain. All this time I thought there was only "Amazing Grace." Absolute pain. You must think I'm as stupid as Jimmy. Sing me one of the others.

Grace, there's something important that I have to talk to you about.

First sing.

It's really very important.

Not until you sing. Nothing until you sing.

Martha puffed a mental sigh, and grabbed for a song.

> *"Come to me my melancholy baby,*
> *Cuddle up and don't feel blue. . . ."*

Once Vince and Martha were inside the synagogue, Costello left the luncheonette to go along East Thirty-second Street checking the blue suits on the barricade, the flak jackets behind them, and the pair of marksmen established in a second-floor office directly across from Beth Hillel. The shooters were both sergeants, Germyn and Chavez, and they were the best in the department. Each was seated before an open window with his weapon mounted on a tripod. Germyn was sighted in on the plate-glass window of the store-front synagogue, Chavez on the open doorway.

Costello stood behind them. He did not like the way he felt. He knew himself to be a cool and capable operator in difficult situations, but he did not feel capable now. He felt jumpy, unsure, and filled with an irrational anger. Anger at himself for summoning Martha back into his life, anger at her coolness, anger at Vince for the oldest and simplest of reasons. He told himself to get a grip, and to lay off the coffee and the cigarets. He crouched down between the two shooters to get their view.

"Can you see them?" he asked.

"All four of them," muttered Chavez, his eye fixed to the scope. "I've got the big perp and the female negotiator. They're off to the right."

"I've got the other perp and the male," said Germyn. "These are very sloppy perps, Captain. Obviously new on the job."

"How do you get old on a job like that?" asked Chavez. "It isn't exactly your long-term career."

"Yeah, but they should know better. They should never show themselves both at the same time. I could take mine out with a head shot right now. Drop him like a rock down a well."

"Mine, too. Like a steer in a stockyard."

"I could douse his lights."

"Flick his switch."

"Pull his plug."

Costello said, "You forgot to say that his ass is grass."

"That, too," said Germyn.

"And what happens to that live grenade when you mow his lawn?"

In an injured voice, Chavez said, "Hey, we were just saying. Academically speaking, you know? The grenade changes everything."

"Everything," said Costello. "Please don't forget that small point."

"Captain, nobody is forgetting anything," said Germyn. "But you get that sucker with the grenade out on the street with nobody around him and I'll take him down like Grant took Richmond."

"Fix his clock."

"Wash his socks."

"Make him history."

Costello's stomach rumbled, and his tongue felt sour. He groped for a cigaret.

Abu said, "Four minutes. You'd better get out of here and take the woman with you. Unless you want to see it happen."

Vince licked his lips. "I'm still hoping that you're not going to do it."

Abu shook his head. He stood over David Krulewich, his pistol pointed down at the back of the old man's neck. Krulewich lay as he had from the beginning, face to the floor and clutching his elbow. Vince stood about ten feet from Abu, and Martha even farther away. Jimmy stood farthest of all, a good twenty feet. His weapon was still pointed steadily at the hostages.

"You staying for the show?" asked Abu.

Vince did not answer. He called, *Martha, better get out.*

Nothing from Martha save, faintly, *All your fears are foolish fancies, maybe. You know dear that I'm in love with you. . . .*

Vince figured moves. It was not within his function as a negotiator to make any moves at all, but he doubted that he could stand by and see a man killed coldly. He measured the distance to where Abu stood. A leap, a grab for the left hand, pushing aside the pistol at the same time. With only Abu it might have been worth a try. Bad odds, but possible. But not with Jimmy in the ballgame. No odds at all that way. Still, something had to be done.

Martha?

Every cloud must have a silver lining. . . .

"Three minutes," said Abu, and to Jimmy, "You ready, kid?"

Jimmy nodded.

"Anybody moves, you use that thing, right?"

Jimmy nodded.

Vince said, "Jimmy, listen to me. Maybe I can talk some sense to you."

Abu said, "Forget it. Jimmy does what I tell him to do. Always. Right, kid?"

Jimmy nodded.

Grace said, *Don't you know any cheerful songs? That one about the melancholy baby was very sad.*

I know hundreds of songs, said Martha. *Look, there's something we have to talk about.*

Hundreds? I'm writhing.

Grace, do you know what Jimmy is doing right now?

How long would it take to sing a hundred songs?

I asked you a question.

He's playing some stupid game with Abu. They're always playing those stupid games with guns. That's another reason why I came down here.

It isn't a game that they're playing this time. They're doing something very bad.

I'm not surprised. I told you that Abu was a creep.

They're doing something that will hurt people. Kill people.

I don't believe that you know a hundred songs. Nobody could know that many.

Grace, I want you to do something for me. A favor. I want you to talk to Jimmy for me.

Certainly not. I told you, I won't have anything to do with that dimwit.

It's very important.

But I don't want to. I came down here to get away from him.

Still, I want you to do it.

Why should I?

Martha showed her why. She showed her the Center. She showed her the young people there. She showed her a life free of the screaming voices. She showed her what her own life could be like. She showed her all of that in a flash, and when she was finished there was a long silence.

Then Grace said, *Those people that you showed me, are they all like me?*

Yes.

And like you?

Yes.

And that place, has it been there a long time?

Yes.

I see. And all this time I've been tending my silly little garden and singing my one silly song, and no one told me about it.

We didn't know you were here.

No one came looking for me.

I'm here now.

Yes. Now. In a sad little voice, she said, *That's my sort of luck, I suppose. What did you want me to do?*

"One minute," said Abu.

Vince shifted his weight to the balls of his feet. He was poised that way when David Krulewich rolled over onto his back, drew his legs under him, and started to get up. Abu kicked him in the side, and shouted, "Get down."

Krulewich ignored the kick. He struggled to his knees.

"Get down or you're dead."

"I think I'm dead already," the old man said, and got to his feet. "So if you're going to shoot me we'll do it standing up, thank you. Which reminds me of a story. Did you ever hear the one about the Jew who went to Texas on the train? Of course, it happened a long time ago. . . ."

Abu whipped the pistol across the old man's face. He staggered back, a gash in his cheek. Vince took off on his left foot, one step and a leap. He was flat out and flying when he hit Abu and knocked him over. They rolled on the floor, and the pistol clattered away. Vince's broad right hand closed over Abu's left, grenade and all, and squeezed like a trap clamping onto an animal's leg. Abu fought to get the hand free. He could not move it. His palm was slowly being crushed into the metal of the grenade, the pin digging into his flesh. His body was jammed against the floor. His eyes were wide.

He screamed, "Jimmy, do it. Kill them. Kill them all."

Jimmy nodded. He raised the gun, but he did not fire.

Abu thrashed around in Vince's grip. "Now, Jimmy, now."

Jimmy looked down at the gun in his hand, and frowned. He looked up. The pain of confusion was on his face. He opened his mouth, but made no sounds. Tears rolled from his eyes.

"Jimmeeee." It was a wail from Abu.

Jimmy's face was a grimace now, his mouth open and straining for words. He sucked in air, his chest heaved, and in the soft, sweet voice of a young girl, he sang:

> "*Amazing grace, how sweet the sound*
> *That saved a wretch like me.*"

He bent over and laid the Armalite on the floor. He sat down on the floor next to it, and put his head in his hands. Martha dropped to her knees beside him. She pushed the gun away, and put her arms around him.

Vince chopped with his left hand at the base of Abu's neck. Abu went limp. Vince rolled over and stood up, dragging Abu up with him. His hand was still clamped over Abu's, securing the grenade.

Can you hold it? Martha asked.

Yeah, but not forever.

Get it out of here.

Vince lifted Abu up with his left arm, his other hand still covering the grenade. He carried Abu easily under his arm. He went through the open doorway and onto the sidewalk.

"Clear the street," he shouted. "We've got a live grenade here."

Uniforms scattered into doorways. The street itself was clear. Costello leaned out his second-floor window, and shouted, "How long can you hold it? We've got a bomb-squad truck down the street."

"Nothing they can do," Vince called back. He hitched Abu higher, carrying him on his hip the way a mother carries a child. He started up the street toward Fifth Avenue.

"What are you doing?" called Costello.

"Going to kill a few alligators."

The first sewer grating that he came to was, typically, stopped up with garbage. So was the second. The third was clear. He tipped Abu up until his hand hung over the grating. He released his grip. The grenade fell free. The pin popped out. The grenade fell through the grating.

Vince sprinted away with the unconscious Abu still under his arm. He counted silently. At the count of eight he dropped Abu, and threw himself flat on the pavement. The muffled explosion shook the street. Smoke came out of the grating.

Vince stood up, collected Abu, and walked slowly back to the synagogue. He left Abu on the sidewalk, and went inside. The place was filled with blue suits. The hostages were up off the floor, dazed, and slumped on benches. Someone in a white coat was working on Krulewich's cheek. Jimmy still sat on the floor, his head still down, Martha's arms still around him. Without moving away from the boy, Martha reached up a hand. Vince took it. She smiled.

"Not bad," she said. "Do you realize how great you could be if you jogged every morning and stopped eating bagels?"

"I'll call Pop and tell him what we've got," he said. "You handle Costello. Tell him he can have Abu, but Jimmy belongs to us."

11

S A M M Y served a hard one to my backhand. I never got my racquet on it. Sammy knew all about my backhand. "Fifteen, love," he said aloud, and head to head, he asked, *Don't you ever have any small problems?*

Not since I was small, I said.

This one is a beaut. Where would you go?

I haven't figured that out yet.

How would you live?

The poker money. I've got enough stashed away.

He served another hard one and came to the net. I was into his head and knew he was coming. I passed him on the right, and all he could do was wave at it. He frowned.

"Fifteen all," he said. *What about ID and passports?*

No problem.

It was warm for April in Washington, and the courts at the Senatorial Club were springy and dry. Immaculate in whites, but with his frizzy hair all over the place, Sammy bounced a ball and prepared to serve.

Ben baby, he said, *you deal in phony papers and you have to leave a trail. It's basic.*

He coiled his short, wiry body into a spring and served one that kicked up chalk. He said, "Thirty, fifteen."

"It was out."

"Bullshit. It hit chalk."

"There's chalk all over the place. It was out." *Sammy, I want to leave a trail, at least for a while. That's part of it.*

He tossed his racquet into the air, caught it on the way down, and glared at me. He played tennis every day that he could at the Senatorial, and he was much better than I was. Every point that I scored was an insult to him.

I said, "I'm your guest, I get the gimmees." *Well, what do you think? Can it be done?*

"Second service," he muttered. *It would be tricky, very tricky.*

He should have given me an easy second serve. Instead, he ripped one at me. I barely saw it go by. I said, *You're being negative.*

"Thirty, fifteen." *It's my function in life to be negative. Look, I'm not saying that it can't be done. I'm saying that as far as I know it's never been done. No ace has ever gotten away with trying to leave the service.*

That's as far as you know. They don't tell us everything.

He put the game away with two straight aces. He batted balls over the net to me. *You want something positive, try this. If you get caught you won't have to worry about the terminal effects of Rauschner's Syndrome.*

You're trying to depress me. Sammy, I need advice.

I'll give you advice. Take tennis lessons.

I needed better advice than that, and he was the only one to whom I could turn. Two weeks after Nordquist's death I came back to New York, and back to the life I had led before I ever had heard of biochips or Bled. Back to the life of reading heads at diplomatic functions, of playing high-stake poker for Carlo Vecchione and Lew Meyerowitz, of drinking too much, snorting too much, screwing most of what came my way, and worshiping Nadia from across a crowded room. The biochip adventure was written off at Langley. It was a tie score: we didn't get it, but neither did the competition. Nordquist was dead, and the chances were that it would be years before anyone else would be able to duplicate what he had accomplished. The Russians, apparently, felt the same way about it, for Nadia was returned to her New York assignment without any blame attached for failure, and once again we were wrapped up tight in our New York cocoon. But this time with a difference. It wasn't enough for us now.

It would be easy to say that Nordquist's death changed our lives, that when he found the solution to all of his problems by walking through the window of Major Mihevc's office he twisted us off our tracks and set us running in a new direction. It would be easy to say, but it would be only partly accurate. The need for change had been there for more than a year, ever since Nadia and I had realized what we meant to each other, what an emptiness our lives were apart, and what those lives might be like in a world that was better constructed than the one with which we were stuck. During that time we batted back and forth the idea of running away from our world of aces and into another where no one would know us, and where we would be able to live what was left of our lives together. Each time we discussed it the conclusion was the same. It could be done, it might be done, but the odds against getting away with it were so high that only a fool would try to buck them. We simply knew too much, and because of that we were guarded so closely by our respective services that flight together was little more than a fantasy. But the desire existed, and Nordquist's death had underscored the need. By walking through that window he had shown us exactly how shallow and silly our lives had become. He finally had shamed us, and after that there were no more games to play, including the game of pretending that what we had was good enough for us. After that, for whatever time was left to us, we wanted more.

I turned to Sammy for advice not because I trusted him any

163

more than Martha, or Vince, or Snake, but because he had always been the one with the brains. I had called him and told him that we had to talk, and he had invited me down to Washington for a day of wisdom and humiliation to be dispensed on the tennis court. The humiliation was expected, for I had never been close to him in tennis, but there wasn't much wisdom being handed out. Nor did the tennis go according to form. Sammy took the first set easily, but he tired in the second. He wasn't reaching the shots he would normally make. He tripped once and fell flat. He was slow getting up, and when he did his face was strained. I came up to the net.

"Get back there and take your punishment," he said.

But his game was off, and when the set was over, he said, "That's it for today, you've suffered enough."

The first signs of Rauschner's were a loss of coordination and a general weakness, and Sammy was our eldest now, but it wasn't something that you talked about. Later, in the clubhouse bar, he said, "About the way I played today, don't let your imagination work overtime."

"It didn't seem like you," I said cautiously.

"This town is full of flu. I've been taking some shots for it from Doc Gregory, and sometimes they get to me."

"You went all the way down to the Center for flu shots?"

He winked. "Like I said, keep your imagination under control." The bar was crowded, and for what he wanted to say next he switched over. *You wanted some words of wisdom from me. First, the obvious question. You've thought this over carefully?*

Of course.

And your Russian friend?

Equally. We've each got less than a year to go, Sammy. What have we got to lose?

Depends on how you look at it. Have you thought about what this would do to Pop?

I've thought about everything. I know what I want. I was hoping I could get some input from you.

I know. He did something unusual then. He put one of his hands on top of mine. He never did things like that. He didn't like being touched. *I know that I haven't been very helpful so far, but here's my word of advice for the day. Don't do anything rash. In fact, don't do anything at all right now.*

That's your advice?

For now. I'm talking about the next couple of days, a week at the most. Don't do anything until I get in touch with you. Let me think about this.

Do you. . . ?

Nothing I want to talk about now, and don't go probing, don't make me block you. Just give me some time on this. Okay?

Okay. I was satisfied. If he was going to put that convoluted brain of his to work, that was enough for me.

Remember what I said. Keep your pants on for the next few days.

A poor choice of words, but I'll do my best.

We did some drinking then. I told him what had happened to Nordquist, and it saddened him. To lighten the mood he told me about the Ipatov defection and showed me the *shen kuei* that he carried on his key chain. We talked about what Martha and Vince had done in New York, and what Snake had done in Afghanistan. We raked up some memories, drank too much, had something to eat, and drank some more. Just before I left to catch the shuttle back to New York we made two promises. He promised to be in touch within a week, and I promised to do nothing until I heard from him. Neither promise was kept. Six days later I got the word that he was dead.

It was Harry who brought me the word. It had to be that way, of course. Harry the raven, the bad-news bird. It was a replay of what happened when Big John Brodski died. I came out of an all-night session at Thayer's suite at the Devon, and

165

Harry was waiting for me in the back of a company car. I walked into the early morning with Jaspers behind me and Childress in front, and when I saw Harry sitting there all I could think of was flu shots. He had said it was flu shots.

I got into the back next to Harry, and said, "Sammy?"

He nodded. "Last night at the Center. Service today. We'll go straight to the airport from here."

"Right," I said, staring straight ahead. "Never mourn."

"Don't give me that stoic shit." I turned to look at him. His face was drawn and his eyes were red. He had done his weeping already. He had also done some drinking. "You don't have to prove any points to me."

He had a bottle of ouzo in his briefcase, and he gave it to me. "Here," he said, "have a drink and cry your heart out if you want to. It won't bother me any, I'm not a member of the club."

He was pretty well shot. I had never seen him that way. I said, "Ouzo? Jesus, Harry, you're the only one I know who would bring a bottle of ouzo to a funeral."

"What's wrong with ouzo?"

"I don't believe it. It's perfect. Sammy would love it."

"I'm Greek, and that's what Greeks drink. Gimme that thing if you're not gonna use it." He took back the bottle and drank from it. He gasped. "Christ, Sammy. Sammy."

"Yeah." I tried some of the ouzo. It tasted awful.

So we took the trip I had made so many times before, New York to Washington to the Center, and I don't remember much of what happened that day. After the ouzo there was a bottle of Wild Turkey that we picked up outside National Airport, and after that a stop on the highway driving down. We both were bombed by the time we got to the Center, but nobody there seemed to notice. Maybe they all were bombed, I don't know. It could have been that way. Nobody at the Center was loved more than Sammy.

We went through the routine at the Center. It was a closed-coffin service, which meant that the terminal effects of the

Rauschner's had been particularly severe. It happened that way sometimes, the skin a horrifying blue and the striation marks like scars, and when that happened they kept the coffin closed. I was just as happy to have it that way. We said all the right words in the mess hall, and later we sat on the lawn and drank the wine that Pop had put out, although most of us were into the hard stuff by then. My gang sat together, not saying much, just drinking. There were only four of us now, and after a while Vince went over to Harry and asked him to sit with us. That made him happy, but it bothered me to see him sitting where Sammy should have been. I knew how stupid that was, but I couldn't help it. You know it's going to happen and you have about fifteen years to get ready for it, but that doesn't mean squat once it happens to one of your own. I looked around the lawn at some of the young ones sitting in their own groups, sedately sipping their wine. I tried to remember what it had been like for me at that age. I couldn't remember, and I decided that I didn't care. It didn't matter now. What mattered was that Sammy was gone, and that the rest of us would soon be right behind him. It was only then that I remembered that he had never called me, and that whatever I decided to do I would have to do on my own.

The next day at noon I sat with Carlo Vecchione, the man who backed my poker action, in a tiny clam bar on Mulberry Street in Manhattan. The place was dark and narrow, and the floor was littered with paper and shells. A sign behind the bar read *Cherrystones—$3.00 a dozen,* and under the sign a fat man in a white apron worked over a pailful with a shucking knife. There were three jars of clam sauce on the bar marked *Mild, Hot,* and *Crazy.* The windows hadn't been washed in months and the sunlight barely filtered through. Carlo's sharkskin suit and Gucci shoes looked spectacularly out of place, but they weren't. The clam bar was the center of an empire.

Carlo listened carefully while I spoke. When I was finished, he said, "You understand, I gotta talk to my uncle about this. It's nothing I can do by myself."

"I figured that."

"This could take a while so make yourself at home." He stood up, and called to the fat man, "Hey, Vito, open a dozen for my friend and bring him a beer." To me, he advised, "Use the mild sauce, the other two could kill you. Tell you the truth, a little lemon juice is all you need."

He went through a door in the back of the room and he was gone for over an hour. The clams were cold and fresh, and when I saw that Carlo wasn't coming right back I ordered another dozen. I put three dollars on the bar but the fat man wouldn't take it. I stared at the pictures on the wall: Garibaldi, D'Annunzio, and somebody else. For all I knew the third one was Carlo's Uncle John. Uncle John Merlo drew a lot of respect in that part of Manhattan.

Carlo came back and sat down. He said, "I spoke to my uncle and he spoke to a couple of people." He saw the look on my face. "No, don't worry, not on the phone. There's another door. We went out."

I nodded, waiting.

"Those certain people, they say it can be done. But it's gonna cost."

"How much?"

"Two hundred and fifty kay." He was watching my face to see if he should have gone higher. When I didn't turn pale, he added, "That's for those certain people, but I gotta figure my own expenses. I gotta get another fifty on top."

"What expenses? All you're out so far is six bucks for the clams."

"Hey, I don't do this kind of thing for a living. You asked me for a favor and I went to my uncle. I'm just trying to help, you know?"

"What do I get for all that?"

"Transportation. That's the name of the game, right? And

silenzio. We do the job and then we forget it. Nobody knows nothing."

"You'll know. And Uncle John."

His face hardened. "You worried about that?"

It worried me plenty, but I shook my head. "That's why I'm doing business with you."

He relaxed. "Okay, then."

"This includes everything? The passports? The people?"

"Everything the best," he assured me. "The papers and the people, too. All good soldiers."

"Carlo, I don't want a couple of your cousins and some neighborhood heavies."

He looked offended. "No, I'm telling you, real good people."

"How long will it take you to put it together?"

"Twenty-four hours. Just give me the word."

"You've got it."

"You understand, it's gotta be cash up front."

"Half up front and half when it's over."

"Hey, come on."

"Carlo, how dumb do I look?"

"Not too much. All right, half and half. How were those clams?"

"The best."

"I told you. Come on, we split another dozen before you go."

I went from Mulberry Street to B. B. Thayer's suite at the Devon. It was well into the afternoon but Thayer was just getting going, still in a dressing gown and his pink cheeks fresh from the razor. We sat at the table where we usually played poker. He sipped coffee with half-closed eyes, and asked what he could do for me.

"A favor," I said. "A big one."

He nodded. He was accustomed to being asked for favors. I told him what I wanted and his eyes opened wide, then narrowed again. He took another sip of coffee, and said mildly, "That's a Texas-size favor, son."

"I know it is. That's why I wouldn't insult you by trying to pay for it."

"I doubt that you could," he said, not unkindly. "Although the way you win at cards you might, at that." He shook his head. "You're a good old fella, Ben, but I can't go lending out my airyplane every time a poker buddy wants to go for a joyride. You'd have to give me a damn fine reason why."

"I might be able to do that. I'm prepared to return the favor. In advance."

"Thought you weren't going to insult me."

"I don't think you'll be insulted." There was a deck of cards on the table. I pushed them over to him. "Would you be kind enough to deal us each a closed hand?"

He raised an eyebrow, but he reached for the deck and dealt us each five cards, face down. I let mine lie. He picked his up and looked at them.

"What now?" he asked.

"You're holding the deuce of spades, five of hearts, seven of diamonds, king of diamonds, and the ten of clubs."

"Son of a bitch." He stared at the cards. He turned them over and stared at the backs. "My own cards."

"They aren't marked."

"The hell you say." He opened a drawer and took out a fresh deck of Bicycles. He broke the seal, shuffled, and dealt again. He picked up his cards.

I said, "Queen, jack of hearts, eight of spades, six of spades, trey of hearts."

"Damn." He went through the same routine of examining the cards. "If these are marked then there isn't a safe deck in New York."

"I told you, they aren't."

He frowned, and shook his head. He cut what was left of the deck, slipped one card out and left it face down on the table. "Call it."

I couldn't, not that way. I said, "Pick it up." He did, and looked at it.

"Nine of spades."

He tossed the card away. "Can you do that with any deck?"

"Yes."

"How?"

I shook my head.

He said unhappily, "You realize that I'll never play cards with you again. Not me, and not anybody I know."

"I expected that. That's the favor I'm returning in advance."

"God damn, but I liked you, Ben."

"Feeling's mutual. Still do."

"But I can't abide a man who cheats at cards."

"Can't say as I blame you. I'd feel the same way in your shoes. Question is, have I returned the favor in advance?"

"I reckon you have, at that." He looked down at the cards on the table, and brushed them away in distaste. "Yeah, you've got your favor. But understand, after this I don't want to see your face, not ever."

"You won't have to. Not ever."

That night, in the North Delegates' Lounge of the United Nations, I stood behind the Vice President of the United States and read his head as he spoke with the Polish Foreign Minister. Nadia was also there, and working. There was a third ace in the room, another Russian. He was monitoring one of the Polish aides, double-checking. I waited until the Pole left the room and the Russian had to follow, and then I called.

Nadia?

Yes, Ben.

I think I have a way to get us out.

Show it to me.

I laid it out for her, not word by word, but in the form of a mosaic with all the tiles in place. She studied it, then said, *Yes, I see it. It could work. It should.*

I think so too.

What odds?

Who knows? Even money if we're lucky.

We're lucky, she decided. *It will work, I have a feeling it will. Actually, those are very good odds for people like us.*

12

I D O N ' T know what New York City used to be like. I'm too young to remember what people call the good old days. They say that back then there was a cop on every corner and the Sanitation Department cleaned up daily. They say that people played radios in their homes, not on the streets, and that the parks were for children and lovers. They say that the bums stayed put on the Bowery, that a junkie was someone who sold scrap iron, and a bag lady was the woman in charge of leather goods at Bloomingdale's. They even say that back in those good old days all the motorists stopped for traffic lights. That's the one I find hardest to believe.

When people complain about the quality of life in New York today they talk about crime in the streets, and the perils of the subways, and the lack of services, but what nobody mentions is the growing number of drivers in the city who no longer stop when the light turns red. From their point of view, why should they? There aren't any police around to stop them, or even to take down a license-plate number. Some of them slow down slightly at the intersections to show how civic-minded they are,

173

but some just bust on through the lights. Like the one that hit me.

It was a blue Toyota going south on Second Avenue. I was crossing the avenue at Seventy-second Street, with the light. It was nine in the evening and there were plenty of people on the street to see what happened. The Toyota went through the light, went through the intersection, clipped me, and kept on going. The left front fender caught my hip and spun me around. I hit the ground rolling, and lay still. I had known it was coming, but the force of it stunned me. I closed my eyes and tried to look limp, but I kept a tight grip on the airline bag slung over my shoulder.

At almost the same moment, a Ford Fairlane went through a light and knocked Nadia down at the intersection of Madison Avenue and East Eighty-sixth Street, almost a mile away. That car, too, kept going. Nadia lay in the street quietly as a crowd formed around her. That was what she had been told to do.

The inevitable crowd also formed around me. Traffic screeched and halted. Voices floated over my head: "Somebody call an ambulance . . . dial 911 . . . get a cop." It was a typical New York accident scene, everyone shouting advice and nobody doing anything. Somebody finally went to find a telephone. I counted off the seconds in my head. Jaspers and Childress came pounding up.

"Slade, can you hear me?" It was Jaspers' voice, close to my ear. "Slade, say something, will you?"

I opened my eyes. His face was above me. "Something hit me. A car."

"Are you all right? Can you move?"

I tried moving my legs, and grimaced. I was only partly acting. Carlo Vecchione had been driving the car and he had cut it a touch too close. I murmured, "My head hurts."

"Listen, just lay there, don't move." He turned to Childress. "Get the car up here and send in a code yellow." Childress went running off.

"Somebody called for an ambulance," I said.

"Don't worry about that, we'll take you in. We're not going to wait for any ambulance."

Yes you will, I thought, you damn well will. The count in my head was close to two minutes. The pavement I was lying on was filthy; I could feel the grit of it under me. There was a sickening mess only inches away from my face. I closed my eyes again to avoid looking at it.

"Hang in there, you're gonna be all right," said Jaspers. "Whoever did it, we'll get the bastard."

I probed his head and found panic. He had been trained to react to attack situations, but a simple accident defeated him. Under the panic was rage. He wanted to shoot someone.

Three minutes. By now, Childress was at their car and trying to understand four flat tires. Four minutes. The average response time for an Emergency Medical Unit was nine and a half minutes. This one was going to be considerably under average. I could hear the siren. Jaspers heard it, too. He stayed crouched beside me. He had unbending instructions for such a situation. Stay with the subject at all times, allow no treatment that included sedation, allow no anesthesia. The siren grew louder; there were two of them. An ambulance and a police car made the turn onto the avenue, roof lights flashing. The ambulance was from New York Hospital, only a few blocks away.

Just about then an ambulance marked Lenox Hill Hospital arrived at Madison and Eighty-sixth where Nadia lay on the pavement, her security men crouched beside her. A police car followed close behind. The orchestration of the knockdowns was timed perfectly.

At Seventy-second Street, two cops got out of the police car and began moving the crowd back. Two men in white jackets jumped from the rear of the ambulance. One pulled a collapsible stretcher through the doors while the other knelt beside me. He was short and sharp-faced, with long, slicked-back hair. He looked more like a water rat than a doctor. He was neither.

He was Carlo's cousin Albie, and he was a flight attendant on Trans-Italia Airlines.

Jaspers had his wallet out and was flashing ID. He said, "I'm a federal officer. This man belongs to me. He can't be touched."

Albie ignored him. He put a stethoscope to my chest, fingers to my wrist, and shone a pencil flash into my eyes. Over his shoulder, he called, "Jerry, we've got a possible concussion. Frame and foam, stat."

"Did you hear what I said?" Jaspers' voice was shaking with anger, and the hand holding the wallet was shaking, too. "I told you to keep your hands off him."

"He has to be treated."

"Look at what I'm holding in my hand."

Albie glanced incuriously at the wallet. "This man may be concussed. His head has to be immobilized before we can move him, and before that he has to be sedated."

"No sedation."

"Get out of my way."

Albie reached into his medical bag and took out a syringe. Jaspers knocked it out of his hand; it rolled on the ground. Albie swung a fist and hit Jaspers on the chin. It was a bulldog snapping at a bull, but it had the desired effect. Jaspers did what he was trained to do. His hand went down, and came up with a pistol.

"*Freeze.*"

The two cops stood over Jaspers, their own pistols drawn and pointed down at him. He stared up at them. A third cop got out of the car and came over. His face was as flat and as broad as a ham, and he wore captain's bars.

"Put that weapon on the ground," he said to Jaspers. His voice was raspy and thick.

"I'm a federal officer." Jaspers jerked his head toward his wallet on the ground.

The captain bent over, peered at it, and straightened up. "Sonny, I don't care if you're the illegitimate son of the sainted

J. Edgar himself. I am Captain Victor Malakoff, and this is my precinct."

"Captain. . . ."

"And nobody pulls a pistol in this precinct without he kisses my ass first."

"Now, look. . . ."

"And I don't see you puckering up. Do I see a pucker, Mister Federal Officer?"

Jaspers stared at him stonily.

"I didn't think so. No pucker, no pistol. Now put down that weapon."

Jaspers laid the gun on the pavement. "You'll hear about this."

"No doubt I will. I've heard it all before." The captain turned to Albie. "Doctor, get on with your work."

Albie put the syringe back in his bag. "We'll do it without sedation," he conceded. "Jerry, let's have that frame."

The attendant brought over a small tank and a round wire framework twice the size of a basketball. He lifted my head off the pavement and pushed a pad under the back of my neck to keep it elevated. He slipped the framework over my head and fastened it at the neck. It was like being in a bird cage. He wrapped the frame with bandage. The heavy gauze went around and around, under my chin, up over my eyes and the top of my head. My world turned white, my head completely encased except for a slit for breathing. I heard the hiss of air from the tank as he sprayed the frame with foam. The foam hardened instantly on contact with air. Instead of a bird cage I was now inside an eggshell. I tightened my grip on the airlines bag slung over my shoulder.

Up on Eighty-sixth Street the team from Lenox Hill Hospital was doing the eggshell job on Nadia. The police officer there had an easier time with her security men than Malakoff had with Jaspers. The Russians were off their turf, unable to argue or try to pull rank. They had to stand there and take it.

"Get him on a stretcher," said Albie.

I felt myself being lifted and placed. I was disconnected from the world by the cocoon around my head. I was wheeled, and then lifted into the ambulance. I heard Jaspers arguing that he had to ride with me.

"Impossible," said Albie. "No civilians in the ambulance."

"Damn it, I'm not a civilian."

"In this precinct you are," said the captain. "You're a civilian who packs a pistol, which is the worst kind. We'll run you over to the hospital in our car."

"Captain, I have my orders."

"Now, we all have our orders, don't we? And we all learn to bend them at times. Into the car, Mister Federal Officer, or would you rather that we left you standing here in the street?"

That was the last I heard of the argument. The ambulance doors slammed shut, the siren whined, and we shot forward. Albie said, "We've got three, maybe four minutes. Jerry, get that thing off him."

I sat up on the stretcher and Jerry went to work on the cocoon with a pair of tin snips. It was awkward work in the lurching vehicle, and he muttered under his breath as he wiggled the shears back and forth. He made one last cut and peeled off the framework. My world turned light again. We screeched around a corner and I grabbed a pole for support. Albie stood in front of me, grinning, while Jerry stuffed the snips and the frame in a case.

"Well, what do you think?" asked Albie.

There were two stretchers in the ambulance. Lying on the other one was a man of my height and build. We were dressed alike. His head was encased in a cocoon of white plaster. He looked enough like me to pass, but that would last only until the plaster came off.

"Twenty minutes is all the lead time we need," Albie assured me. "Malakoff can stall them that long."

"He's getting paid enough." I nodded at the man on the stretcher. "What happens to him?"

"All he knows is that a car hit him. He sticks with that story. Maybe he takes some heat, but that's what he gets paid for."

"Any word from the other team?"

The driver answered from the front seat. He was linked up with the other ambulance by radio. "Team two is rolling, heading for Lenox Hill."

"Any problems?" asked Albie.

"Going smooth."

Jerry called, "Almost there. Get ready."

I lay down under the stretcher and they draped a sheet to cover me. We pulled into the emergency driveway of New York Hospital. Albie and Jerry opened the doors and lowered the other stretcher to the ground.

"Here's your prize package, safe and sound." It was Malakoff talking to Jaspers.

"He damn well better be."

"Out of the way, move it." It was Albie's voice, high with urgency. "Let's get this man inside."

There were the sounds of feet, and of wheels on concrete, and then silence. The voice of the driver drifted back to me. "Lie still. Couple of minutes, that's all."

I counted off three of them, and then there was the sound of feet again, the slam of the doors, and Albie saying, "Move out."

The ambulance rolled. I came out from under the stretcher, and asked, "Where did you leave him?"

"Emergency room. He's Malakoff's baby now. Don't worry, the captain can handle it. Jerry, how we doing on time?"

"Nine thirty-six. Okay so far."

"What about the others?"

"Rolling from Lenox Hill, on their way to the airport."

We went back on Sixty-ninth to York Avenue, up York to the entrance to the FDR Drive, and then we were heading up along

179

the river to the Triboro Bridge. While we were rolling, Albie and I changed into light blue trousers, white shirts with black bow ties, and blue jackets. The jackets had a shoulder patch with the logo of Trans-Italia Airlines, and around the cuff the single stripe of a flight attendant. Albie clipped an airport ID card to his lapel, and handed me mine. The name on the card was Enrico DiLauro. There was an Italian passport with the same name in my flight bag.

"This woman," said Albie, "how good is her Italian?"

"Same as mine. Perfect."

"Jeez, I hope so. I don't want any screw-ups on the other end."

By the time we changed clothing we were over the Triboro and onto Grand Central Parkway on the way to LaGuardia Airport. We were about a mile short of the airport entrance when we saw the Lenox Hill ambulance up ahead of us.

"Pull in behind him," said Albie. "We'll go in together."

We took the curving approach road into the airport, both ambulances turning away from the terminals and out along the service road lined with hangars and warehouses. The Lenox Hill ambulance pulled into an alleyway next to the Consolidated Catering Company. We followed it in. Albie opened the back doors, and jumped down. I waved to Jerry and the driver, and jumped after him. The alleyway was dark, and there was the constant roar of engines.

"We move quick now," said Albie. "Try to look like you belong."

I nodded. I was looking at Nadia. She had gotten out of the other ambulance and was walking toward me. She, too, was dressed as a flight attendant: blue jacket and skirt, and a perky cap. In the faint light I could see her high cheekbones and the deepset eyes. She came close to me, face to face. We had never been that close before. We kissed lightly, a first touch.

Albie said impatiently, "Let's go, we gotta be quick."

Consolidated Catering prepared thousands of airline meals each day. The warehouse was a cavernous shell with crates stacked high against the walls. The rear of the building opened onto the working area of the airfield. There were dozens of vehicles moving about: forklifts, cars, and vans. One of the vans was waiting for us, the driver pacing nervously.

"You sure cut it close enough," he complained as we piled in. "They been calling for this load for ten minutes."

Albie said, "Shut up and move it."

The terminals seemed far away, but it took only minutes to get to them. Precious minutes. By now the cocoons had been cut away at the two hospitals and the substitutions had been discovered. By now Jaspers had notified Harry, who had pushed all the buttons. By now the alarms had gone out to all the proper authorities, and by now there were surveillance teams posted inside these terminals and all the others. And by now the Russians, no doubt, had mounted their own operation to find Nadia.

We passed the terminals of the major airlines and into the world of the charters. Trans-Italia was a charter outfit flying six times a week to Rome and Milan. Their DC-10 was parked away from the terminal. The van pulled up next to it, and Albie went over the set-up with us. We were three flight attendants traveling deadhead to Milan to pick up a flight there. We did not appear on either the crew manifest or the passenger list. We were bureaucratically invisible. If there were any questions, Albie would handle them.

"But there won't be any questions," he said. "It's all taken care of. Just sit back and enjoy the trip."

Nadia said, "You sound as if you've done this before."

"What can I tell you?"

"Never any problems?"

"Never. Relax, it's as smooth as silk."

"That's comforting," she said, but I felt her warning. She was in his head. I took a look. It wasn't pretty, but it wasn't any more than what I had expected. There was nothing to do about it now.

We boarded, and worked our way to the rear cabin. The aircraft was filled, and ready for takeoff. There were three attendants in the cabin. They nodded to Albie when they saw him, old friends and partners. There were three separate, vacant seats. We took them, settled in, and minutes later the aircraft moved out onto the runway. At 11:06 P.M. Trans-Italia flight number 21 took off for Milan. Estimated flying time was seven hours and fifty-five minutes, which would get us there about 1:00 P.M., Central European Time.

We flew through the night. Nadia sat four rows in front of me and one aisle over, close enough so that our minds could touch. We let the tendrils of our thoughts reach out, and after a while we slept. It was a needed sleep, a release from strain, but it did not last long. Just as two lovers asleep in the same bed will awake at the same moment and turn toward each other, we came up from sleep and reached out again.

Ben, what happens now?

As planned. No changes.

Did you take his head?

Same time you did.

You saw?

Sure. They turned us in.

Swine.

Betrayal is an art form to these people. Actually, I don't think Albie did it himself. Uncle John Merlo couldn't exist without ties to the Feds. As a guess, I'd say that Uncle John dropped the dime on us as soon as this plane got off the ground.

They'll be waiting for us in Milan. Your people, certainly. Maybe mine.

No question about it.

When will they make their move?

Not until Albie collects from me. That's the way Uncle John would set it up. First the money, then the heat. They'll wait to hit us in the terminal.

What bastards.

I wouldn't have it any other way. It wouldn't work any other way. Better get some sleep now. We'll be busy later.

Of the two airfields servicing Milan, Malpensa is less frantic and less sophisticated than Linate to the south. We landed there at 12:45 P.M., local time. Nadia, Albie, and I stayed in our seats while the other passengers disembarked onto busses that would take them across the field to the terminal.

I wish we were closer, said Nadia. *I can't pick up anything from here.*

They're in the terminal, believe it.

Albie came over. "Listen, we got some business to settle."

"In the terminal."

"Hey, no. We do it here."

"What's the difference?"

"Uncle John said I get paid on the plane."

If I needed any confirmation, that was it. I looked around. The attendants were the only ones left. I headed for the lavatory. "Step into the office."

The second half of the deal, a hundred and fifty thousand wrapped in two bricks of bills, was in my airline bag. I handed them over. "Tell Uncle John I said thanks for a first-class job."

"I'll tell him." He stuffed the bricks into his own bag. "You're on your own now. Good luck."

"Thanks." I probed him quickly. He was laughing at me.

"We better not go together," he said. "I'll go first. You and the woman wait for the next bus."

"Sure, we're in no hurry."

As soon as he was gone we ripped the Trans-Italia patches off our jackets. I put them into a plastic bag together with the passports and the ID that Albie had provided, and left the package in the lavatory for our friends to find. We left the DC-10 and went down the steps and onto the tarmac in the thin sunlight of an April afternoon. We watched Albie's bus rolling across the field.

"I hated to give him all that money," said Nadia. "Such a waste."

"Poker money is meant to be wasted. Let's go."

We hurried across the tarmac to the twin-jet Quadstar parked down the line. It didn't look big enough to cross an ocean, but it could, and easily. The rear ramp was down, and a man in uniform was waiting there. He threw us a casual salute as we came up.

"Mister Slade?"

"Yes. Mister Thayer's aircraft?"

"Yes sir. My name is Conway, I'm the steward. The pilot is ready to take off as soon as you board."

We went up the ramp and settled ourselves into the lap of B. B. Thayer's luxury. We took off at once. The flight lasted another eight hours, directly back to LaGuardia Airport in New York, the only place in the civilized world where no one would be looking for us. We arrived there at 3:30 P.M., local time, and cleared controls using passports I had bought in Times Square. They were cheap, but effective, good enough for one shot. We probed the area as we went through. It was clean. That's the way their minds worked. I knew, I had lived among those minds long enough.

We took separate taxis to the airport Holiday Inn, and took separate rooms there, as well. Those separate rooms were the hardest part of the gig, but it had to be that way. We were too close to take chances and so we stayed apart, although our rooms were close enough so that we could rest with our thoughts entwined. Actually, it was the way that we knew each other best.

We ate in our rooms and stayed within them for two days. That was as long as I figured it would take the Agency people to bounce back from Milan and latch onto Thayer. I had no illusions about Thayer's silence; he owed me nothing. On the third day we checked out at noon. We left the Times Square passports in our rooms for our friends to find. At the Pan American terminal I bought tickets in the names of Karl and Erika Gottfried, the names on our third set of passports. The passports were West German jobs, bought on Halsey Street in Brooklyn, near the Navy Yard. They came complete with supporting ID, and they were the best you could get. You always get the best near the navy yards. We used them for our tickets, and one hour later we departed on Pan Am flight 009 bound back to Malpensa Airport in Milan. On that particular day it was the only place in the civilized world where no one would be looking for us.

We cleared the airport as Karl and Erika Gottfried. The place was clean. We rented a car and drove north from Milan, leaving behind the permanent brown cap of industrial smog that hangs over the city. The countryside was flat and unattractive until we passed Sesto Calende and started up the western shore of Lago Maggiore. There the landscape gave way to tree-covered slopes of deep green and silver. We drove with the water below us on our right and, rising high on our left, the sub-Alpine peaks that pocketed the lake like the setting of a jewel. All of that country was gem-like, carved out over the centuries first by nature and then by man.

We stopped when we came to Cannero Riviera, just short of the Swiss border, and stayed at the Hotel Park Italia. It was not yet the high season and the place was almost empty. The managers were a young Swiss couple who welcomed our company. We told them that we were looking for a house to rent, and they found one for us. It was old, but it was well-built, furnished solidly, and it fronted on the lake. There was a stretch of pebbled beach, and a rickety boat house with a dory. There were chunks of marble in the ground, and pine trees growing next to palms. It was a world away from East Seventy-fifth Street, the Lucite and the chrome. It was a home.

"This is the place," Nadia said when she saw it. "This is where we stop and where we stay."

It was a home, and more. It was the place for us to live out the rest of our lives together. That was in the middle of April, and I figured that we had until Christmas.

13

THREE years later I celebrated my thirty-third birthday and I never felt better in my life. Nadia felt even better than I did. She was pregnant.

It was a time of wonderment for us, and a time of elation that grew every day. Three years after leaving New York, and more than a year after we should have been dead, we were in the best of health without a sign of Rauschner's Syndrome. We had no idea why we had lived so long, but we accepted the blessing without searching for the reason. In reflection, I realize that we must have known, or at least suspected, what had happened. The reason was there for us to see, but we did not want to see it. We preferred to live our lives from day to day on the shores of Lago Maggiore, content with what we had and confident that things would work out for us now that we had broken through the statistical barrier. We took Nadia's pregnancy as a happy omen, as if some cosmic physician had used it to signal our salvation.

The life that we led was a simple one, and as orderly as the winds that blew over the lake. In the early morning the *tramontana* came down from the north, after ten the *inverna* came up from the south, and all day long the *mergozzo* blew into the Gulf of Pallanza from the west. In the same orderly fashion we drove into Intra in the mornings to do the day's shopping, and on Wednesdays we would cross over the lake to Luino where the vegetables and the fish were fresher. Wednesday was market day in Luino and the trip by ferry took only half an hour, but often we would borrow the power launch from the Hotel Park Italia and make the crossing by ourselves. The launch was built for comfort, not speed, but the trip was always an adventure.

The shopping was even better in Brissago on the Swiss side of the border, but we did not go there. We were supposed to be dead, and so we assumed that we no longer were being hunted, but we took no chances with borders and passport controls. Even when we borrowed the launch we kept to the Italian part of the lake. It was an inconvenience because the newspapers and magazines were more recent in Brissago, but I told myself that I could live without the latest news from the outside world. I had my own world now and it was enough for me.

In the afternoons I worked on my memories. I did not call them memoirs. Memoirs were meant to be published, and these were not. They were recollections of the years I had spent working for the Center, and, by extension, for the Agency; and in terms of security they were explosive. Even then, years after the events, they would have caused high heads to roll, and so each installment was carefully deposited in my box at the Banco Ambrosio in Milan. It was a form of insurance, but it was also a way of bringing the past back to life for me and, in the process, bringing back to life the four people who had been dearest to me and who now were gone. Along with Sammy, the others had to be dead by now, and although I had lived all of my adult life in expectation of their passing, I felt their absence deeply. I put down as much as I could remember about Sammy's sharp mind and cutting wit, Martha's unaffected compassion,

Vince's strength, Snake's tenacity; and they lived for me again that way.

That was how we spent our days, and we did little else. When the weather was good we would borrow the launch from Aldo at the hotel and go out on the lake. Other days we walked along the shore and collected the small chunks of marble that lay all around. We went each week to the *cine* in town, and after the show we treated ourselves to a meal at the hotel. We spent a lot of time in bed. It was a quiet life, but we had had enough of the other kind, and if what we had was idyllic it was also marred by one blemish. We were running out of money. We never had expected to live so long, and the poker stash was almost gone.

There was only one way for me to make money, and that was by playing cards. If there had been any other road I would have taken it, but gambling, my kind of gambling which was not gambling at all, was all I knew save for the tricks that had been taught to me. I had no market for those tricks anymore, and so I went looking for a game.

It wasn't easy to find what I wanted. There were several casinos in the lake area, but roulette and dice were beyond my control, and in baccarat and chemmy my edge was too thin to guarantee a profit. I finally found it over in Como, a private game for a gang of businessmen from Milan who fancied poker American style. They played every Sunday night in a room above the casino, and it wasn't difficult to get into the game. All that was needed was money, a lot of it, and I had enough left to buy my way in for one night. One night was all that I needed. The next week I was back in business with a steady income. I played it the same as I had in New York, winning, but taking care not to bruise any feelings. I thought that my money problems were all taken care of until one of the regulars came up from Milan one Sunday and brought along an American guest who was looking for some action. It was B. B. Thayer.

There he was walking into the room, pearl-grey Stetson low on his head, the man who once had sworn that he would never again sit at a table with me. The only man in that part of the world who knew me as Ben Slade.

There were several ways I could have handled it. One way was to get up and leave before he recognized me. Another way was to take him aside and ask him not to expose me. The third way was to face him squarely. Of the three options, the last was least likely to succeed and, of course, it was the one I chose. I was being stubborn and prideful, but nobody was going to run me out of a game, and I wasn't going to beg for a favor.

Thayer came over to the table with his friend from Milan. The friend introduced him to the people sitting there. When it was my turn, he introduced me as Karl Gottfried. Thayer's eyes narrowed when he saw me. He started to smile, and thought better of it. I could see the memories on his face. Before he could say anything, I stood up.

"This gentleman and I have met before," I told the others. "We have an old superstition. We don't play in the same game. Thayer, I have a proposition to make to you." I put a deck of cards on the table in front of him. "I'll cut you for the territory. Whoever wins sits down and plays. Whoever loses walks away and keeps his mouth shut. How does that hit you?"

Thayer pursed his lips, thinking. He had a lot to absorb. He hooked a thumb into his vest pocket. He scratched the back of his head. He said, "Well now, I don't exactly see what's in that proposition for me."

There was a stack of chips in front of me, my working capital for the night. I pushed it all forward. Thayer let himself smile. He said, "Chicken feed."

"Maybe so, but that's what I've got and that's my stake. You're a gambler. I've never known you to pass up a straight proposition before."

That amused him. "Straight?"

"As straight as it can be."

"Do tell." He picked up the deck and hefted it. "I do believe you mean just that." He made his decision, turned to his friend from Milan and handed him the cards. "Paolo, would you?"

The friend, mystified, shuffled the deck, cut it, and placed it on the table. Thayer motioned to me. "Go ahead."

I cut deep and came up with the jack of diamonds.

Thayer cut. He turned over the king of hearts.

I nodded to Thayer and to the others, and walked out of the room. I stopped just outside the door, and listened. I heard the clatter of chips and the murmur of confused conversation from the other players. They were trying to figure out what had happened. Thayer did not let them wonder for long.

"Well, gentlemen," I heard him say, "you've just seen the last of Mister Ben Slade, one of the slickest card sharps it has ever been my misfortune to encounter. I hope old Ben didn't take you for too much."

I didn't wait to hear any more. It was time to go home and tell Nadia what had happened, time to decide what had to be done. Actually, the decision was out of my hands, but at that point I did not know it. With my name out in the open, it took the Agency only seventy-two hours to find me again.

Harry Kourkalis showed up at my front door three days later. It was a cold November morning with mist rolling in off the lake, and he wasn't dressed for it. No coat or gloves, and his face was pinched and red. He stamped his feet and blew on his hands. He was shivering. He smiled apologetically.

"I thought it was always warm here," he said. "Fir trees growing right next to palm trees. I never saw that before."

"Come in," I said. "There's a fire going in the sitting room."

"You aren't surprised to see me?"

"I caught your head as you turned into the driveway."

I took him inside and sat him in front of the fire. It really wasn't that cold outside, but he groaned with pleasure. I asked, "How did they find me?"

"That poker business in Como. You're blown. So is she." He

gave me that doggy apologetic look again. "Before anything else . . . it's good to see you. I never thought I would again. You know?"

I told him that I knew. He wanted to start right in with what he had come for, but I told him to hold it. I wanted Nadia there. I went out back to where she was changing the butane tank for the kitchen stove. She was doing things like that more and more, proving points about pregnant women. I told her about our visitor. I had told her before about Harry.

She said, "I don't understand it. They sent a mouse."

"No, he's more than that."

"If they sent someone like that it has to be a trick."

"We'll see. Come inside and we'll have some coffee."

"As soon as I shift this tank."

When she came into the sitting room with the coffee tray, Harry got to his feet. "I'm pleased to meet you, Mrs. Slade," he said. "Or do I call you Nadia Petrovna?"

"Around here it's Signora Gottfried," she said, setting out the cups. "It doesn't make any difference what you call me. We aren't going to be friends."

His face turned pinker. "I'm sorry. Maybe we can avoid being enemies."

"Maybe," she said noncommittally.

He took a sip of coffee, then another, and sighed. "That tastes good. Been flying all night. Checked into a hotel and drove up here from Milan. Ben, the past few days . . . total chaos at the Center. We couldn't believe it when we heard it. That you were alive."

"I figure to stay that way, Harry."

"Of course you do." Then he understood what I meant. "You don't have to talk that way. There is absolutely no need to talk that way."

"You mean that nobody ever wanted me dead?"

"You're talking Agency. I'm talking Center."

"Dead is dead."

"That's history, anyway. Things are different now. I have a message for you."

"Let's hear it."

The message was simple. They wanted me back without conditions. They wanted us both. There would be no penalties for what I had done, and there would be no attempt to debrief Nadia. There was nothing political in it. They wanted us for only one reason. Somehow, we held the key to the cure of Rauschner's Syndrome. They wanted that key, and they were willing to grant us total immunity if we would help them to find it.

I asked, "Who sent the message?"

"Personal from Pop to you."

"What about the Agency?"

"I won't kid you. I couldn't if I wanted to. The offer is good for a week. That's all that Pop could get them to agree to. I've got six more days to bring you in. If I don't, then it's a brand-new ballgame and the Agency gets to play."

"What the hell does that mean?"

He spread his hands wide. "Who knows with those people? I guess it means that you either come in with me or they come and get you. I don't know. I'm just the messenger."

He finished his coffee and put down his cup. He looked at Nadia hopefully. She smiled, despite herself, and refilled the cup. Then she went into the kitchen and came back with a plate of cookies. It was that doggy look of his.

"That's the message," he said, munching. "You'll want to check me out so I'll shut up now. Go ahead, take a look at my head. I won't try to block anything."

He was kidding himself. He wouldn't have been able to block either one of us for more than ten seconds. We spent the next minute scampering through his head like two field mice in a haystack. He was clean. There was no sign that he was lying, or concealing anything pertinent. The major impression that I caught was his sincere desire for me to come back home to where I belonged, to rejoin the family, and to bring my wife with me. That was Harry, all right. He cried at everybody's wedding.

Nadia, too, found him clean. She thought, *Ben, he means it.*

He believes what he's saying, I agreed. *That doesn't mean very much. They could have sent us a dodo.*

Could he possibly be a dodo? At his level, wouldn't he have to know too much?

It's a good point, one I can't answer. First reaction?

Negative. You?

Tending toward positive.

Then we have to talk.

All of that took seconds. I said to Harry, "Look, you're going to have to give us some time. You said that you have six days. We need some of that to think about this."

He frowned. He had been hoping to wrap it up on the spot. "Let me make two points," he said. "The first is about the Rauschner's. This is a personal appeal from Pop. You're holding the fate of a lot of people in your hands, people just like you. I don't think you can turn Pop down on that."

"Point noted."

"The second point is about immunity. All we can guarantee is the Agency. We don't know what Nadia's people have in mind. The sooner you come in, the sooner she'll be safe from them."

"Also noted, but we'll still need the time. Where are you staying?"

"The Belvedere."

Again, that was Harry. With the Agency paying expenses he could have stayed anywhere in Milan, but he had to pick a place like the Belvedere. I wrote down the telephone number and told him that I would get to him as soon as I could. He wasn't happy about it, but he knew enough not to press me. He left reluctantly, thanking Nadia again for the coffee and the cookies. When he was gone, she took the cups and plates into the kitchen and I heard her banging them around in there. She had to be upset to abuse the crockery.

"Don't break anything," I called. "Come in here and we'll talk it over."

"We can talk on our way to Luino," she said. It was Wednesday, our day for shopping on the other side of the lake.

We walked up the road to the hotel and asked Aldo if we could borrow the launch. He took the keys off a hook in back of the desk, and tossed them to me.

"Go quickly," he said, winking. "Two of the guests were asking to use it, but I thought that you might come by."

"Thank you, Aldo, but guests come first. We'll take the ferry."

"No, take it. They are unbearable people, a woman and her son, quite disagreeable. If this were July I would have turned them away." He shrugged. You took what you could get in November.

"Are you sure?"

"Without a doubt."

The launch was a twenty-footer with an engine that clunked. We cruised out past the ruins of the Malpaga castles, each on its own tiny island, turned up-lake as far as Brissago, and then ran down and across toward Luino. The *inverna* was blowing up from the south and I kept the bows into it. Nadia was at home on the water and the roughness did not bother her, not even now in the fifth month of her pregnancy. The sun was out, burning the mist off the water and turning the day warm. We kept our thoughts to ourselves during the crossing. In Luino, we shopped for tomatoes, and cheese, and the little white fish that fry up as crisp as sticks of candy. Only when we were on the water again and on our way home did I say what was on my mind.

"We have to face the fact that we've been blown," I said. "We have to make a move and the Center is the quickest and safest place for us."

"Safe?" she said angrily. "How can you trust people who would have killed us a few years ago?"

"I'm not putting my trust in those people. I trust Pop. The Center is my home."

"The Center is an institution. I don't want my baby born in an institution."

"That institution is also a research center. Think of what we would be doing for the others."

"Think of what we would be doing to ourselves."

"If we don't go in it means that we're on the run again."

"I'd rather be on the run than be in jail. Because that's what it is. It's a prison that they're talking about. It always is. Every time you submit to authority it means going to jail, one way or the other."

It was an exaggeration, but not by much. It sounded like something that Sammy would have said, and I told her so.

"Good," she said firmly. "You think of him so often and you admired him so much. Ask yourself what he would have done if he were here."

I knew the answer to that without posing the question. In my situation, Sammy would not have gone back. What Harry had delivered, despite the sweet promises, was an ultimatum, and Sammy would never have given in to it. It was the best point she could have made, and once she made it I knew that we weren't going. She read the decision in my mind, and smiled her relief.

"If we're running," she said, "the sooner the better."

"Harry said six days."

"I know, but still. . . ."

"All right. We'll have to travel light."

In all ways but one. There was no way of traveling light with what she was carrying. She caught that thought too, and smiled brilliantly. "He won't be a burden. More like an inspiration."

"He?"

"I've decided." The smile faded. "What direction are we running in?"

"Switzerland first. Figure things out from there."

We clunked our way back across the lake toward home, the launch shuddering with the vibration of the ancient engine. There was little traffic on the lake in that season: a few fishermen and, hugging the near shore, a stubby freighter. It occurred to us both in the same moment that if we were going to Switzerland, all we had to do was put the helm over and head north up the lake. We could go ashore above Brissago and be in Lugano by evening.

"What do you think?" she asked.

Her voice was neutral, but I knew that she did not want to do it that way. We both were dressed in jeans, shirts, and light nylon jackets. Between us we had about a hundred thousand lira plus the three thousand Swiss francs that I always kept in the back of my wallet. There were bank cards in the name of Gottfried, but that name was no good to us now. Doing it that way we would be starting with nothing, and from where we were we could already see our house and the strip of beach in front of it. In the house were the material things that could start us properly on our way: clothes, papers, a cash reserve.

In that same neutral voice, she said, "I could pack a few bags in twenty minutes. Another twenty minutes in the car and we'd be over the border."

"All right."

"Unless you think. . . ."

"No, that's all right. We'll do it that way."

I pulled the old clunker off her heading for the hotel and pointed her at our beach. "I'll drop you off and bring the launch back to the hotel," I said. "You get it together and pick me up there. Twenty minutes, right?"

"Make it thirty. Is there anything you want me to get for you?"

Sad eyes staring. We were walking away from three happy years in that place; running, not walking, away from what once had been our haven. And now, a memento. . . ? A chunk of marble? A palm frond for a fan?

"Just the essentials," I said. I touched her arm lightly. "Do it quick and clean. Don't look back."

"I know. Pillar of salt."

I ran the launch up onto the beach and held the nose pointed into the gravelly bottom while she scrambled ashore. She reached over the gunwale for the basket of shopping. She stared at the fish, and tomatoes, and cheese, and put the basket back. We would not be using it.

"Give it to Aldo," she said. She turned, and ran toward the house.

"Thirty minutes," I called after her, and she waved.

I brought the launch into the mooring in front of the hotel, maneuvered alongside the stone waterwall, and nosed up against the hanging rubber fenders. The wall ran along the shore below the lawn that sloped down from the hotel. The afternoon sun had turned pale, and the air was raw again. There were only four people in sight. Two men walked along the wall, coming toward me from the right. I could not see their faces. They wore anoraks and jeans, and they walked briskly. There were wooden, slatted chairs up on the lawn to the left of me. Two people sat there, and they looked as if they might be Aldo's guests, the unbearable mother and her son. The mother was built like a bulldog, and was bundled in sweaters. The son looked to be in his late teens, large and bulky, and wearing jogging clothes a size too small. Mother and son were bent over magazines.

The boy looked up, saw the launch, and jumped to his feet. He called excitedly, "Hey, Ma, the boat's back. Come on, it's our turn now."

The mother put down her magazine. "All right, don't go getting yourself all in a dither."

"Ma, come on, *please*." They spoke in English.

I idled the engine and went up to secure the forward lines. I stood on the coaming with the lines in my hand, ready to jump ashore. The two men changed from a walk to a trot when they saw me, running down the waterwall. I could see their faces now: Jaspers and Childress. Harry, you bastard, you said six days. I put my foot against the rubber fenders and pushed off again. The bow began to swing out slowly. I leaped for the cockpit and kicked the engine up. It groaned, sputtered, and raced.

"Slade," Jaspers called. He and Childress were running hard. I hunkered down in the cockpit and put the helm over hard.

Up on the lawn the boy saw the two of them running toward the launch, and let out a whoop. "Ma, look. Hey, you two, cut it out. We're next on the boat."

"Hey now, stop that fussing," said the mother.

"They're gonna get in ahead of us. That aint fair."

"Well, you just go down there and tell them that. There's no need to shout."

The boy didn't see it that way. He sounded another whoop, grabbed a beach bag from beside his chair, and went charging down the lawn, yelling, "Hold on there, you sons of bitches, that boat is ours."

Jaspers and Childress ignored him, but his mother gave a scandalized squawk. She might have been built like a bulldog, but she came out of her chair like a greyhound and went running after him. Within a few steps she was right behind him, the two of them sprinting over the grass.

She called, "Damn it, you quit that this minute, you hear? You're gonna embarrass me right out in front of everybody."

But the boy had his head down. He kept running, pounding

along the waterwall with his beachbag banging against his thigh, his mother close behind. Jaspers and Childress came running from the other direction. The bows of the boat were still turning out from the wall, much too slowly as the engine missed repeatedly. There was a foot of water between the launch and the wall, then another, and another. I had the wheel hard over, and I pounded the throttle with the palm of my hand. The movement of the boat was painfully slow.

The boy made it to the mooring first. He stared in dismay at the widening gap between the wall and the boat. He called to me angrily, "You can't do that, you just came in. It's our turn now."

He backed up a few feet from the edge of the wall. Jaspers and Childress had stopped running. Jaspers reached under his anorak and came out with a pistol. The boy ran forward and jumped awkwardly for the boat. Jaspers fired while he was in the air. The boy twisted, hit, and fell into the cockpit. His mother stood at the edge of the wall, her mouth open and her eyes wide. Jaspers fired again and half of the mother's face disappeared. She pitched forward into the water. The engine exploded into full power and the bows of the boat came up. Jaspers shifted his target, sighting in on the boat. Childress grabbed his arm. I couldn't hear their voices, but I was close enough now to get into their heads.

No more shooting.

Easy target. Put a couple below the waterline.

No, you might hit him. Let the others. . . .

The launch moved away from shore, spray hitting the windscreen. I put her up on her boards, turning tightly and heading back to the house. Jaspers and Childress turned and ran toward a car parked on the esplanade. I went cold. There was only one place they would be going and there was no way in which I was going to get there first. I was well away from shore now and coming around the islands of the two Malpaga castles. I bent over the boy. His eyes were closed, but he was breathing.

He wasn't a boy, but a young man with a very young face. I went into his head, but found nothing. He was out cold. He had been hit in the right shoulder, and the shock of it had put him under. I didn't much care. I just wanted to get back to the house. I pulled a tarpaulin over him, and the beachbag he still clutched in his arms. I straightened up and saw the others then.

Let the others. . . . That's what Childress had said.

The power boat came out from behind the larger of the Malpaga islands with two of them in it. One was crouched at the gunwale, and one stood at the wheel. I knew them both. Their names were Hoffman and Petofsky, and they belonged to the same outfit as Jaspers and Childress. Hoffman, at the gunwale, held an automatic weapon. Their boat was larger than the launch, and much faster. It came up on me quickly, and circled around. I put the wheel over, but the other boat kept pace, crowding in. Petofsky, at the wheel, waved and then, in a broad gesture, drew a finger across his throat. It took me a moment to realize that he wasn't being macabre. He wanted me to cut the engine and heave to.

Instead, I turned in toward him. There was a cracking sound as the two hulls touched, and came apart. Hoffman stood up and fired into the boil of my wake. I turned away again.

Petofsky raised a bullhorn, and spoke into it. "Mister Slade, you know who I am. I have orders not to hurt you, but I'll sink you if I have to. Come alongside."

I put the wheel over hard and turned away, but I didn't have the speed for it. Petofsky came around quickly, herding me like a collie working on sheep. I slammed at the throttle, trying for an extra jolt of speed. He kept pace easily. He raised the horn again.

"Mister Slade, I can keep this up all day, but I'm not going to. Unless you heave to at once I am going to fire into your hull."

There wasn't any choice. I cut the engines to an idling murmur. The swells caught the launch and tossed it as Petofsky worked around under my lee. We came together and Hoffman slipped a fender between the two hulls. The two cockpits lay side by side with Petofsky only a few feet away.

"Come aboard, Mister Slade," he said. "You're coming with us."

I didn't move. "What about the launch?"

"We're leaving it here. Someone will spot it and pick it up."

I shook my head. "Can't be done. I have a wounded boy on board, badly wounded. He needs a doctor's attention at once."

"You have a *what?*"

"A civilian. Jaspers shot him."

"Sweet Jesus." He leaned over to look into my cockpit. From where he stood, all he could see were the boy's feet and the tarpaulin over him. "Jaspers did that?"

"Not only that, he killed the kid's mother."

"Ah, no. Ah, shit." I saw the anger in his eyes, and the indecision as well. Up until then he had had a relatively clean operation going. Now he had a corpse, plus a wounded civilian floating around in the middle of Lago Maggiore. He could take the chance of leaving a corpse behind, but not someone who could still talk. He made his decision. He said, "Throw him overboard."

"Maybe you didn't hear me. I said he was alive."

"I heard you all right. Roll him over the side."

"Negative."

"Do it or you're going down, Slade. I can't leave him."

"That's your problem, not mine. You want to tell Hoffman to shoot, go ahead. You're supposed to take me in one piece. I'm not going to do it."

"Son of a bitch." I wasn't sure whether he meant Jaspers or me. He said to Hoffman, "Watch him. I'm going over."

He climbed onto the railing of his boat, balanced himself, and jumped down into my cockpit. Both craft rocked wildly. He bent over the boy and pulled off the tarpaulin. The boy stared up at him. He had his beachbag in his arms, the muzzle of an Uzi poking out of one end of it. He fired up at Petofsky and blew him over backward. He sat up quickly, swung the weapon in a short arc, and killed Hoffman. He slumped back, his face white and pinched.

He opened his mouth, and the voice of a young girl said, "This is absolutely the last time I get involved in something like this. I loathe violence, don't you?"

I managed to nod.

"If people would only sit down and reason with each other, these things wouldn't happen. Don't you agree?"

I nodded again.

"Well, I've had enough of it, thank you. I'm going down to the garden and tend to the azaleas. I find gardening so restful, don't you?"

"Look, who the hell are you?"

"Grace. Just call me Grace. *Amazing grace, how sweet the sound. . . .*" The voice trailed off, and his eyes closed.

I punched the throttle and the launch leaped forward. The lurch of it slammed the boy against the boards, but I couldn't worry about that. I had to get home. The engine wheezed and clunked. I cursed it, and at one point I kicked it. The *inverna* was still blowing and I had to push the launch through it to work my way down the lake. It took me almost half an hour to get there. I jumped from the boat as it hit the beach, and raced for the house with the sand sucking at my shoes.

I called her name as I came through the door, but I got no answer. I called again, and my voice echoed. I ran through the rooms. Someone stood in the livingroom doorway, his arms spread wide to keep me from coming in. He caught me, and I struggled.

He said, *No, Ben, you don't want to go in there.*

It was Vince Bonepart. He held me in a grip I could not break. I did not stop to wonder how he could be there. I kept on fighting him.

"Ben, ease up," he said aloud, "it's me."

"Let him in," said someone else. "You can't keep him out forever."

The grip on my arms relaxed and I pushed into the room. The place was wrecked. There was blood all over, and there were bodies on the floor. Sammy Warsaw sat on the edge of an overturned chair, his head in his hands. Martha sat sprawled on the floor, staring vacantly at the ceiling. The bodies belonged to Jaspers and Childress. Snake stood over them, a weapon slung from her shoulder.

I looked around for Nadia. She was on the couch. They had put her there. I knelt beside her. Her face was white, and there was a bullet hole in the side of her head. She was dead.

Sammy stood over me, a hand on my shoulder. In a sad, strained voice, he said, "We were late. They came to kill her, and we were late." He paused. "If it means anything, they're dead, too."

It meant nothing. They were dead, and she was dead, and what she had carried was dead, and for what was left of my life I could have been dead, as well.

14

Y o u go to sleep at night, and you get up in the morning, and somehow you get through the day. You keep on going. You do that for one day and another, and then a week and another, and before you know it a month has gone by. Then two months, and three, and five. You keep on going, but you never stop thinking about her. You hang on desperately to thoughts of her, afraid of how it might be if you were to forget things like the way that she would smile when she was surprised, or that catlike stretch of hers each morning. It's bad enough to be without her, irrevocably alone, but you know how much worse the emptiness would be if the memories started to fade. So you hold on to what you can remember despite the extra grief it brings. The grief serves a purpose. It holds you up, stiffens your back, and pushes you forward. It lets you know, like a bleeding wound, that you are still alive. It reminds you that there are scores that will have to be settled.

You go to sleep at night, and you get up in the morning, and your brothers and sisters are all around you. Their thoughts are with you, literally, inside your head and adding strength. They cannot take the grief away, they cannot absorb any part of it for you, but they can keep you from howling each night at the moon, and from running off in search of blood. They can keep you sane, and at the same time they can answer the questions that have to be asked throughout the sad winter. You ask, they answer, and you try to put the pieces together. Some of it seems so obvious now, unbelievable that you hadn't been able to figure it out yourself. Some of it is unbelievable still, impossible to accept, except on faith. But all of it, the obvious and the unlikely, finally falls together and makes sense. Deadly sense.

They had to kill her, just as they will have to kill you. And Snake, and Martha, and Sammy, and Vince. And even Jimmy Abdul. Because you were the ones who got away.

Get it through your head, says Sammy for the twentieth time. *There is no such disease as Rauschner's Syndrome. It's a myth, a piece of fiction that the Agency invented. It doesn't exist.*

Wearily, you counter with, *But how do you know that? What about the medical books? We've all read them.*

Martha gets into it gently. *Do you think that the Agency doesn't have the money and the talent to print their own books? Have you ever seen Rauschner's mentioned in a textbook outside the Center?*

Of course not. It's classified material.

It's classified bullshit, says Vince. *There's no such thing.*

And Martha again. *Ben, dear, we know how you feel. We all felt the same way when Sammy first told us. We couldn't believe it.*

But how do you know? What about the doctors who lectured to us about Rauschner's at the Center?

Agency doctors like that bastard MacGregor, says Snake. *For Christ's sake, look at yourself in the mirror. You're thirty-three and you were supposed to be dead years ago. Isn't that enough to convince you?*

But how do you know?

No Rauschner's Syndrome, they tell you. The aces were no

more fated for an early death than anyone else. We died early, but not from any disease. We died from a set of fabricated symptoms, followed by a discreet needle that shuffled us off without any fuss or inquiry. We died for the simplest of reasons. After more than a decade of service to our country, we knew far too much to be allowed to live. And so our country decreed that we had to die. From a fictional disease called Rauschner's Syndrome. That's what they tell you.

But how do you know?

And Sammy says, *Do you really want me to answer that?*

And, on reflection, you're not sure that you do. Because along with the grief comes another companion, a deep, raw, and unreasoning anger that cuts across you like another bleeding wound. It's a general rage at first, but it soon becomes specific, focused on those who made this happen. The Agency, Delaney, and all the callous bastards who kill so casually. It's a mounting anger that feeds on itself and grows to encompass all of the world that does not bleed as you do. It is an anger of unstable fire, ready to spill in any direction, and so, on reflection, you are not at all sure that you want to know the answers to all the questions. You dare not know any more than you do, because the rage knows no reason and could easily turn on the ones you love most. For they've known about this for three long years and they haven't done a damn thing about it.

And so when Sammy says, *Do you really want me to answer that?* you reply, with caution, *Not now, but someday.*

Let me know when, he says. *Until then, take it on faith. We know.*

So you go to sleep at night, you get up in the morning, and an entire winter goes by that way with your brothers and sisters keeping you sane. Keeping you from taking on the Agency single-handed. Keeping you cautious. Caution is the word that winter. There's nothing you can do about it now, they tell you. Now is the time to play it cool, the time for caution. We know, we've been living with this thing for three years, and they've been years of caution. And you listen to them because you trust their judgment. You learn to live with your grief and hide your rage, but then a morning comes when you wake and you know that the time for caution is over. The winter is done, the spring has come, and it's time to make a move. It's time to ask that question.

That's the way it was for me that winter, crisscrossing through the southern part of the United States with Sammy's circus. That's the way I led my life until a morning in April when I woke in a fairgrounds outside of Greentree, Virginia, with the rage a roar in my head. Perhaps it was because the Center was so close by, less than one hundred miles away. Perhaps I didn't need a reason. Perhaps the time had simply come. It was time to howl, and strike out at anyone who did not bleed like me. It was time to raise scalps, draw blood, and race wild through the night. It was finally time to move away from grief and into anger.

I was sharing Vince's camper then, and I rolled out while he was still asleep, heading for a dawn cup of coffee at the pie wagon with the sounds and the smells of the circus all around me. The Top was up, and the cleaning crew was already at work mucking out the ring from the night before. There was nickering all along the horse line, and down on Menagerie Row the big cats muttered their displeasure. There was a white mist close to the ground and the cats resented the damp; they would mumble and grunt until the sun came up and burned the ground dry.

It was a short walk to the pie wagon for my coffee, for there wasn't all that much to Sammy's circus. It was small, old-fashioned, and frayed at the edges. The menagerie consisted of two huge but weary elephants named Bull and Rosie; two camels, two tigers, two lions, and a bear. There were eight rosinback horses for the equestrian act, and the riders doubled as clowns. Vince did the Strong Man, Snake threw knives, Martha helped out in the fortune-telling tent, and Amazing Grace puttered around with the floral arrangements. The aerialists were also the jugglers, two of the girls from the sideshow had an act jumping poodles through hoops of fire, and another of the girls was Snake's target for the knives. The sideshow, itself, was minimal. There was a Fat Lady, a Crocodile Boy, a Strong Man, a Gypsy Fortune Teller, and the girls who were part of the come-on. They danced to music piped through loudspeakers from a tape deck in Sammy's camper. There was a mechanical steam calliope in the camper, but it wasn't good for much. All it could play was "The Entrance of the Gladiators," which, traditionally, was all it was supposed to play. Sammy was enough of a traditionalist to use it for the opening of each performance, but at all other times he used tapes. He was a traditionalist, but he drew the line at feeding musicians.

The name of the outfit was the Jenner Brothers Southland, and it was one of the last of its kind. It did not play in air-conditioned city arenas, or faceless suburban shopping centers. It didn't travel on the railroads, or advertise on television. The Jenner Brothers Southland pitched its tents on the meadows outside of tiny towns from Florida to Pennsylvania, wheeling and dealing its way through local zoning and health regulations, and winding its way through the night from one date to the next in a caravan of three dozen campers, trucks, and station wagons filled with the paraphernalia of the past. Everyone in the business knew that you couldn't make money with that sort of a tent-show circus anymore. The money lay in the city arenas with comfortable seating, elaborate lighting, and per-formances geared to the smooth familiarity of a television spectacular. Yet at the end of every season, Sammy's circus showed a modest, but adequate, profit. The Jenner Brothers Southland brought something to the small towns of the Atlantic seaboard that could not be found on the tube: the raw and earthy side of a circus where the blasé kids of the television age could actually smell the lions and tigers, flinch from the roar-ing, and watch the daredevils fly through the air without the safety net of electronic editing. The circus was a cultural anachronism that Sammy cherished. He had bought it from the Jenner brothers almost three years ago, pooling his money with Martha, and Snake, and Vince, and for those three years it had provided the perfect cover for a bunch of aces on the run. They all owned it, but Sammy ran it. Many of the people who worked for the circus were Lowara gypsies, and they had taken Sammy as one of their own. In the way of the Rom, they would have died rather than betray him.

One of them was Stevo, who once had been the ringmaster, and who nodded to me as I passed by the rear of his camper, and murmured a greeting. The sun was not yet fully up, but he sat behind the camper in the shade of a tent flap. He would sit there through most of the day. He was in mourning, and had removed himself from the mainstream of the circus life. His wife had been Dunicha, the fortune-teller, and she had died at Lago Maggiore playing the role of Jimmy Abdul's mother. Stevo had wanted to leave the circus entirely for at least six months in the custom of the Lowara, so that the people around him would not be burdened by his grief, but Sammy had persuaded him to turn over his ringmaster's job to his cousin Bendigo, and to stay on among those who loved him. He had done that for Sammy. Dunicha had died far away, and for reasons that Stevo did not understand, but he had never blamed Sammy for her death. He adored Sammy to the point of worship. All of the Lowara with the circus did. They liked Martha, they respected Vince, they were afraid of Snake, they marveled at Jimmy Abdul, and they were just beginning to accept me. But they adored Sammy.

I was finished with my first cup of coffee and was working on a stack of wheats when Sammy came into the pie wagon. He wore beat-up riding breeches and boots, a jacket with most of the buttons missing, and a crimson *diklo* around his neck. Except for his hair, he looked like a Rom. He slid onto the stool next to me, muttered, "Morning," and sipped his coffee silently. His eyes were still puffy from sleep and his frizzy hair was pointed in all directions.

I waited until he had gotten some caffeine into his system, then said, "You told me once that when I was ready to ask that question, you would answer it. Well, I'm ready now."

He nodded sleepily. "You sure? Look, if I answer that question it doesn't stop there. It opens up a whole can of worms. You might not like what you hear."

I knew damn well that I wasn't going to like it, but I tamped the anger down, and said quietly, "I know that, but it's time. I want to know."

He finished his coffee, slid off the stool, and stood up. He didn't look sleepy anymore. "Let's get out of here."

We left the pie wagon and walked along the tented area of the sideshow and down to the waterpoint where a couple of local kids were getting the thrill of a lifetime hauling buckets for the livestock. Sammy walked silently, his hands behind his back and his head down.

I said, "I'm waiting. How do you know?"

He lifted his head. "I have to go back a couple of years. Do you remember Big John Brodski's funeral?"

"Yes, of course." I remembered it well, walking up the hill with Pop after the service, and the conference with Delaney about Nordquist and the biochip.

"Well, it all began then. It was a practical joke."

It took Sammy's sharp, curious, and irreverent mind to question the unquestionable, to wonder why the aces had to die so young. For him to do that was akin to a convinced communist questioning Marx, or a fundamentalist Christian questioning the validity of the Resurrection. Rauschner's Syndrome, a short and merry life and a ticket out before the age of thirty-two . . . those were the tenets of our faith, and no one in the history of the Federal Center for the Study of Childhood Diseases had ever doubted them until Sammy put his mind to it. Still, for all of that, it started with a practical joke at the funeral of Big John Brodski.

Big John, himself, was the joker. He had always been known as one at the Center. When we were kids, he was the character who short-sheeted your bed, and put shaving cream in your shorts; and it wasn't by accident that those pet raccoons of his had feasted on Martha's shoes. His joking was legendary at the Center, but it was only one of two notable aspects to his personality. The other was his love affair with the state of California. He had been born there. Well, we were all born someplace, and Big John, like the rest of us at the Center, had not seen his home since the age of twelve when Pop had plucked him out of an impossible family situation. But the fact that he was a Californian in name only never deterred John from preaching the virtues of the place. Give him half a chance and he would back you into a corner and bore you stiff with a spiel about California's mountains and valleys, its deserts and beaches, its climate and its glorious golden people. The trick, when cornered, was to escape as quickly as possible. No delay, you ran like hell. If you didn't, what you got was a detailed rundown of the Forty-Niners' chances for the Super Bowl, an analysis of the Dodgers' pitching rotation, a report of skiing conditions at both Heavenly Valley and Mount Shasta, and the exact times when the surf would be up off Malibu. We all ran from Big John Brodski when the California mood was on him, leaving him staring after us wistfully. He was both puzzled and hurt by our indifference, and could never understand why we did not share his passion. It was an attitude that stayed with him all of his life, and the reason why, in the spring of the year in which he died, he called Sammy and said that he wanted to ask a favor.

"A big one," he said over the telephone. "When can we get together and talk?"

"I'll be at the beach house this weekend," said Sammy. He had a place near Cape May on the Jersey shore. "Come out on Sunday. We'll drink and we'll talk."

They both did a fair amount of drinking, but Big John did most of the talking that Sunday afternoon, sitting on Sammy's patio with a stretch of dunes before them, and beyond that the choppy waters of Delaware Bay. John had brought along a tape player and a single audio cassette, but before he played it he had his favor to ask.

"You know, I don't have much time left," he said over the first drink. "Six months at the most."

"I know," said Sammy, frowning. He was right behind Brodski in age, and he wasn't in the mood to think about that on a Sunday afternoon at the shore.

"All right, we've both been to enough of those services at the Center so we know what's going to happen when I go. A lot of horsing around, some speeches, and then everybody gets plastered, right?"

"Right."

"And all the time I'm just lying there in the coffin doing nothing with my skin all blue, and my face twisted up, and those marks on my neck like a strangled chicken. Right?"

"Right," said Sammy, wondering where this was leading. He had seen enough of those faces stamped with the final symptoms of Rauschner's Syndrome, and he did not need any reminders of how he, himself, would look someday.

"I'm out of it. You see what I mean? It's my party, but I don't get to have any fun."

Sammy refilled his glass. "That's the way it usually works."

"Doesn't seem fair, does it?"

"Maybe not, but I don't see what you can do about it. It's sort of a tradition, Big John. At a funeral the dead guy just lies there."

"Not this time," said Brodski, a touch of triumph in his

voice. He showed Sammy the tape machine and the cassette. "That's the favor I'm asking. I want you to smuggle this into my coffin. Hide it someplace where it can't be seen."

"What's on it?"

"You'll see." Brodski gave him a small black box. "This here is a remote control. What I want you to do is, when you figure the time is right, like when everybody is feeling sort of bad about me, that's when you press the button and start the tape. What do you say?"

"I don't know," said Sammy, staring at the black box doubtfully, and recalling the long parade of practical jokes for which Brodski had been responsible. "It isn't going to blow up, is it?"

"Shit, no."

"Dirty songs? The *Internationale?* The sayings of Chairman Mao?"

"Nothing like that," Brodski assured him. "You can listen to it now if you want to."

"I definitely want to," said Sammy, pressing the button.

At first there was music, an orchestral arrangement of "California, Here I Come" that segued into "Hooray for Hollywood," and then there was Brodski's voice, loud and clear, saying:

"Good morning, you rotten bastards. I've finally got you, haven't I? I could never do it while I was alive, you always ran away from me, made me feel like shit. Yes, you did, and don't try to deny it. You all did. But not this time, you sons of bitches. This time I've got you nailed to the floor. This is a funeral, you can't walk out on me, and before you bury me I'm going to say just a few more words about the golden state of California.

"To begin with, did you know that the state flower of California is the golden poppy? Did you know that the state bird is the valley quail? That the state animal is the grizzly bear and the state fish is the golden trout? Did you know that the state insect is the dog-face butterfly? Did you know that California was first sighted by the Spanish explorer Juan Rodríguez

214

Cabrillo in 1542, and that the first mission was established at San Diego in 1769? Did you know that California became a U.S. Territory in 1848, and that gold was discovered in. . . ."

The tape rolled on with Brodski's voice proudly declaiming the history of the state of California. He kept it up for almost ten minutes before the music started again. Then, his voice hushed, he wound it up by saying:

"That's it, boys and girls, the final words of Big John Brodski. I finally got you to listen to me. You can go on with the party now. Go out on the lawn and drink yourselves silly, and don't worry about me. I've had one hell of a perfect day, and I want you all to know that at this very moment I'm not in heaven and I'm not in hell. I've done a lot better than that. I've gone back to California."

The tape clicked to a stop. Brodski looked at Sammy expectantly. "What do you think?"

"Neat."

"Will you do it?"

"Glad to."

Brodski grinned broadly. "Thanks, *tus*, you're a buddy. Listen, I was wondering. Do you think we could rig some kind of a gadget so that when you pressed the button my body would sit up? A lever, or something like that. That way it would look like I was really talking."

"Jesus, John, you'd scare them half to death."

"What the hell, it's a funeral, isn't it?"

"No, it wouldn't be fair to the troops," Sammy decided. "Not before they had a crack at the booze. I'll take care of the tape, but that's it. No more tricks."

Which was why, several months later, Sammy stood in the chilly morgue of the hospital at the Center, staring down at the corpse of Big John Brodski laid out in the usual bronze coffin. It was early in the morning, a good two hours before the coffin would be transported to the mess hall for the funeral service. Getting into the morgue had not been difficult. Security within

215

the complex was of the simplest sort compared to the tight cordon around the outside of the Center, and besides, who would want to sneak into a morgue?

Sammy had wanted to, and had done it easily. Now he stood with the tape recorder in his right hand, and with his left hand slipped under the corpse's neck. His lips were compressed in distaste at the sight of Big John's face. He had seen the ravages of Rauschner's before, but never this close up. The skin was a light, fluorescent blue, the features were twisted into a grimace, and the striations around the neck looked like the marks of a hangman's noose.

Sammy used his left hand to lift Big John's head away from the satin pillow under it. The tape machine was ready to roll; the power was on and the volume was set high. All that was needed to put it in motion was a command from the remote panel in his pocket. He was about to slip the machine under Brodski's head when he realized that the fingers of his left hand felt odd. They were slick and wet. He looked at them, and felt the icy touch of shock at the base of his spine. His entire left hand was blue, the same fluorescent blue that covered Big John's face.

He slipped the tape machine back in his pocket, looked at his fingers again, and rubbed them together. They were stained with a thick and oily cosmetic. He stood still, lost in the moment. He took a handkerchief from his pocket, wiped his hand clean, and gingerly touched a finger to the marks on Big John's neck. His finger came away black. He touched the cheek and saw that the terminal grimace of Rauschner's Syndrome had been painted onto the skin. He felt weak. He looked for a place to sit, but there was none. He leaned against a slab.

Something was very wrong. People put cosmetics on corpses, sure, but to make them look better, not worse. Why paint on the symptoms of Rauschner's Syndrome? His mind bounced from point to point. If *this* was so, then *that* had to be . . . and so on down an inexorable line of reasoning that brought him up against the unthinkable. He was wrestling with that when he heard footsteps, and the door opened. It was Doc MacGregor. He started with surprise when he saw Sammy.

"Warsaw," he said. "What are you doing here?"

Sammy did two things at once. He applied a look of melancholy to his face, and he jumped into MacGregor's head. What he saw in that head stunned him. It was a vision of horrors. And then, suddenly, there was nothing. The vision was gone so quickly that he wondered at what he had seen, or if he had seen it at all. MacGregor was staring at him intently.

In a soft voice, Sammy said, "Hi, Doc. I thought I'd just sit here with John for a while. We were pretty close, you know."

MacGregor seemed relieved. His eyes measured the distance between Sammy and the coffin. "Never mourn," he said automatically. "You really shouldn't be here. This place is off limits except to medical personnel."

"I'm sorry," Sammy said contritely. "I just wanted to spend a few minutes . . . you know?"

"I understand, but you should go now. I really can't make any exceptions."

"Sure, Doc. I was about to leave anyway." He walked to the door, the tape machine in his pocket swinging against his hip. Before he left he looked back and said to the corpse, "Sorry, John. You'll have to make it back to California on your own."

MacGregor said, "What was that?"

"Private joke," said Sammy, and left quickly.

"He went into MacGregor's head," said Martha. "I could never have done that."

I nodded my agreement. It went against all tradition.

"Normally, neither would I," said Sammy. "Remember, I was shocked, I was surprised, and when he walked through the door I just jumped. I had no time to think."

217

"What did you get?" I asked.

"Enough. Not all of it, but enough to know that they were killing aces. That they had always killed them. That it was Agency policy. He was wide open for a couple of seconds, and then he clamped down. He throws a damn good block for a normal."

"He's had enough practice," said Martha.

"Couldn't you break it?" I asked.

"With enough time, sure. He didn't give me the time."

Martha had joined us as we sat in the front row of seats under the empty Top, watching Bendigo, the replacement ringmaster, working a new horse. I was just getting to know Martha again after three years. There was an edge of reality to her now that tempered the bouncing optimism. The others had changed as well. It was as if, given the knowledge that they were going to live normal lives, they had modified the roles they once had chosen. Vince had grown more within himself. Snake had softened somewhat, and Sammy . . . I hadn't quite figured out what the change was in Sammy, but it was there.

Bendigo stood in the center of the ring as the new horse went round and round in an easy canter. His long whip flicked out from time to time to keep the pace steady. The rosinback would have to work with three other horses in precise rhythm as the equestrians jumped from one to the other. The new horse was lathered, but he kept up the pace.

"He's working him too hard," Sammy muttered. "Stevo never pushed a horse that way." He called to Bendigo in Romany, "Take it easy, give him a rest."

Bendigo waved cheerfully, and called, "Sure thing, boss," but he kept the horse working.

"Fucking gypsies, they can drive you crazy," said Sammy. There was a depth of affection under the words. They had saved his life, and they had kept him safe for years.

"He's pushing the horse because you're watching," said

Martha. "He wants you to see how hard he can work. He's still competing with Stevo."

Sammy looked at her in surprise. He stood up. "You're probably right. Let's go." On our way out, he yelled at Bendigo, "*Apo miro dadeskro vast,* by my father's hand, if you break that horse I'll break your back."

Bendigo smiled, unperturbed. He knew an empty threat when he heard one.

We left the Top, and walked slowly down to Menagerie Row through the warm and dusty morning. There was the strong smell of the animals in the air, and the sounds of the birds that always flocked near the cages. The two elephants, Bull and Rosie, were staked out in the open near the water trough. They were spraying each other, and the ground around them was trampled into mud.

Vince was there, helping the keeper to shift bales of hay. We sat on the bales to watch Bull and Rosie complete their morning dust-off, and Vince came over to join us. He went into our heads to see what we had been talking about. He frowned and said, "MacGregor, huh?"

Sammy said, "I've been laying it out for Ben. He decided that he wants to know."

"Have you told him how you kept it from us for months? That you didn't tell us until it was almost too late?"

Sammy shook his head impatiently. "Come on, there's no sense dragging that up."

Martha said softly, "If you're telling it to Ben the way it was. . . ?" She left the point hanging.

Sammy turned to me in appeal. "How could I say anything? I had no proof, all I had was that quick fix on MacGregor's head. I had a load of questions, and no answers to them. How did they induce the symptoms of Rauschner's? How did they do the actual killing? And how about the other aces? The Russians, and the French, and the others. If the Agency was

219

doing it, then why did the others die too? I had to figure it all out before I could say anything. You can see that, Ben, can't you?"

Instead of answering that, I said, "Open up and let me take a look at it."

He nodded. I went into his head and saw what he had gone through in those weeks after Brodski's funeral. He had read every medical text available, he had consulted an impressive list of authorities, he had charted the death of every ace he could remember. He had questioned the tenets on which his life had been constructed, and most of all he had sat and thought. Again, if *this* is so, then *that* must be. Not should be. Must be. He had done this all during the time when he was working on the Ipatov defection, and while I was in Bled, and by the end of that winter he had come to some conclusions.

"It's easy to sit here now and tell me what I should have done," he said. "But all I had were some theories. I wasn't *sure* of anything."

Vince picked up a large round stone and rolled it along the ground to where the elephants were standing. Rosie investigated it with her trunk, then ignored it. Vince said, "She's not so smart. Every morning I roll a stone like that at her, and every morning she checks to see if it's something to eat. You'd think she'd learn."

Sammy said, "I still had no proof, but it was pretty clear that the symptoms were induced during the quarterly checkups that they gave us. The next ace on the list got the symptoms, and once that happened he got shoved into the hospital."

"And after that it was adios," said Vince. He rolled another stone at Rosie, and she sniffed at it. "And I said that she isn't so smart. Christ, how dumb we were. Not just us, but all of the others. Thirty years of aces marching to their deaths like good little soldiers."

"How did they do the killing?" I asked.

"What difference does it make?" asked Vince. "They could

have used any one of a dozen different toxic substances. The simplest way would be an injection from an empty syringe, an air bubble straight to the heart."

"Once you hold it up to the light and look at it," said Sammy, "it all looks simple. Even the business with the other aces. Every intelligence organization operates essentially the same way. If the Agency had to get rid of its aces, then the KGB had to do the same, and so did all the others. And they had to protect each other, too. If any individual ace lived too long then the whole structure would have been compromised. Remember how superior we used to feel because we lived a year longer than the Russians did?"

"I remember," said Martha. "It seems so childish now."

"Don't be ashamed of the feeling," Sammy told her. "We were children, and we were deceived by our parents. There was no mystery to it. The Russians simply chose a different terminal age than our people did. Remember, they had to cover for each other. All the aces had to die, no matter what."

His next words were for me. "That's why the Agency had to kill Nadia, and that's why her people would kill us if they could. They're all in it together."

He was going to say more, but a small boy came running up, his bare feet kicking dirt. His name was Yanali, and he was Bendigo's son. He said to Sammy in Romany, "Please, you are to come quickly. Terlina was throwing the knives and I think she has killed someone."

"Killed?" said Sammy. "Who?"

"The *gajo* she was using for a target."

"Holy shit, she finally did it," said Vince. He slid off his bale and started for the back lot, running hard.

We all followed. Terlina was the name that Snake went by in the circus. Sammy had gotten us all Lowara names and papers. The way the gypsies worked the ID game made the guys who peddled the papers around the Navy Yard look like amateurs.

Snake had been complaining for weeks that her knife-throwing act needed something to liven it up. Traditionally in the circus a man threw knives at a female target, and Snake had continued the tradition by using one or another of the girls from the sideshow. That, she decided, was the problem. A woman throwing knives at another woman wasn't exciting enough for the audience. She needed a man for a target, and it had not been easy to find one. For a while I had thought of volunteering myself, but despite my faith in Snake I could not get myself to do it. The gypsies, of course, would not hear of it; it would have been an insult to the manhood of the Rom. Snake had finally talked a local into playing target for her. He was a state trooper with a reputation for taking risks, and today was their first day of practice.

We found them on the back lot. The cop was strapped to the target board, arms and legs spread wide. His body was outlined by the silver knives that Snake used in her act. His head was slumped over and his eyes were closed. Snake stood in front of him, slapping his face.

Sammy got to her first and grabbed her arm. "Cut it out," he said. "It looks like you won this round already."

Snake pulled her arm away. She hauled off, slugged the cop as hard as she could, and screamed, "You son of a bitch."

"I don't think he can hear you," Sammy observed. "Where did you hit him?"

"I never touched him, the miserable bastard." She kicked the cop in the leg.

"Scared him to death?"

Snake whirled on him. She was dressed in the loose trousers and long shirt that she had learned to wear in Afghanistan. "What the hell are you talking about?"

"He isn't dead?"

"Of course not, the little wimp fainted on me." She kicked the cop again, and he groaned. "Does that sound like dead to you?"

Sammy nodded at Yanali who stood about twenty feet away, his eyes wide. He seemed disappointed that the *gajo* was still alive. "The youngster thought that you iced him."

"Wishful thinking, that's all. Anything to screw a *gajo*." She called to Yanali, "*Na may kharunde kai tshi khal tut,* young one. Don't scratch where it doesn't itch. When I kill somebody you'll see the blood."

Yanali stuck his tongue out at her and made a quick sign with his fingers. They were all afraid of her, but he was far enough away to run.

"Help me get him down," said Snake. She and Sammy unstrapped the cop and laid him on the grass. He was coming around now, and making sounds deep in his throat. Snake shook her head at the sight of him. "I'll have to go back to using the girls. There isn't a man around here with the balls for the job."

She was looking at me. I smiled, and shook my head.

"Chicken," she muttered. She turned to Vince. "How about you?"

"Sure," he said casually. "Glad to."

"You will?"

"Of course. The essence of knife throwing is mutual trust and confidence. I trust you, *tus.* That's all there is to it."

"Terrific."

"I said mutual. You have to trust me, too." He grinned evilly. "We'll alternate. First I'll throw at you, then you throw at me."

"You're crazy."

"Not at all."

"You're no knife thrower."

"I've been watching you. It's not that tough." He plucked the knives from the board. There were twelve of them. He arranged them in a fan, points down, in his left hand. "Come on, stand in there. I'll throw first."

"You're serious, aren't you?"

"Dead serious. You've been talking about balls. Let's see how good you are."

She stared at him long and hard. "And if I do it you'll let me throw at you?"

"Deal."

She marched over to the target board and stepped onto it, her feet in the stirrups. She spread her arms wide. Vince said, "Sammy, strap her on. I don't want her moving."

Sammy started for the board, but Snake stopped him. "I don't need the straps," she said. "You know damn well I won't move."

"Suit yourself," said Vince. He turned and paced off thirty feet from the board. At that distance, thrown hilt first, the knife would turn over two and a half times and land on the point. "Ready?"

"Ready." Snake stood with her back pressed against the target board, her eyes locked on his.

Vince selected a knife, drew back his arm, sighted, and threw. It landed point first in the grass at Snake's feet. "Don't panic," he said. "Just warming up."

He sighted, and threw again. The knife went into the board two feet above Snake's head. The next one was in the grass again. The next was so wild that it missed the board entirely and glanced off a tent pole. Vince drew back his arm again, but Snake wasn't waiting for any more. She bailed out, diving off the board and onto the grass, her hands over her head. She looked up at Vince angrily.

"That's it," she said. "Now I throw at you."

Vince shook his head. "Sorry, *tus*, the deal is off. Mutual trust and confidence. I couldn't work with somebody who didn't trust me."

She came off the grass and jumped him, her small fists bouncing off his shoulders and chest. He held her off, laughing, and then went down on the grass, taking her with him. They rolled over and over with Snake trying to get her hands around his neck. She was laughing, too. Martha jumped in and tried to pull them apart. It was very jolly and totally phony. They were putting on an act, and it was all for me.

"Mutual trust and confidence," I said.

"It was never a question of trust," said Sammy. He wasn't talking about knife throwing. He was three years back in time, during those months when he had kept what he knew to himself. "Of course I trusted you, all of you, but I wasn't sure. My whole world was coming apart and I didn't know what to do about it. I still didn't want to believe it. Crazy, right? I didn't want to believe that I could lead a normal life. It was more important to . . . I had to know the truth. I needed some sort of confirmation, and I didn't know how to get it."

I remembered the day we played tennis. "Those flu shots."

He nodded. "I used every excuse I could to get down to the Center, just to nose around. It was a waste of time. I never got close to MacGregor, never got another chance to get into his head. After a while I realized that there was only one person who could tell me what I wanted to know."

"Pop?"

"Sure. The day we played tennis I told you not to make a move until you heard from me."

"The next thing I heard was that you were dead."

"I went to see Pop that night. I had to. I told him everything: Brodski's corpse, MacGregor's head, everything I had read. I begged him to tell me the truth." A long pause. "Are you sure you want to hear this?"

I wanted to hear it, but I didn't need the performance that was going on in front of me. The other three were still on the grass rolling over and over. It was supposed to remind me that we were all together again, that we had a good deal going, and that caution and cool were the words to remember. It was supposed to temper my anger.

Enough, I told them. *You don't have to do that. You've made your point.*

It was like throwing a switch. They stopped wrestling, stopped laughing, got up and came back to where Sammy and I were sitting. Unembarrassed, they smiled at me as they brushed themselves off. They weren't even breathing hard.

"Better," I said, and to Sammy, "Go ahead."

One of Pop's graces was the exquisite courtesy with which he treated his kids, always as equals and as guests in his home. That evening he sat Sammy down, gave him a drink, and listened patiently. His face grew sad as the words came pouring out. He never interrupted, save to prompt gently whenever Sammy faltered. He did not seem shocked or surprised. He let the words flow until he was sure that Sammy was finished.

"What is it you want me to tell you?" he asked.

"The truth. That's all I'm asking."

"You won't like it when you hear it."

"Maybe so, but that's what I want."

Pop sighed, and poured them each another drink. Slowly, reluctantly, he said, "The truth of it is that I've been dealing with sensitives for thirty years, and you're about the twentieth person who has come to me with this story. I'm sorry, son, but that's the unvarnished truth. I've heard it over and over. It's always about a plot to kill the aces, to keep them from leading normal lives, to protect the security of the organization. It's always an ace near the end of the line who comes to me with the story, and I have to tell you that the details never vary. I've heard it all before."

Stiff-faced, Sammy said, "You don't believe me."

"I didn't say that," Pop protested mildly. "I said that I've heard it all before. The first time I heard it was almost thirty years ago. I checked it out and there was nothing to it. I heard it again a few years later and there still was nothing to it. Every time I hear it I check it out, and I've never found any substance to it. It isn't that I don't believe you, I know how real it seems to you. But it isn't real. It never has been."

"Are you saying that I imagined all this?"

"I'm saying that what you have is a life wish, a fantasy, a last explosive effort of the mind to battle with reality. It's entirely understandable, but that's what it is, a fantasy. The cosmetics on Brodski's face, the things that you think you read in Doctor MacGregor's mind . . . all part of the fantasy. As I said, I've heard it all before. Many times."

"I know what I saw on Brodski's face, and I know what I scooped from MacGregor. That paint on my hand wasn't any fantasy."

"Not to you, it wasn't. I know that. Look, son, there's only one way to settle this, and I've done it before. Let me ask you this. Do you think that I'm lying to you?"

"No, sir." The words came automatically.

"Do you think that something like this could go on around here without me knowing about it?"

This time the answer was not automatic, but it was the same. After a moment, "No, sir."

"Very well then, you have your choice. You can either accept my word for it, or you can take a look at my head and satisfy yourself that way. Which will it be?"

"You mean . . . probe you?"

"That's right. You have my permission if that's what you want."

"I couldn't do that."

"Nonsense, of course you can. I'm aware of all the traditions against it. I helped to establish those traditions, but this is one time when your peace of mind is more important than any custom. I invite it, Sammy. Go ahead."

Sammy shook his head. "No, I could never do that. Never."

"Then I don't know what more I can say to you."

"Neither do I," said Sammy, totally confused now. "I believe you. I have to now. But I know what I saw and what I heard."

He looked hard at the man he had known as a father for the past twenty years. He saw the familiar lined cheeks, the pale

227

blue eyes, the corded neck, and he saw something else that he had never seen before. He saw tears in those eyes and on those cheeks. He had never known Pop to cry, but he was crying now. Not because a young man was going to die young. That was part of the game. But because a hope had been kindled, and his job had been to extinguish the spark.

"Pop." Sammy put out a hand to touch the old man's arm.

"Yes. Well." Pop cleared his throat. "It's like a bad joke, isn't it. One last kick in the pants from the fates."

"It isn't any joke."

"No, I suppose it isn't. Sammy, go home. Put this out of your head and do the best you can with the time you have left. Go up to that beach house of yours, have a couple of drinks, and get a good night's sleep. Maybe things will look better tomorrow. Will you do that for me?"

"Yes, Pop. And thanks."

He pressed the old man's arm, and left. He made the long drive up to the Jersey shore, and once he was there he sat outside on the patio with the wind and the water, toasting his fantasy. He was still confused, but, somehow, he felt more at ease with himself. He finished half a bottle of cognac, drinking to a dead dream, and pleased now that he had kept his suspicions to himself. He fell asleep in a deck chair, the night deep around him, thinking of how lucky he had been to have had a man like Pop in his life.

They came to get him in the middle of the night. Six of them, from the Agency.

15

Sammy slept curled in the canvas sag of the deck chair, his arms across his chest, and his knees drawn up. The early part of the evening had been warm with an off-shore breeze and a clear quarter-moon, but after midnight the wind had shifted around to come in from the sea and had brought with it an invasive damp and a scudding of clouds that made the moon a sometime thing.

Sammy shivered in his sleep, but he did not wake. Despite the damp, his sleep was peaceful, and he dreamed. Not unreasonably, his dream was of a very old man with a beard and a crown, who sat on a throne. He was a kindly, smiling old man, and he was surrounded by children who loved him. They sang sweet songs to him and wove garlands of flowers for him to wear around his neck. They were all adorable children, except for one little boy who refused to sing or weave flowers. Instead, he skulked at the edge of the crowd and threw stones at the throne. The stones never hit their target, but they always came close, and whenever one whizzed by his head the old man would shake his fist, and yell:

"You little bastard, I'll get you for that."

And the other children would nod knowingly, and say, "He's going to get him, the little bastard."

Sammy's dream was the sort in which the dreamer could observe the action, know that he was dreaming, but also know that there was nothing he could do to change the course of events. Sammy stood in the midst of his dream, and observed. He was not a fool and he knew that the dream was symbolic, but he could not decide what role the old man was playing. He could have been Pop, of course, but he also could have been Sammy, himself, grown old in defiance of disease and surrounded by descendants of his own. It didn't matter to Sammy. Either way, he was enjoying the dream, except for the kid who was throwing the rocks. Sammy wanted to grab him and shake him, and talk some sense to him. He wanted to tell him that you didn't throw rocks at nice old men. He wanted to ask him why he couldn't be like the other children. He wanted to warn him that he was doing something both foolish and dangerous. But he never got the chance. The boy threw one more rock that hit the old man on the cheek, and drew blood.

"That did it," said the old man. "Now you're going to get it, you little bastard."

"He's going to get it," the children whispered.

The old man wasn't nice anymore. He was an angry old man with an ugly look on his face, and a knife in his hand. He jumped off the throne and ran after the boy, pushing his way through the crowd of children who screamed with excitement. The old man reached him in a couple of strides, grabbed him by the hair, and lifted him off the ground. He held the edge of the knife to the boy's throat.

"I warned you," he said. "I told you not to throw those rocks."

"He warned you," chanted the children. "Now you're going to get it, you little bastard."

"He warned you," said Sammy, who felt a deep satisfaction in knowing that the boy was about to be punished. "He's going to slit your throat, you little bastard."

"You little bastard," screamed the kids.

. . . the little bastard . . .

. . . don't worry, we'll get the little bastard . . .

Bravo Two, back of the house.

Roger, Bravo. Moving.

Beach report.

Delta Two in place.

Delta One?

Roger, Bravo. In place.

Roadblock, report.

Fox One and Two in place.

Now all teams hold. Bravo One going in the front.

. . . no lights . . . sleeping . . . don't worry, we'll get the little bastard.

"Little bastard," Sammy murmured, and awoke. He woke quickly and clearly with the thoughts of others in his head, and knew at once that there were men nearby who had come to get him, men with murder on their minds.

He rolled off the chair and onto the cement of the patio deck. His fingers touched something cold and hard: the half-empty bottle of cognac. He placed it aside carefully. He lay still and waited for his eyes to adjust to the darkness, and at the same time he filtered the voices in his head, counting and tagging them. There were four men within range, and two more blocking the road that led from the house to the highway. Part of what he was getting were head thoughts, and part were the echoes of walkie-talkie chatter. The head thoughts were murderous, and the radio talk was in the jargon of professionals. The mental voices that he heard were familiar to him. They all belonged to members of the security service at the Center.

"A fantasy," he said under his breath. "He said it was just a fantasy."

He reached for the bottle of Martel, uncorked it, and took a quick swallow. He replaced the bottle upright on the deck. He did not know why he had taken the drink. From the way that he felt he knew that he was still half-bagged from the earlier cognac, and the last thing that he needed now was a fuzzy head. But he also knew that he needed the drink, and he took it. He listened to the thoughts of Bravo One inside the house, working his way from room to room in the darkness. He was searching for Sammy, and when he found him he was going to kill him.

Bravo One to all teams. Search completed. No sign of occupant.

Somebody broke radio procedure, and said, *He's gotta be in there, Mickey. They said he'd be home all night.*

Roger that, but still no sign.

Leader, this is Bravo Two. We'll have to use a light.

Negative.

Come on, Mickey, he could be hiding in a closet or something like that. We'll never find him in the dark.

There was a moment while Bravo One considered, and then, *Delta One, move in toward the back of the house and give us cover there. We'll go through the house again with a light. If we flush him out the back, he's all yours.*

Roger, Bravo One. Moving in.

Sammy raised his head, and looked around. The darkness was almost complete, the quarter-moon hidden for the moment by the scudding clouds. He placed the positions of the six men. The two Bravos were in the house. Delta One was at the back door. Delta Two was somewhere on the beach between the house and the water. Fox One and Fox Two were covering the front of the house, the garage, and the road. It was an efficient blanket. The house stood on a triangular piece of land that jutted out into Delaware Bay, and they had cut off the base of the triangle. There was no chance of getting to the car, or getting down the road on foot. The only way out was the sea.

He knew then why he had taken the drink. He had known from the first moment that he was going to have to go into the water, and he had reached on instinct for the antifreeze. He did not want to go into the water. He was a strong swimmer, but the tide was running out and he did not think that he could swim against the set of it. All he could do was go out into the current and let it take him down as far as Gunner's Point. One of two things would happen there. Either he would round the point and be able to swim up the bay, or he would be swept past the point and be pushed out to sea. He figured that the odds were on the side of the sea, but he could not see an alternative.

Bravo One to all teams. Interior search is negative. Repeat, negative.

Mickey, he's got to be outside someplace.

Yeah, I sort of figured that out for myself. All teams now converge on the house. Make a thorough search of the grounds. Remember, if the subject is located he is to be terminated at once. No questions, just do it.

Roger, Bravo One.

"Ah, Pop," murmured Sammy. "God damn it, Pop. You sweet old murdering son of a bitch."

He allowed himself a moment of outrage and anger, another of regret, and another of the sadness that comes with wisdom. The moments were gone in as many heartbeats, and then he was ready to run for his life.

He came up off the concrete deck into a crouch, and then a leap, and then he was off the slab and onto the sand, racing for the waterline. The sand was hard-packed, and he could run on it. His mind reached out for Delta Two, the one on the beach. He found him off to the left, and then his eyes picked him up as well. He was walking slowly toward the house, feeling his way in the dark. Sammy cut to the right, veering away, but in that moment he felt the alarm in the other man's mind and he knew that he had been seen. He heard the threatening *spit* of a silenced shot, then another, and then the hail.

233

"He's on the beach. Delta Two, on the beach."

"All teams." It was Bravo One, up at the house. "Fox team, hold your point. Everyone else on the beach."

Sammy cut left, then right, then left again, waiting for another of those spitting sounds. Instead, he heard pounding behind him. Delta Two had given up shooting in the dark and was trying to outrace him to the water. Sammy stopped the zigzag and made straight for the phosphorescence of the rollers pounding in on the shore. He knew that he was running awkwardly, but he didn't know why. Then he realized that he still had the bottle of cognac in his hand and was swinging it stiffly as his arms pumped up and down.

Drop it, you idiot, drop it, he told himself, but he didn't. He saw the edge of the water ahead of him, and then he was into the shallows, up to his ankles, and his knees, and then he was fighting his way through the surf. The bottle was truly a hindrance now, but he still would not drop it. He stuffed it inside his shirt, and then threw himself forward, diving under the first of the rollers.

Arms extended, fighting the flow, he thought: I told you not to throw those stones. I warned you, but you wouldn't listen.

He came up for air and glanced quickly over his shoulder. No sign of Delta Two on the beach. He should have been there, popping away. He went down again as another roller came crashing in. He was still under water when a hand closed over his ankle. He gasped, and took in water. He kicked, but the hand held firm. He fought to the surface and Delta Two came up with him, still grasping his ankle. They were face to face, and Sammy knew him. Arnie something, his hair plastered down and water streaming from his face. He twisted Sammy's foot and flipped him over. Sammy's head went under again. He struggled under the surface, thrashing, and the weight of the bottle dragged at his shirt.

Will you please get rid of the fucking bottle? he asked himself. Now? Please?

He reached in his shirt and grabbed the bottle by the neck. Still thrashing, he felt himself being lifted as Delta Two swung his body around by the leg. The lift raised him up, and his upper body broke the surface. Delta Two was right in front of him.

"Listen," Sammy gasped, "do we have time for a drink?"

Delta Two's eyes widened. "What?"

Sammy swung the bottle like an axe. It hit Delta Two across the right temple. There was a grunt, and the grip on Sammy's ankle loosened. Delta Two slid under the water. The bottle was unbroken.

Some people, thought Sammy, simply cannot handle the hard stuff.

Something kicked up water nearby. He looked back toward the beach. The other three were standing there, dim figures. He could not hear the sound of firing, but their arms were extended and he knew that they were shooting at him. He shoved the bottle back inside his shirt. There was no thought now of throwing it away; they had come too far together. He kicked up his legs and dived deep. He stayed under for as long as he could, stroking out to sea. When he came up the three of them were still there, but he doubted that they could see him now. He let himself float, only his eyes and nose above the water. He reached for their heads, hoping that he was still within range. He got them faintly.

Jesus, Arnie went under.

Can't see anything now.

We blew it. The little bastard got away.

There's a bitch of a current here. Should carry him south to the point.

Could he make it back in here?

Not once the current gets him. It could take him straight out to sea, too.

We can't count on that. We'll have to cover the point and all of the surrounding area.

Just us?

You kidding? It's a code green now. We'll need all the help we can get.

They faded out then, but he had gotten enough. For a code green they called out everyone except the marines. That meant more Agency personnel, plus the state police, the locals, the Coast Guard, and anyone else they cared to enlist. They'd need a cover story, but they were experts at that. Escaped murderer, rapist wanted in six states, armed and dangerous, shoot on sight. They could make it anything they wanted to, and they could make it stick. There was no limit to the resources behind a code green.

He felt the tug of the current then, the first pull southward, and at the same time the clouds opened up enough to let the edge of the moon show through. The shore receded rapidly, and soon it was only a blur. He turned onto his back and let the current take him. The water was cold, but bearable, and the surface was smooth. He was not concerned about keeping afloat; he could stay that way for hours. The first crunch would come when he came to the point. There the current would either sweep him out to sea, or curl him safely into the bay. The second crunch would come if he made the bay. He would have to go ashore then, and he did not know what would be waiting for him there. The result, for the moment, was out of his hands. He let himself go and drifted.

Three hours later, cold, wet, and shivering, Sammy lay flat on marshy ground and watched three gypsies doctor a horse. He lay concealed by a hedge that bordered a hollow. The gypsies had built a small fire of brush and twigs in the hollow, and the smoke from it hung heavily in the damp air. It was four in the morning and the clouds concealed the moon once more.

The horse was down on its side, and only one of the men was actively caring for it. The other two sat with their backs against trees and watched from under hat brims pulled low over their eyes. They offered occasional comments on the horse, passed a bottle back and forth, and turned a crude spit on which were impaled several slowly charring lumps of meat. The third man crouched beside the horse. He rubbed its heaving flanks with bunches of straw, and wiped away gobs of bloody foam from its lips. Every once in a while he put a pail of dark liquid to the horse's muzzle and spoke softly and compellingly to the animal, but the horse refused to drink. He was a very old and sick horse, and two of the three men did not expect him to live through the night.

Sammy lay without moving. He had been that way for half an hour, ever since he had crawled ashore and had staggered his way through a mile of marshland apparently inhabited only by croaking frogs and clouds of gnats. The offshore float and the swim around Gunner's Point had done much to exhaust him, and the trek through the bog had completed the job. He had been close to collapse when he had seen the dim shapes of the circus wagons, the caravans, and the campers parked alongside a country road, and had circled around them cautiously. They had been dark and dead in the night, offering him nothing, and he had stumbled on another hundred yards before coming across the fire in the hollow. For the next half-hour he had lain behind the hedge, listening to the talk of the three men sitting there, and digging at their heads. He had done that sort of digging often enough in the past, and now he did it with urgency. He figured that he had until no later than daybreak to get under some sort of cover. By dawn the area would be swarming with an army of cops and agents, and Sammy Warsaw would have to disappear.

He dealt first with the language that the three men spoke. Romany, the universal tongue of gypsies, and a distant derivative of Hindi. He had never encountered Romany before, but he was trained to assimilate language on the spot, and he drew huge chunks of it from the minds of the three men. He took more than words from them. Along with the language came the names of people and places, the memories of births and deaths, love and laughter, good times and hard. Lying there, he gulped their culture.

Their names were Stevo, Bendigo, and Zurka; and they were Rom of the Lowara tribe, part of a *compania* that worked for the circus encamped down the road. Men in their thirties, they were cousins to each other, and all were related in some way to the other members of the *compania*. They held different jobs with the circus, but all of them worked with horses. Stevo was the ringmaster, responsible not only for introducing the acts under the Top, but for the care of all the horses and the training of the equestrians. Bendigo was his assistant, and did much of the actual work. Zurka, the youngest, was a farrier by trade, master of the disappearing art of horseshoeing. The animal on the ground was his. The horse was known simply as Black, and in the haphazard way in which the Rom told time he was somewhat over twenty years old. He had belonged to Zurka since childhood, and was a *grast* of the heart, well-beloved. Now he was dying, and Zurka could not bring himself to shoot him. His cousins had told him that he was being foolish and impractical, but he had insisted on nursing the horse through one more night. They had brought him to the hollow to keep him away from the prying eyes of the Jenner brothers, owners of the circus. Like all *gaje*, the Jenners had an overdeveloped respect for laws and regulations, and would have insisted on veterinarians and police reports. This was not the way of the Rom, who loathed paperwork as much as they were indifferent to the workings of authority. A man took care of his horse, and when that horse died he disposed of the remains without any help from the police or from men in white coats. If there were two types of the *gaje* that the Rom despised most, they were cops and medicals, and it was a point of honor to trick them both whenever possible. Life, to the Rom, was little more than a constant challenge to survive, and tricking the *gaje* had always been a basic form of survival.

This business of tricking the *gaje* was something that each of these men believed in down to his bones; it was bred into all of them just as was their love of horses. So Stevo and Bendigo were quite in agreement with their cousin's desire to take his horse off to a quiet spot and dispose of him there. What they had not counted on was Zurka's insistence on nursing this particular animal right down to the last puff of breath in his body. All the Rom knew that few horses died a natural death, and that a helping hand was almost always required to ease the old friend over to the other side. To deny a horse this simple act of kindness and keep him alive against all odds seemed to them an unmanly thing to do. Stevo and Bendigo had come with shovels prepared to bury a dead horse, and instead they had been forced to sit through the night, sip bad whisky, and watch a soft-hearted man keep alive a horse that was ready to die. They respected Zurka's love for this horse, but to them what was going on in the hollow was no act of love. It was indecent, and it was also impractical. The circus was due to get on the road not long after dawn, and whatever happened to the horse would have to be accomplished before then. Still, a certain delicacy was required in discussing the subject.

"This horse Black is a sizable horse," said Stevo, looking at no one. He took a tiny bite of raw whisky and passed the bottle to Bendigo. "A horse this size will require a very large pit."

"Very large," Bendigo agreed. "Such a pit would take an hour to dig with three men working." He took a sip of his own. There wasn't much left to the bottle. "At least an hour."

"And it is now close to dawn. Jenner has said that we must be on the road early."

"That whore of a man. Perhaps if we got some help the pit might be dug more quickly."

Stevo wagged his head slowly. "To bring more people here

would be to invite an unhealthy attention. Also, it has been my experience that if it takes three Rom one hour to dig a pit, it will take six Rom the same length of time."

"True," said Bendigo, "but only if there is whisky. There is very little whisky left in this bottle."

"There is always wine," Stevo pointed out.

"Also true. Perhaps then . . . just perhaps, it might be best to start digging the pit right now. What do you think?"

Stevo did not answer at once. He was busy inspecting the lumps of meat on the stick above the fire. Six hedgehogs with their quills shaven off had been rubbed with wild garlic and pepper, and put up to roast.

"These hogs are almost ready to eat," he announced, and then casually, "Yes, we could do that, I think. We could mark the ground with sticks and get a start on the digging."

Zurka looked up from what he was doing. "There is no need for that yet. This horse is still alive."

"But not for long," said Bendigo. "No disrespect was intended for your noble stallion, but time grows short."

Zurka shrugged. "I care nothing for time."

"Neither do we," Stevo assured him, "but Jenner cares for time and he is the one who pays the money."

"I spit on his money."

"No doubt," Bendigo said dryly, "but if we don't make an end to this horse pretty soon you will have to cover him with brush and leave him here."

"Never," Zurka declared. "I will stay behind with him."

"You will not," said Stevo, "and you know you will not. You will go with us when the time comes and your horse will be abandoned. Really, cousin, it is time to finish this business. You must put an end to him decently and then we will bury him in a pit. Do it now, we can't wait any longer."

"Do you know what you're asking?" There were tears in Zurka's eyes. "This animal carried me when I was only a boy."

"We know that."

"He gave me wings."

"We know that, too."

"He was the friend of my childhood, the companion of my youth, the partner of my manhood. . . ."

"Bullshit," said Stevo. "He is a sick old horse and it is time for you to shoot him."

It was at this point that Sammy, lying behind the hedge, decided that he had heard enough. He was interested in the fate of the horse and how the three men would handle it, but he had an urgency greater than theirs. He stood up, forced his way through the hedge, and strode into the light of the fire. The three Rom stared at him, startled. Stevo and Bendigo reached into their pockets for knives, while Zurka produced a pistol from under his shirt.

"*Na daran Romale wi ame sam Rom shashay,*" said Sammy. "Take it easy, you Rom, I'm one of you myself."

Nobody moved.

"Put the weapons away," said Sammy. "Don't you recognize Romany when you hear it?"

Zurka looked at the pistol in his hand as if surprised to find it there. He made it disappear. Bendigo took his hand from his pocket, empty. Only Stevo was unimpressed, his eyes still narrowed with suspicion.

"Who are you?" he said. "Where do you come from?"

Sammy spread his arms, palms up. "Well, I'll tell it to you straight, my brothers, and without any sweet talk. I'm on the run from the *gajo* police and I need a place to hide."

"But who are you?" Stevo insisted.

"My name doesn't matter," said Sammy. "I'm asking my brothers for help."

"You're no brother of mine," said Bendigo. "I don't have a Tshurara for a brother."

Stevo shook his head emphatically. "No, he's not a Tshurara. He talks like a Lowara, just like us, but he doesn't look like any Lowara I ever saw. Are you Kalderasha?"

"I'm a Rom in trouble," said Sammy. "That should be enough. Are you going to help me?"

"What did you do?" asked Zurka, his horse forgotten for the moment. "Why do they want you?"

"Does it make any difference? The *gaje* always want you for something." He moved closer to the fire and squatted next to it. He nodded at the meat on the stick. "You don't want to cook those hogs much longer. They look done to me."

Slowly, his eyes still fixed on Sammy, Stevo took the spit from the fire and pulled free one of the chunks of meat. He handed it to Sammy. The appeal to hospitality had been too blatant to be ignored and, also, it served as a test. He had never met a *gajo* who could eat a hedgehog without gagging.

"My thanks," said Sammy. He chewed on the meat and spat bones in the fire. He licked his lips and grinned at Stevo. "As you can see, I've been in the water. Hot food helps."

"I would offer you something to drink," said Stevo, "but the bottle that we have is empty." It was only a small lie.

"That's all right, I have my own." Sammy reached inside his shirt and took out the bottle of cognac. He gave it to Stevo. "Help yourself."

"Martel," said Stevo, looking at the label. He was finally impressed. "Where does a Rom with rags on his back get the money to buy a bottle of Martel?"

Sammy said jauntily, "Who said that I bought it?"

It was the right answer. Stevo allowed himself the tiniest of smiles. The bottle went around, and when it came back to Sammy there was only a sip left. He finished it off and tossed the bottle behind the hedge.

"Now," he said, "how are we going to hide me?"

Stevo said flatly, "We're not. If you're on the run, mister, you better keep on running. Don't stop here."

Bendigo stirred, about to say something, and then subsided. Zurka, too, looked unhappy. Helping a fugitive was part of their way of life, a necessity if the Rom were to survive in the world of the *gaje*. To turn away a brother was unthinkable, but Stevo was running the show and he seemed to know what he was doing.

"You won't help?" asked Sammy.

"We're not looking for any trouble here."

Sammy said softly, "Sometimes you don't have to look. Sometimes it comes and finds you. They don't want me for stealing some chickens, brother, and they don't want me for wiring some car. They want me for something big, and in a couple of hours this place is going to be full of cops. All kinds of cops, FBI and people like that. I'm telling you, it's big."

"If you're trying to sell me something, that isn't the way to do it. We don't want little trouble, and we don't want big trouble, either. You better get going."

Zurka finally said, "Look, we can't just turn him away."

Stevo snorted. "You. You just worry about that horse of yours, that's what you better do."

Bendigo said, "Stevo, he's right. You got to help another Rom."

"What Rom? The only Rom I see here is the three of us. You think this one is a brother because he can talk the language and eat a hog? What do we know about him? We don't know his name, we don't know his *tzerha*, we don't know anything about him. Rom, my ass. You think I'm gonna hide a *gajo* from the cops, you're crazy."

Three pairs of eyes turned on Sammy. He felt them. He summoned up words, and the words that he finally spoke would be remembered by the three men in the hollow for the rest of their lives; remembered and repeated beside campfires and caravans wherever they wandered. They were the words that would open up a new world for Sammy, make him a member of it, and bind him in loyalty to it. They were the words that would give him his name in Romany, change his life, and save it.

"What a strange world it is that we live in now," he said. "A world in which every man's hand is turned against his brother. So, you insist on knowing my name and my *tzerha* before you will help me. Very well, what else do you want to know? Shall I tell you the name of my dog, or of my uncle's aunt? Do you want my fingerprints, my blood type, a piece of my flesh to prove who I am? All right, you ask me these questions, and I'll ask you one in return. Tell me, brothers, what is a Rom?"

The three men muttered unhappily, and Sammy held up his hand.

"Think about it. The answer isn't as simple as it seems. What is a Rom? In the outside world, the *gaje* see the Rom as a master of deception, as a petty thief, as a mindless buffoon who feasts on chicken one day and feathers the next, as a lazy brute who sends his women to fool the unwary with the fortune-telling trick. Is that how you see yourselves, is that the Rom you are? No, of course not. You know that you are Lowara, and therefore you are Rom. Just like the Tshurara with their horses, they are Rom. And the Kalderasha with their copper kettles, they are Rom. As are the Loautari with their violins, the Kastari with their hammers, and the Anasori with their pots of tin. You call all of them Rom.

"But I ask you, is this all that there is to the meaning of the word? If you think that, then I am wasting my breath here. I cannot reach the hearts of those whose eyes cannot see a world beyond the caravan, and whose ears cannot hear anything more than the sobbing of a gypsy violin. For I tell you, brothers, that there is a piece of the Rom in the hearts of many men. Wherever there is a man who refuses to bow to authority, there you will find the Rom. Wherever there is a boy who would follow the caravans down some dusty forest road, there too will you find the Rom. You will find him wherever there is a man who insists on living free and is willing to carry the burden of that freedom, and you will find him wherever there is a man who respects women, cherishes children, and is not afraid to wear only his pride as a cloak against the cold.

"You will find a tiny part of the Rom in the heart of every strong man, and in the eyes of those who follow the flight of the wild goose winging across an autumn sky. *Vadni ratsa*, the wild goose of our stories and our songs, the bird that comes and goes by his own design, never resting for long in one place. Do you still need a name for me? Very well then, call me *vadni ratsa*, the bird of our dreams and of our fancies. Here I am, the wild goose in flight, and who can be more of a Rom than that? They are after me, brothers, they wish to clip my wings. Will you let them do this, or will you keep me safe? I leave it to you."

Crickets crooned and frogs barked in the night. Stevo hawked, spat, and looked away. Bendigo rubbed his nose and ran his fingers through his drooping mustache. Zurka turned to his horse and petted his muzzle.

"*Shashimo Romano*," said a woman's voice. "The truth is told in the language of the Rom."

The woman strode into the clearing. She was big and broad, and not quite young. Her dress was a deep purple and it trailed along the ground. Her name was Dunicha, and she was Stevo's wife.

"What are you doing here?" asked Stevo.

"I came to see why it takes all night to put one sick horse out of his misery," she said tartly. "I did not expect to hear great words spoken."

"How much did you hear?"

"All of it. *Shashimo Romano*. How are you going to hide him?"

"You believe what he says?"

"I believe what my heart tells me. I believe that we must hide him."

"You believe that he is Rom?"

Dunicha said in a pleasant voice, "You are my husband and so it would not be proper for me to call you a fool in front of these men, but let me ask you something. Did you hear a single word he said?"

245

"I heard."

"And were you not moved?"

Stevo admitted grudgingly, "I was moved."

"Well then?"

"All right, woman, all right." He turned to Sammy. "*Vadni ratsa*, the wild goose. You got any more of that high-class brandy, Goose?"

It was a token of acceptance. Sammy let out breath. "Sorry, that was the end of it."

Stevo searched around his feet for the whisky bottle, found it, and held it up to the light. He offered it. "There's maybe a drop left."

Sammy shook his head. Stevo finished it off, and sat looking at his hands, brooding. "Lots of cops, huh?"

"They'll be all over the place. They'll look everywhere."

"Christ, what a mess." Stevo looked at his wife. "Okay, we gotta help him, but what can we do? There's no place to hide him from an army of cops."

"There's one place," said Dunicha. She stood with her hands on her hips and looked defiantly at her husband. "What's the matter with your head? Too much cheap whisky?"

"Get me some money and I'll buy good whisky," said Stevo. He was not angry with her. "What one place?"

"The Sebastiani trick."

"Sweet fucking Jesus, are you crazy, woman?"

"It's the only way. They'll never find him."

"Yeah, but. . . ." Stevo looked at his cousins. They were as surprised as he was. "Did you hear what she said?"

Bendigo said thoughtfully, "The Sebastiani trick, been a long time since I heard that somebody tried it. Stevo, it's crazy, but it might work."

"Question is, could he do it?" said Zurka.

Dunicha said, "He's the right size."

"You gotta be strong to do it."

"He looks strong enough," she insisted.

"I mean strong in the heart."

Stevo said, "He's right. If our *vadni ratsa* gives up on the trick, if he quits halfway through it, then we're all in the shit with him."

Dunicha had been standing near the edge of the hollow. Now she crossed the clearing to come closer to Sammy. To do that she had to pass between Zurka and Bendigo, which would have been *marhime*, the highest form of tabu. Using the traditional phrase, she said, "*Bolde tut, kako*, please turn aside," and when they did she advanced to the fire. She squatted in front of Sammy, taking care that her skirts did not touch him, for that, too, would have been *marhime*.

"Well, my little wild goose," she said, "do you think you can do the Sebastiani?"

Sammy had no idea what she was talking about. He looked into her head to see what was involved. He did not like what he found there. It turned his stomach and made him feel faint. He said, "Is there any other way?"

Dunicha shook her head.

"Then I'll do it. And don't worry about quitting. I'll do it all the way."

She looked at him intently. "Yes, I think you will." She said to her husband, "Well, what are you waiting for?"

Stevo let out a deep rumble of a sigh. "Waiting for you to get out of the way so we can get to work."

Dunicha nodded, satisfied, and moved to the edge of the clearing. With the decision made, the men stirred into motion. Stevo said, "Zurka, I guess it's time that you did what you should have done a couple of hours ago."

Zurka knelt close to the head of his horse. He stroked the muzzle and said a few words softly. He took out his pistol, put it in the horse's ear, and pulled the trigger. A sharp crack, a shudder, and the horse lay still. Zurka went across the hollow and sat with his back against a tree, his head in his hands.

Dunicha said, "No time for that. Start digging."

Zurka and Bendigo took shovels and began to dig a shallow pit. Stevo knelt beside the horse. He took out his knife and examined the blade. He plunged the knife into the horse's belly and opened it from stem to stern. The horse's intestines came spilling out, and with them a smell so strong that Sammy gagged and retched. He did not want to, but he had no control over what he was doing. He turned away when he saw that Stevo was grinning at him. After a while, he forced himself to turn back and watch.

Stevo gutted the horse expertly. Everything came out including heart, lungs, and liver. By then the shallow pit was dug, and the offal was shoveled into it. The pit was filled in with earth, pressed down, and the fire was spread over it. More wood was added and the fire blazed up, scorching the earth around it.

"More digging," said Stevo.

They dug another pit, this one big enough to bury a horse, and then Dunicha went back to camp and returned with a short length of iron pipe, a large, curved needle, and a ball of twine. She also brought a bottle of wine. The men dragged the carcass of the horse into the pit, and then, with most of the heavy work done, they washed themselves in pools of marsh water and sat together on the edge of the horse's grave with their feet dangling over. They drank the wine and ate what was left of the hogs, and when they were done an edge of the sky was pale.

"Time to move," said Stevo. He jumped down into the pit and looked up at Sammy. "So, Goose, are you ready to do the Sebastiani?"

The Sebastiani trick, named after a Rom on the run in another century. On the run from what? As Sammy said, what difference? When did the *gaje* ever need a reason to hound a gypsy? Perhaps a few chickens were missing, or an absentminded pig had wandered off. Perhaps that most durable of myths had cropped up again, the innocent child abducted. Whatever the reason, the *gaje* came looking for Giulio

Sebastiani with pitchforks and fowling pieces, rolling across an Umbrian countryside with torches flaring. They searched the wagons of every Rom they found, scattered the *companias*, vented their anger on anything untamed . . . and found nothing.

Not quite nothing, of course. They found fortunes of gold coins sewn into skirts. They found dozens of women to brutalize. They found stores of brandy and beer. They found ailing horses, true jades, that had been clipped, and painted, and groomed into the simulacra of health. They searched diligently. They even found a dead horse just expired and about to be buried, one of those jades that not even gypsy skill had been able to save. But they never found Giulio Sebastiani, curled up inside the carcass of that horse and breathing through a tube in the equine anus.

For over a day, Sebastiani lay inside the horse while the *gaje* ravished the countryside in search of him, and when it was finally safe for his people to take him out they found him half dead, but triumphant, and the legend of the horse trick was born.

Sammy slid down into the pit and stood beside the carcass. He looked around at the skies and the trees. There was time for a few deep breaths, and then Stevo gripped his shoulder.

"Now," he said.

"Right," said Sammy.

He placed himself in the belly of the horse and they sewed him up inside of it. Like Giulio Sebastiani, he stayed there for over a day while the *gaje* came to scour the countryside. They came in many forms: plain clothes, state cops, local heat, FBI, and a variety of the military. They searched through the Jenner Brothers Southland Circus, shook it apart, and found nothing.

Not quite nothing, of course. They found a few bags of grass, an old moonshine still, a camper with out-of-date tags, and a Mexican boy without any papers; but they never found Sammy Warsaw, and when it was time to take him out of the horse he was half dead, but triumphant. Stevo pulled him out,

249

stood him on his feet, poured whisky down his throat, and called him his little wild goose. Dunicha stood beside her husband, smiling knowingly. Sammy managed to smile back. He had done the Sebastiani trick, and he had entered into the world of the Rom.

It took him three days to get back on his feet, and by then the circus was in western Pennsylvania. By then, as well, the Agency had listed him as dead from Rauschner's Syndrome, and there was the closed-coffin funeral at the Center. They had no choice but to say he was dead. They were hoping he was. The day after the funeral he got in touch with Martha, Vince, and Snake; and twenty-four hours after that they were all together, out of the cold and under the cover of the Jenner Brothers Southland.

All except me.

16

I T took them three years to find me, and it could never have been done without the help of the Rom. The gypsy world contained within it the essentials of a superb intelligence-gathering organization. It was a world of secretive people with a loyalty only to each other, and bound by a language which only they spoke. It was a world well accustomed to deception and intrigue, and one in which a favor was always returned. It was a world of the underdog whose ear was always pressed to the ground. In the old days the illiterate Rom had left their signs by the side of the road as warnings to the caravans behind them, arcane arrangements of stones, or rags, or the bones of a bird. Now the world of the Rom was bound by the long-distance telephone lines into a network of safe numbers. A café in Paris, a coppersmith in Sarajevo, a gas station in Los Angeles: each with a repository of messages to be passed down the line. The messages flew back and forth across that world, the business of the tribes conducted from telephone booths, and a prudent Rom never failed to carry a roll of quarters as part of his every-day needs.

From the very beginning the word went out that Stevo

251

Vedelshtshi, a Lowari in America, was looking for a particular *gajo*. We don't have much to go on, was the word. We can't tell you his name, because he will be using a false one. We can't tell you his passport, because that too will be false. We can't even tell you what language he will speak, because he speaks so many with ease. But this much we can tell you. Whenever he needs money he plays cards. He plays poker like the devil himself, and he wins. He wins so often that he has to be cheating, but he has never been caught. Not much to go on, but find this poker-playing *gajo* and you will have won the eternal friendship of Stevo, the grandson of Vedel.

"The odd part," said Sammy, "was that it wasn't some bigshot Rom who turned you up for us, it was a sixteen-year-old kid. He was working as a dishwasher in that casino at Lake Como and he heard the stories about the *gajo* who was winning all the money at poker. Then he heard that you had been kicked out of the game for cheating and his mind went clickety-click." Sammy wiggled his fingers. "Clickety-click, like that. He called a number in Milan, and somebody else made a call to Putzi in Miami, and he got hold of Stevo. You have to give them credit, they worked pretty quick."

"But not quick enough," said Vince. "We figured that if the Rom had the word, then the Agency and the opposition would have it, too. We knew that we had to move fast, but we were late. We screwed up."

"We came as soon as we could." Snake's voice was high and tight, defensive about what had happened. "We just couldn't move as fast as the other people. We didn't have their logistics, we didn't have their staffing. All we had was poor Dunicha to smooth the way with the Rom for us."

"Thank God we did," said Martha. "She got the weapons for us, she played her part . . . and she died. For you, Ben. Not one of us, but a gypsy woman."

It had taken them all of the morning to bring me up to date, and now we sat in Martha's fortune-telling tent with the sounds of the circus growing outside as the early arrivals strolled through the sideshow. Martha was dressed for work in a long dress of garish blues and greens. She wore a *diklo* on her head and chains of gold around her neck. She had taken over the fortune-telling gig after Dunicha died, and she was good at it. She did not have the theatrical flair that the gypsy women brought to the job, but she was honest about it. The wives of the Rom were not. Fortune telling to them was just another trick to play on the *gaje*. It was not to be taken seriously, and it was never practiced among themselves. It was a scam, and a constant source of amusement to them. Martha, however, treated those who came into her tent with respect and sincerity. She looked into their heads, tapped into their dreams, and tried to guide them toward some form of fulfillment. She made many of them happy, but just as many went away disappointed. She lacked the gypsy flair.

We had sat together through the morning while Sammy had told me his story in a low and quiet monotone. It was almost all Sammy, although each of the others had put in quick words and phrases of explanation, spare brush strokes on the canvas. Now, with the mention of Lago Maggiore, we were more or less up to date and each of us was left with his own thoughts of what had happened next: the flight up the lake into Switzerland and the retreat back to the states under the cover of the ID that the Rom had provided. Then had come the winter just past, the winter of my sadness and my anger, the winter of their caution and their cool. That anger had been building through the morning, and now it was a roaring in my head so strong that I was sure it showed. It did to one of them, at least. In some ways, Jimmy Abdul could be more perceptive than any of the others.

Martha's tent was a dimly-lit rectangle divided in two by a sagging curtain. The front half of the tent was for business: tables, chairs, astrological charts, a length of black velvet, and a crystal prism. Behind the curtain was a sofa, another table, and a Primus stove on which to make tea. Jimmy Abdul sat there during the days, not doing much. He read the magazines that Martha bought for him, brewed her tea, and hummed his single tune. Sometimes Grace came up from her garden for a visit, but most of the time it was just Jimmy. He was totally devoted to Martha, and she had insisted on bringing him with her when the time had come to go under cover. Now, for the first time that morning, he spoke, leaning forward to look at me intently, and when the words came out they were in the little-girl voice of Amazing Grace.

"Ben, you're angry, aren't you?"

"Am I, my little cherub? I hadn't noticed."

She liked the part about the little cherub. I could hear it in her voice as she said, "Yes, you are. Definitely angry. I can feel it."

"You're too sharp for me, kid." I threw up my hands in mock surrender. "You're right, I'm sore because you didn't bring me a flower from your garden. You always promise, but you never bring me one."

She giggled. "You know there really aren't any flowers."

"Not even a daisy. Not even one red rose."

"You don't really mean that." She said to Martha, "He doesn't, does he?"

"No, he's just kidding," Martha assured her.

"Is that all it is?" asked Sammy. He sat on a rickety kitchen chair tilted back on two legs. He rocked forward and the front legs came down sharply. "Just kidding, Ben? Not angry about anything?"

"Should I be?"

"I don't know, but Grace is right, I get the same feeling. You asked some questions and you got some answers. Is there anything else I can tell you?"

"Maybe." It was time to let it out. "Maybe you can tell me what you've been doing for the past three years besides playing with this toy circus of yours."

254

His face, usually so mobile, was suddenly still.

"Maybe you can tell me how many aces have died while you've been making like a gypsy."

Still as stone.

"Maybe you can tell me how many more are going to die."

"Ben. . . ." Martha, of course.

"Maybe you can tell me why Nadia had to die if you knew about this all along."

Martha again. "You're being unfair."

"Am I? Then tell me why you haven't done a damn thing to stop the slaughter. Not just Sammy, all of you."

"I was afraid this was going to happen," said Sammy. "You asked some questions and I tried to give you some answers. I told you that you might not like what you heard."

"You're damn right I don't like it. All I've heard so far are the daring adventures of Sammy Warsaw. Now I want to hear what we're going to do. I've been holding this in all winter because you told me there was nothing I could do. You told me that the time wasn't right. Well, the time is right for me now. I'm ready to kick some ass. I'm ready to kill some people."

"You want revenge." He made it sound like a dirty word.

"Of course I do. Am I supposed to be ashamed of that? They killed the woman I loved and I want blood for that. But more than that, I want to stop the killings. They're murdering our people, Sammy. Don't you care about that?"

"I care," he said stiffly. "We'd all be dead if I hadn't cared."

"Not me, I made my own move. And don't tell me about the past. What are we going to do now?"

I looked around the tent. Grace had fled, and Jimmy Abdul stared at me vacantly. The others had trouble meeting my eyes.

Sammy said softly, "Nothing."

"You don't mean that."

"I do. We're going to do nothing because there's nothing to do. What did you have in mind? Do you want to bomb the

Center? Do you want to take out Delaney? Do you want to declare war on the Agency? And the KGB? And every other outfit that's killing aces? Is that what you want?"

My thoughts had not gone that far. I knew only that something had to be done. I said, "You've always been the leader, Sammy. I figured you'd know what to do."

"Then listen to what I'm saying. There is absolutely nothing we can do. Look at it realistically. We got out and we're safe. We've got a good deal going for us here. That ought to be enough."

"And what about the others that they're killing?"

"I can't allow myself to think about that. You called me the leader before. Well, it's always been a funny sort of leadership, but as long as I'm in charge I've got only one responsibility, and that's the safety of the group. Just the five of us, plus Jimmy now. I'm not going to jeopardize that safety by making some sort of idiotic gesture against the Agency. Not for any reason. You've got the best of reasons, but not even for you."

"Final words?"

"Final."

I looked around the tent again. Vince nodded his agreement with Sammy. Snake was slower to do it, but she nodded too. Martha finally met my eyes, cool and clear, and she nodded along with the others. She did not have to say that she was voting for Jimmy, as well.

"You've changed," I said. "All of you. Three years ago you would have taken on the world, no matter what the odds."

There was a long silence. Someone had to respond to that, and it was Martha. "All right, we've changed," she said. "Three years ago we had no future. Today we do. I guess we want to keep it."

There was no need for a nodding of heads this time. I could feel the agreement coming off them, a wave of desire for a life without risk, colored only by a thread of regret for days gone by. Days of their youth. At thirty-three, they were middle-aged.

I stood up. "If that's the way it is, then all I can say is thank you. Thanks for coming for me. Thanks for keeping me sane this winter. Thanks for trying."

Vince growled, "You don't have to thank us for something like that."

"Yes, I do. Because I'm leaving."

Sammy said, "Where to?"

"Home. The Center. It's the place to start."

He shook his head. "Suicide."

"Maybe."

"You gonna walk up to the front gate and ring the bell?" asked Vince.

I grinned at him. All of us knew half a dozen ways to sneak into the Center. We had done it regularly as kids.

"Yeah, getting in is easy," he agreed. "How about getting out?"

"I'll worry about that when I get there. Thanks again. For everything."

I walked to the flap of the tent. Sammy got there before me. He wasn't exactly blocking the exit. He said, "It isn't just revenge. It's Pop. You can't accept what I told you."

"What you told me isn't proof. I have to find out for myself. I have to be sure."

He scratched his chin absently. "Look, we like what we have here, and we don't want to lose it. If you get into the Center and they take you, you'll talk. And when you talk this all goes down the tubes. The circus, the life we have, everything."

"I won't talk."

"Everybody talks."

"Then that's just a risk you'll have to take, isn't it?" I waited for him to move aside. He didn't. "You going to try to stop me, Sammy? Is that where it's at now?"

Our eyes met. He looked away. He moved.

I went back to the camper and packed a bag. There wasn't much to put in it. Once I was ready, I sat and waited. One of them would show, and I wondered which one it would be. I was betting on Martha, and I was wrong. There was a knock on the door, and Snake walked in. She didn't waste any time.

"You're going to need wheels," she said. She handed me the keys to her car. "The registration is in the glove compartment."

"Thanks. Feel like coming along?"

She was tempted for a moment, but she shook her head. "You were right, we've changed. Softer, maybe. I'm sorry, Ben. Good luck."

She leaned over and kissed me. She had changed, all right. The last time she had kissed me we were twelve years old. She was halfway out the door when she stopped and looked back.

"There's a compartment under the back seat," she said. "It isn't easy to find. It isn't supposed to be."

I took my bag out to the car. It was parked at the end of the lot. If I hadn't known that the compartment was there I would never have found it. Even knowing, it took me ten minutes to get it open. There was an Uzi in it, a dozen clips, and an assortment of knives. I closed the lid and lowered the seat over it. I drove out of the lot against traffic: people coming in for the afternoon performance. I left without looking back. It was Sammy's circus, not mine.

It was less than a hundred miles from Greentree to the Center, and I could have driven it in a couple of hours. Instead, I did it in two days. I dawdled along side roads, looked at trees and fields, and the curve of the land. I looked at horses grazing and horses cavorting, at the lines of barns against the evening sky, and at those smoky horizons that have always spelled Virginia for me. I looked at ripening vines and blossoms. I had a good idea of what was waiting for me at the Center, and now that I was in motion I was no longer in a hurry to come to it.

Because Sammy was right. He might have lost a step on his youth, but there was nothing wrong with his brain. He knew me better than any man alive, and he knew what was calling me home. He knew that I was not essentially vengeful. The blood was up and the lust was there, but given some time they both would have vanished. He knew, as well, that despite my concern for murdered aces past and future, I was not a man for crusades. Justice had to be done, but not necessarily by me. He knew that I was, at the very bottom, a man most concerned with his own center, touched by the particular, not the abstract, and that all that truly pushed me homeward was the compelling need to look just one more time into a pair of ancient eyes and to hear from well-worn lips some reassuring words. Sammy was right. I could not accept the judgment that he and the others had made on Pop. I had to see for myself. No matter what else, until the conviction was nailed to my brain, Pop was still the man who had given me my life. He had made me, and I was his, until convinced of his betrayal. Once convinced, of course, I would kill him.

So I dawdled that first day, stayed the night in a motel, and on the second day came into the outskirts of Fredricksburg. I found a shopping mall where I bought, at various places, a pair of black chino trousers, a black jersey, and a pair of crepe-soled shoes. I bought a coil of nylon rope and a rotating hook and eye. I bought a square of tarpaulin and a pair of wire cutters with insulated handles. I found another motel and settled in to wait out the night. At three in the morning, dressed in black, I left the motel and drove the familiar roads that skirted the borders of the Nathan Bedford Forrest Military Reservation until I came to the fence that marked the western edge of the Center. It was a high, chain-link fence, and it was electrified. I followed the curve of it into wooded country and found a place to leave the car. I took the Uzi from the back-seat compartment, hitched up the rest of the gear, and struck out into the woods, still following the fence.

In the end, I did not need the gear I had bought. There were several ways in that I remembered, all of them drainage ditches which, in theory, were protected by the fence. In practice the burrowing of small animals and a natural erosion had enlarged the ditches enough to allow for the careful passage of a teenager underneath the electrified links. The first two that I came to were still large enough for a teenager, but not for me. The third had been blocked up with rocks. The fourth was open, and was deep enough for me to use without clipping the wire or jacking it up. I went in on my back, the hot wires inches above my nose. The ditch was slick with mud, and when I climbed out on the other side I was slick with it, too.

Familiar territory, coming home after so many years away. No security inside the Center, only at the perimeter, and in the hour before dawn the place was silent, the buildings only eerie outlines of the shapes I knew so well. The quarters for the aces and the deuces, the compound where the new kids stayed, the mess hall and the lounge, the hospital, and after that the double-winged complex where Pop lived and worked. Beyond his building was the main gate through the fence, and on the other side of the gate were the squat and functional structures of the Agency: barracks and motor pool, security office, and the maintenance hut that housed the generators. There was a single pool of light at the gate, and in it I could see the shadows of two guards. That light was the only sign of life in the place, but I knew that another light would be shining in Pop's quarters. He never slept more than an hour or two at a time, and just before dawn he was sure to be awake.

I went up the stairs to the second floor, and down the corridor to the door of his private office. The darkness was complete, but I knew that hallway well enough to navigate it easily. The door was closed, but it opened to the touch. I stepped into the reception room. It was dark, as well, but the door to Pop's room was partly open and a shaft of light showed there. I unslung the Uzi, and moved forward silently on the thick carpet. I got to the doorway and stopped there, hidden in the shadows.

Pop sat at his desk. I had expected to see that, but I had not expected to see Roger Delaney sitting across from him. Pop looked well: a little older, a touch frailer, but unmistakably Pop. Delaney looked the picture of the smooth, high-level Agency operator that I remembered, although his patented plaid suit was badly rumpled and his collar was open. It took me a moment to realize why they were sitting across from each other that way. They were holding cards in their hands, and they were playing gin rummy.

It's hard for me to explain what happened then. I had come to the Center prepared to face Pop and to ask him some questions, knowing from the beginning that in order to be sure of the answers I would have to go into his head. I was prepared to do this, prepared to do what Sammy could not bring himself to do, prepared to break the tabu, although I knew that the doing would be difficult. And then in that moment, I did it and it wasn't difficult at all. I popped right into his head, but I wasn't looking for the answers to any questions. It was the cards that made it easy to do. After so many years of playing cards and reading the hands of the other players, what I did then was automatic. I went into both Pop and Delaney, and read the cards that they were holding.

Pop had four fives, four nines, and two jacks.

Delaney had three aces, the six-seven-eight of spades, two deuces, and the other two jacks.

Delaney drew a card. It was the deuce of diamonds, giving him three of them. He fingered the two jacks in his hand. He did not want to throw either of them. He knew that they were hot cards, but he did not know how hot. He hesitated. It was either throw a jack, or break up his hand. A pro would never have hesitated, and never would have thrown the jack, but Delaney could not get himself to break up the melds he already had. He tossed the jack.

Pop picked it up.

Gin, I thought, without thinking.

Gin, indeed, thought Pop. *Come on in, Ben. We've been waiting up all night for you.*

To Delaney, he said aloud, "He's here."

Something hard poked into the small of my back, and a voice in the dark behind me said, "Nice and easy, mister. Just let your arms hang loose."

Hands plucked the Uzi from me, and then ran over me, checking. There were two of them behind me. They edged me forward into the light, and then into the room. Pop smiled at me, the familiar beaming. Delaney looked at me curiously, then looked at his cards.

"You got me with ten," he said to Pop. "Serves me right for playing gin with a sensitive. You knew I was holding those jacks, didn't you?"

"Of course."

Delaney scribbled on the scorepad. "That's forty-three fifty I owe you."

"Plus ten," said Pop, and added, *Roger bet me ten dollars that you wouldn't show up tonight, but I was sure that you would. After all, I should know my own people, shouldn't I?*

I did not answer. I did not know what to say. I was speechless and thoughtless.

Cat got your tongue? asked Pop.

How . . . I mean, since when . . . ?

All my life. Just like you.

But you never . . . why . . . ?

Many reasons, son. Many good reasons.

Delaney said, "Are you two communicating?"

"After a fashion," said Pop. "Ben is having some trouble adjusting to the idea that he's not the only ace in the room."

"Oh, that. Well, talk out loud, for Christ's sake. That other crap makes me nervous."

"Of course," said Pop. "Ben, come in and sit down. We have a lot to talk about. Don't be concerned about the two men in back of you. They're only a precaution, and we can dispense with them now. Don't you think so, Roger? This conversation should be private."

Delaney took a pistol from a shoulder holster and held it on me casually. To a point over my shoulder, he said, "You two wait outside."

I heard them go out of the room, and heard the door close. I crossed the room and took a chair by the window. I turned around to face the desk. Delaney's pistol followed me.

"How did you know I was coming?" I asked.

"You were rather obvious in your shopping yesterday, you left a trail all over town," said Pop. "We've been expecting you ever since that sad day in Italy. We knew that you'd come looking for blood."

"That's not all I'm looking for. I'm looking for information."

They glanced at each other, and Delaney said, "That means he knows. Question is, did he figure it out himself, or did somebody tell him."

"As a guess, he was told," said Pop. "Warsaw, probably. Is that it, Ben? Has Sammy confided in you?"

I did not answer. I had a high, hard block up.

"That's an answer in itself," said Delaney. "Where is he?"

I shook my head.

"Do you know how long it would take me to get that out of you?"

"Roger, let's do without that sort of talk," said Pop. "Sammy's whereabouts can wait. Before anything else we could all use some breakfast. We've waited for it long enough." He picked up a telephone and said something into it quietly.

"Nothing for me," I said.

"Nonsense, it will only be coffee and rolls, and it will all be out of a common pot. Nothing to fear."

A moment later the door opened, and someone came in with a large tray. He laid it on the desk. He was wearing hospital whites, and at first I thought he was an orderly. It was Harry Kourkalis. He had lost a lot of weight since Italy, and the whites hung on him. He had changed in other ways. His face was a blank, and his eyes were still, with nothing behind them. He laid out coffee and a basket of rolls, and stepped back like a professional waiter, waiting.

"You remember Harry, of course," said Pop. "Harry, you remember Ben."

Harry nodded. He looked like a zombie.

"You might say hello to Ben."

Harry looked at me. He had a hard time doing it. He said, "Hi."

"Hi," I said, and asked Pop, "What's wrong with him?"

"He hasn't been the same since Italy. He's been . . . withdrawn. You see, he feels guilty. He feels that he betrayed you. He didn't, of course. His offer to you was genuine. He said what he was told to say, nothing more. But still, he feels guilty."

"You used him."

"He was used," Pop conceded. "Since you understand that, you might tell him so. It would mean a lot to him."

I tried to catch Harry's eye, but it was impossible. Speaking to the air, I said, "Nobody's sore at you. It wasn't your fault."

He nodded again. If it meant a lot to him he wasn't showing it.

"Ever since then I've kept him close to me," Pop said. "It's the best place for him right now."

"What have you got him on?"

"Nothing much. A little something now and then to keep him going." He looked up. "Thank you, Harry."

Harry walked over to the far side of the room, and sat down. He walked like a zombie, too. There wasn't much left of him.

I waited while Pop and Delaney had their breakfast. I didn't touch mine. Not in that place, despite Pop's assurances. When Pop was finished he patted his lips, brushed crumbs from his shirt, and said, "You wanted some information."

"Yes."

"Let's dispose of that first. My mind is open to you. Help yourself."

I went into his head and it was all there. Sammy was right.

The old man had always known and had always approved of what was being done to the aces. He had approved of Nadia's death. He was, in Sammy's words, a sweet old murdering son of a bitch.

But there was more than that arranged in his head for me to see. There was an explanation, and a plea for my understanding. There was also a strong sense of righteousness, for no sane man thinks of himself as being truly evil. He dares not. Every man who slaughters and sins has a rationale for what he does. He tells himself that he is fighting fire with fire. He tells himself that you can't make an omelet without breaking eggs. He tells himself that the ends justify the means, that might makes right, and that the tools of the devil have their uses. He tells himself, and truly believes, that the hand of God appears in the works of all men, and thus in his. He tells himself all this to support the buffer between man and his deeds, for without that buffer men would stand alone, and answerable. And that would never do. Precious little evil would get done, and how would the works of man progress without the grease of sin to spin the wheels?

That was what he showed me as I surveyed his head. Sometime early in his association with the Agency he had convinced himself that this efficient necessity, the killing off of young men and women in the name of national security, was, in fact, a blessing to them. He had rescued them from chaos, made them whole, and had given them their one perfect day. Having done this much, who could deny him the right to close out that day with a sunset of his choosing? By his lights, he was granting them the boon of eternal youth, and insuring that they would never decay by way of age or envy. By his lights it all made sense, and he begged me to understand that.

He had more begging to do. He wanted me to understand why Nadia had to die. It was a favor done for the Russians. She was past her time, she had to go, and they asked for the favor. And properly so. He had learned long ago that there was never a need to bear evil alone. There was always someone eager to share that burden, and in every part of the world where aces were used in the national interest there stood a man with an axe prepared to chop them down in their prime. That was the system, it could not be fought, and he begged me to understand that. It was evil, of course, but it was good, as well, in the sense of the greater good. It was this greater good that he had always served, and over the long years of service he had come to understand that he had to fight fire with fire, and that he couldn't make an omelet without breaking eggs.

This is the way I have lived my life, he told me. *Sad about some of it, proud about most of it. The very human mixture of sin and redemption, and I know now that I never could have lived it any other way.*

"Can you understand that?" he asked aloud.

"Yes," I said, coming out of his head. I understood it very well. It was the same old weary rationale, and it meant nothing to me, but I understood it. I also understood that I would have to kill him.

"I'm glad," he said, "because that makes what comes next easier to say."

"Next?"

Delaney said, "Why do you think we've been waiting for you? Why do you think you're still alive? We have a job for you."

I didn't understand. "What job?"

"My job," said Pop. "I should have retired years ago. We want you to take over the Center."

17

I T made all the sense in the world by the terms of their twisted logic. Who else could take over from Pop? He was the only director the Center had ever had. They wanted an ace for the job, just as Pop had been an ace, although none of us had known it. They wanted someone who knew the system inside out. They wanted someone who had been forged in the fire. They wanted someone daring enough to have bucked the system once, but wise enough now to accept the fact that the system could not be beaten. They wanted someone with failed ideals, with the sense of a cynic, and with the calculating amorality of a professional card sharp. They wanted me, and to confirm their conclusion they had fed my data into Cyber. The computer had agreed. Ben Slade was the man for the job. That's why they had sent for me at Lago Maggiore with orders to bring me back alive, and that was why I was sitting where I was, unharmed.

"You didn't have to come in under the wire," said Delaney. "You could have walked in through the front gate. We were hoping that you would."

"Let me get this straight," I said. "You want me to run this place? As the director?"

"Effective on Pop's retirement," said Delaney. "You'll have the same authority that he's always had. You'll be reporting to me, just as he has."

He was smiling as he said it. They both were. They were acting as if it were Christmas time and I was the kid with the stocking full of goodies; and I confess to a feeling of profound shame at that moment. I was into both their heads, and the shame deepened as I realized that the offer was sincere. They really wanted me, and it seemed to them to be a matter of casual importance that they had killed Nadia, and that they would willingly kill my friends on sight. That part of it was supposed to be water over the dam now. As practical people, we would put that behind us and go forward. They were that sure of me, and I was ashamed to think that they saw me that way.

"Well," asked Delaney, "what do you have to say?"

"Easy, Roger," said Pop. "He's stunned, give him a moment. We've been living with this, but it's all out of the blue for him."

It was all of that, and more. It was an absurdity. Still . . . questions came springing to mind.

"I assume you've thought this all out," I said, "so would you mind telling me how you're going to explain a new director who was supposed to have died of Rauschner's more than three years ago?"

"You were never listed as dead," said Delaney. "What made you think that you were?"

"I assumed it."

"No, not you," said Pop. "Sammy and the others were, but not you. You see, even then we had plans for you."

I was supposed to be flattered by that. "You'll still need an explanation for the people here. Why am I still alive?"

"There will be an explanation," Pop assured me, "and it will be the best news they ever heard. We've discovered a cure for Rauschner's."

My heart jumped, which shows how conditioned I was. I had

lived for so long with the threat of Rauschner's that I could still think of it as real. "A cure for a phony disease?"

"Take a look at it," said Pop, laying it out for me in his head. It was a neat little piece of chicanery, framed in the form of a memorandum.

(1) Four years ago the research staff at the Center finally isolated the virus believed to cause Rauschner's Syndrome, and the serum for a potential cure was developed.

(2) Extensive tests for the serum were required.

(3) After discreet inquiries, Benjamin Slade was chosen as the sensitive on whom those tests would be performed.

(4) The tests were conducted secretly over a three-year period at a secure government facility in Abilene, Kansas.

(5) The tests have proven to be totally effective in the case of Benjamin Slade, and he is no longer at risk from Rauschner's Syndrome.

(6) Slade has been returned to active duty at the Center.

"What do you think?" asked Delaney.

"It's workable," I said. I felt somebody at my elbow. It was Harry with a fresh cup of coffee.

"You didn't drink yours," he said. "You let it get cold."

I still didn't want any, but I took it from him, and said, "Thanks."

He looked at me closely. "You're Ben, aren't you?"

"Yes."

"I thought so. Your wife makes good cookies." He went back to his corner and sat down.

The poor sad bastard, he still remembered those cookies. I said to Pop, "Does this mean a change in Center policy? Does everybody get the cure?"

Pop and Delaney looked at each other silently. Delaney answered. "Not everybody. The line will be that the cure worked for you, but that it's still in the experimental stage. We estimate

that in the foreseeable future it will have a positive effect on
. . . ah, very few of the people involved. Very few, indeed."

"I see. And those few will be aces in low-level jobs? Those
without access to highly-classified information?"

"Exactly."

Which meant, in essence, no change at all. Most of the aces
would continue to die, those who were allowed to live would
pose no security threat, and a new dimension of hope would be
added to the life at the Center.

"Is that supposed to be a sop to my conscience?" I asked.

"It's progress," said Delaney. "It gives you something positive
to talk about when you take over."

"That's assuming I take the job."

Delaney's eyes narrowed. "Are you saying that you don't
want it?"

"What would happen if I were to say no?"

He shrugged. "I can't imagine the possibility, but if you said
no . . . well, obviously we couldn't let you live."

"That makes it easy for me to say yes, no matter how I feel."

"I don't think you understand," said Pop. "Once you give us
your answer I'll have to go into your head. I'll have to see if
you've accepted our terms unconditionally. I'll have to be convinced that you are committed to the program we've laid down.
You won't be able to block me, Ben. You'll have to let me in."

"And if he isn't convinced by what he sees," said Delaney,
"then it doesn't make any difference what your answer is. Don't
think you can string us along, laddie. What we're after is total
commitment, right here and now. We want you on our side, but
we want you all the way. If you don't have that commitment,
then you're not the man we thought you were. And if you're
not, then you're dead."

I stood up. Delaney's pistol came up with me. I said, "I need
to stretch and I need to think. Stop waving that thing at me."

I walked to the open window and looked out. The sun was
well up, and there was haze on the hills. I could smell the grass

freshly mown, the cloy of magnolia, and the sharp bite of wood-smoke from somewhere. There was birdsong, and the hum of traffic from the highway, and a strain of music faintly winding through the trees. There was movement in the compound where the new kids lived. They were always the first to be up and around, as eager as puppies for the new day. By now the mess hall was open and the resident aces were shaking out the fog and lazily stretching toward the morning. Breakfast, classes, midday meeting, lunch, classes, and on such an April day there might be a softball game in the late afternoon. Early dinner and study for the kids; later dinner and beer for their elders. The unchanging routine of the Center, so much a part of my life. And they were giving it all to me. The works, all of it. All those people down there, mine to shape, mine to lead, mine to care for . . . and eventually mine to kill.

I leaned out the window, breathed in the air of my youth, and listened again to that strain of odd music floating downwind.

Kill or be killed, it was as simple as that. Join them, or die, and I wondered which it would be. I truly did not know. I wanted no part of them, but I did not want to die. Just that. I did not want to stop ticking. I told myself that I had never figured to live this long. I told myself that with Nadia gone I didn't have a hell of a lot left to live for. I told myself that the others had turned their backs on me, and that now I was truly alone. None of it helped. I still did not want to die.

And with that I wondered how much I had left of the ideals that we all begin with, the standards so quickly eroded by age and disappointment. I remembered Nadia white and dead, and I wondered at how I could even think of working with her murderers. I remembered Big John Brodski, and all the other aces they had slain. I remembered Nordquist walking through that eighth-floor window in Ljubljana, and I wondered if I had the strength to walk through this window of my own. I breathed deeply of the morning, and wondered again at the strangely familiar music on the breeze. I teetered on the edge of decision,

271

not knowing which way I would fall, and then the decision was taken from my hands.

"Don't do it," someone said.

I turned from the window. Harry still sat in his corner, and he still had the look of a zombie, but his eyes were brighter and his voice was firm. He said it again. "Don't do it."

"Harry, be quiet," said Pop.

Delaney muttered, "Get him out of here."

Harry stood up and came across the room to me. Close to him now, I could see that the brightness in his eyes were tears. They ran down his cheeks. Whatever they had him on was at a thin point, almost worn through. He said, "You're Ben, aren't you?"

"Yes." I kept my eyes on him, but my ears were tempted away by the music outside.

"I thought so. You're not going to do it, are you?"

"I don't know."

Pop said, "Harry, take the breakfast things back to the kitchen."

Harry ignored him. "You don't want to be like them, Ben. They're not like us."

"I know." That music.

"They kill people."

"Yes."

"They killed her."

"Yes."

"She gave me those cookies, and they killed her. Are you going to kill people, too?"

There it was, and there was only one answer. I put my hand on his shoulder. The music was loud in my ears. "Don't worry," I said. "I'm not going to do it."

"Ah, Ben," Pop's face was a mask of disappointment. "Do you know what you're doing?"

"I know," I told him. "I'm making an omelet without breaking any eggs."

"I hope you enjoy it," Delaney said sourly. He, too, seemed

more disappointed than angry. "It's going to be your last meal. Are you sure about this?"

"Dead sure."

"Dead as a doornail. You're finished, laddie."

"Maybe." I knew the music now. It was "The Entrance of the Gladiators," merrily piped on Sammy's steam calliope. I turned to the window. It was all down there before me. I said over my shoulder, "Come take a look. The circus just came to town."

The Jenner Brothers Southland Circus came winding up the road from the highway and into the parking lot outside the gate. The elephants led the way, Bull and Rosie in trappings of purple and gold, swaying howdahs perched on their backs. Sammy rode on Bull, and Vince on Rosie. Behind them came the camels led by trainers, then the string of rosinback horses with standing riders. The menagerie cages came next, the big cats staring out solemnly, then the side show tents, then a gang of gypsy women led by Martha and Snake flashing the brilliant colors of their skirts and banging on tambourines. Jimmy Abdul tagged close behind Martha, jumping up and down with excitement as the acrobats turned cartwheels down the length of the line, and the clowns in full costume juggled sticks and stones that they had picked up from the roadside. Vibrant and spangled, busy and loud, the circus spread a cloud of dust and noise as it filed into the parking lot and went about setting up tents.

Love a parade? I loved this one, and what I loved about it most were the television people stalking along the flanks with cameras rolling. I saw the logos of the three major networks on their trucks, plus two from local stations in Washington and Richmond. They were recording every move and every minute.

"Oh my God," said Delaney in back of me.

I turned around. He was staring, transfixed, at what was happening below us. Pop was on the telephone, speaking urgently. The two guards at the gate had turned out the reserve from the barracks, and now there were a dozen of them in the parking lot trying to turn away the trucks and wagons. It was like trying to sweep back the sea with a broom. The trucks came on and on, parking in their accustomed rows and letting down their sides to set up shop.

"I don't care what you do," Pop was yelling to someone. "Get those people out of here. Use force if you have to."

"No force," snapped Delaney. "Are you crazy?"

"No force," Pop repeated, "but I want all those cameras confiscated and I want every inch of the tape that they've shot. Tell them national security, tell them anything you please, but . . . what?"

"What?" said Delaney.

Pop looked up, his face stricken. "Some of those people are broadcasting live. Live, right now."

I crossed the room to the television set in the far corner. Delaney's pistol did not follow me this time. I doubt that he remembered that he had it in his hand. I pushed the button and, sure enough, there was the scene in the parking lot, and the round and smiling face of WCTU's Bill Roeder.

" . . . lovely April morning here on the grounds of the Federal Center for the Study of Childhood Diseases, a little-known government facility south of Washington. As you can see behind me, the circus people from the Jenner Brothers Southland road show are busy preparing for today's performance. It's a benefit in the oldest traditions of the circus, a free show for the young people here, all of whom are suffering from rare and incurable ailments. It's a case of the mountain coming to Mohammed, since all of the children here are confined to the Center on a full-time basis for observation and treatment. This means that their only form of entertainment is television, and even we in the industry are quick to admit that there is no substitute for the real thing. So today, thanks to the generosity of Jenner Brothers Southland, these kids at the Federal Center are going to be treated to a dose of old-fashioned circus, complete with bareback riders and cotton candy. Even now, so early in the morning, they are beginning to flock to the. . . ."

He kept on talking as the camera panned to the fence that separated the lot from the grounds. The kids were there, all right, along with the older aces and some of the staff, all of them pressed against the barrier that kept them away from the electrified fence. Waving and mugging for the camera, they had no idea what was going on.

Neither did Delaney. He pulled his eyes away from the television, and said to me, "Do you know what this is all about?"

"You've been looking for Sammy Warsaw for three years," I told him. "You never found him, but he just found you."

"Sammy?" said Pop. He put down the telephone. "Sammy?"

"There seems to be some confusion with the security guards," Roeder was saying, "but that should be sorted out shortly. In the meantime the animals are moving into place and. . . . Hold it, Scotty, hold it. Get that shot over there."

The camera panned to the elephants. I went back to the window. It was easier to watch it from there. Bull, with Sammy on his back, had sidled up to the cement-block maintenance shed and was leaning against it. The structure shuddered. Bull leaned again and blocks began to slip. One more push and the shed went over in a pile of dust and rubble. The generator for the Center went with it. All the lights in the Center went out, then came on again as the emergency generator cut in. Bull picked his way delicately through the pile of blocks and bricks, and walked all over the second generator, crushing it. The lights went off for good, and with them the current for the electrified fence. Bull walked up to the fence and crashed through it, Sammy urging him on. The rest of the circus parade, led by the horses, saw the opening and followed the elephant through. Bull came across the lawn at a stately pace, heading for the administration building. I leaned out the window, and waved. Sammy saw me, and waved back. He kept on coming.

Delaney saw the bottom line at once. He was a bureaucrat accustomed to the shifting of fortune, and he knew better than to waste time defending a losing position. As soon as he saw the circus come pouring through the fence he knew that the old ball game was over and that a new one had begun. The Center was on the very edge of public exposure, and he was looking at a massive breach of Agency security. He was also looking at the end of his career.

He turned to me, and said, "I don't know what's happening, but it has to be stopped. Can you do it?"

"It can't be stopped, but it can be controlled."

"Will you?"

"I'm not sure that I want to."

"What good will it do you to blow the Center wide open?"

"No good at all, but it won't hurt me any, either. What's in it for me?"

He smiled, and his face relaxed. He was on his own ground, talking his own language. "Let's deal. We made you an offer earlier. Perhaps it can be renegotiated."

"Perhaps." I thought quickly. "There are four points, but they're not negotiable."

"Go ahead," he said cautiously.

"No more killing. You'll announce a total cure for Rauschner's. The aces will live out their normal lives."

"Do you realize what you're asking?"

"I'm not asking anything, I'm telling you how it has to be."

"The complications would be enormous."

"Not compared to the alternative. Take a look at it."

His eyes flicked down to the scene below, Sammy coming across the lawn on Bull, the rest of the circus mob following, and the television crews behind them.

He said, "You've got it. What else?"

"The entire medical staff of the Center has to go. They're not doctors, they're butchers. They have to be replaced, top to bottom."

No hesitation this time. "Agreed. What else?"

"No matter what you people thought, no matter what the computer said, I'm the wrong man to run this place. I'm not tough enough, I'm not sharp enough, and I'm not crooked enough. The man you want is out there on that elephant."

"Warsaw? Are you serious?"

"This invasion wasn't my idea, I knew nothing about it. Sammy is the one who shafted you, and he's the one to run your shop."

"You really don't want the job?"

"Sammy is the logical choice. Your computer would have told you that, but you had him listed as dead."

"Will you be around?"

"I'll be . . . available."

"Very well then. Agreed."

"No question on those three points?"

"None."

"All right, hold still now. I'm going to do to you what you were going to do to me. I'm going into your head to see how much of this you really mean. If you're just playing for time then the deal is off."

I went in. He was straight. He meant it. I came out. "It's a deal," I said, "on those three points."

"You said there were four."

"There are. The fourth one is Pop. I want him dead."

There was a sudden stillness in his eyes. He turned to look at Pop, and I turned with him. The old man was standing near his desk, a faint smile on his face.

"Bloodthirsty, Ben?" he asked.

I ignored him. I remembered what Snake had told me about Afghanistan. He was dead, and you don't talk to dead people.

Delaney said, "How necessary is this? It seems extreme."

"He owes me."

"You mean the woman? You can't lay that all on him, that was a mutual. . . ." He saw where that was leading and he backed off from it.

"A lot of people were involved, including you," I agreed, "but I have no quarrel with you. People like you are filth, but you're

277

necessary. You keep the wheels spinning. But not him. He started out on the side of the angels."

Delaney ignored the part about filth. Words like that didn't bother him. He remembered the pistol in his hand and he hefted it, staring at Pop.

Pop said, "Selling me out, Roger? So easily?"

"For the greater good, Pop. Always for the greater good." He held out the pistol to me, and said, "He's yours."

I did not take the pistol. I walked over to Pop and stood in front of him. He was still smiling. He said, "Are you really going to kill me?"

"Yes," I told him. "God damn you. Yes."

I put my hands around his neck. He did not try to stop me. The skin on his throat was cold and dry, and the bones there were fragile. I squeezed. He tried to say something, but he had no voice.

He said to me, *Ben.*

I squeezed harder. His face changed color.

Son.

I squeezed harder. His eyes popped.

I loved you all. I really did.

I squeezed once more and felt the bones snap. His head flopped over, and he was dead. I opened my hands and he fell to the floor. I looked around. Delaney was staring pointedly out the window. Harry's eyes were on the floor. He would not look at me.

Without turning around, Delaney said, "There are things to be done."

"Yes."

I went downstairs and out onto the lawn. Sammy was off the elephant, and running toward me. Snake, and Vince, and Martha were through the fence and close behind him, racing across the grass. I ran to meet them with my arms open, and just for that moment there was something close to joy within my sadness, something close to peace.

HERBERT BURKHOLZ *is a native New Yorker who has lived much of his adult life in Spain, Mexico, Italy, and Greece. He is the author of eight books, including the critically acclaimed novel* The Spanish Soldier, *and his articles have appeared in* The New York Times Magazine, Playboy, *and other publications. Formerly Writer-in-Residence at The College of William and Mary in Virginia, he now lives in Woodstock, New York.*